F I V E   S K I E S

Also by Ron Carlson

Stories
News of the World
Plan B for the Middle Class
The Hotel Eden
At the Jim Bridger
A Kind of Flying: Selected Stories

Novels
Betrayed by F. Scott Fitzgerald
Truants

For Young Readers
The Speed of Light

FIVE SKIES

RON CARLSON

VIKING

Succor: Susan and Walter DeMelle, Jay Boyer, Lyn and
Steve Farmer; Support: Marianne Merola, my dear friends and
students at Arizona State University; Advice: Josh Kendall;
G.E.C.; Equation: my father Ed Carlson 1922–2004.

VIKING
Published by the Penguin Group
Penguin Group (USA) Inc., 375 Hudson Street,
New York, New York 10014, U.S.A.
Penguin Group (Canada), 90 Eglinton Avenue East, Suite 700,
Toronto, Ontario, Canada M4P 2Y3
(a division of Pearson Penguin Canada Inc.)
Penguin Books Ltd, 80 Strand, London WC2R oRL, England
Penguin Ireland, 25 St. Stephen's Green, Dublin 2, Ireland
(a division of Penguin Books Ltd)
Penguin Books Australia Ltd, 250 Camberwell Road, Camberwell,
Victoria 3124, Australia
(a division of Pearson Australia Group Pty Ltd)
Penguin Books India Pvt Ltd, 11 Community Centre, Panchsheel Park,
New Delhi – 110 017, India
Penguin Group (NZ), 67 Apollo Drive, Rosedale, North Shore 0745, Auckland,
New Zealand (a division of Pearson New Zealand Ltd.)
Penguin Books (South Africa) (Pty) Ltd, 24 Sturdee Avenue,
Rosebank, Johannesburg 2196, South Africa

Penguin Books Ltd, Registered Offices:
80 Strand, London WC2R oRL, England

First published in 2007 by Viking Penguin,
a member of Penguin Group (USA) Inc.

1 3 5 7 9 10 8 6 4 2

Publisher's Note
This is a work of fiction. Names, characters, places, and incidents either are the product
of the author's imagination or are used fictitiously, and any resemblance to actual persons,
living or dead, business establishments, events, or locales is entirely coincidental.

ISBN 978-0-670-03850-3

Printed in the United States of America
Set in Palatino
Designed by Abby Kagen

For Gail Hochman

FIVE SKIES

IT WAS A COLD MAY in all of Idaho, and as the month began there were only a few short stacks of lumber and construction gear on the plateau above the remote river gorge, along with all the game trails and the manifold signs of rabbits who were native to the place and who now moved cautiously around the three men sleeping on the ground.

The first time Arthur Key saw the plateau at the far edge of the ranch called Rio Difficulto, he was lying in a sleeping bag in the frigid open air at dawn, or a little before it, in the deep gray light through which so many creatures jostled in the sage. He was a big man and had slept in rough sections, shouldering the oversize Coleman sleeping bag up over his right arm and then his left by turns. A screaming rabbit had woken him, the cries thin and shrill in their extremity sounding only like a woman to him, only like a crime. They beat into the fading darkness like a two-note whistle, then suddenly stopped, and Arthur Key lifted his head and scanned the area. At first he didn't know where he was, which rooming house, but he knew the low black line of the crenellated mountain horizon was a hundred miles distant. The large Ford flatbed—still loaded—was parked off in the sage, cocked unevenly because of their having let so much air out of the tires the night before. Beside it he could see a small open army surplus jeep with a winch on the front bumper, and behind that a pile of material, a stack of large lumber in stays, the small tractor, a blue portable john still in its rough wooden crate, the frost on everything silver in the new light. There was nothing else, no building, no tent, no small trailer across the work yard. He closed his eyes and smiled. Darwin had said *room and board*.

Arthur Key put his hand on his head and felt the frost in his hair. In the new silence, he could now hear another sound which at first he assumed to be some pressure in his head. Then as he yawned and cleared his ears he guessed it was the flat high harmonics of an intercontinental flight, San Francisco to Boston, but as the vibration persisted he sat up and listened again. There were fluctuations in it like those in human speech, and a rhythm as if a generator were running somewhere a half mile away. He wanted it to be a generator, the gas-driven generator that would be running the galley trailer where coffee would be ready, hot coffee and absolutely anything else.

In the past six weeks, mornings had been kindest to him. He had saved himself for two things: waking and having some coffee, and then, of course, the day caught up with him and he put his head down and worked, whatever it was. He'd just finished two weeks in Pocatello working cement on the foundations for new storage units. He told himself he was trying to regroup, to get a grip, but he now knew, after this time away from the life he had ruined, he wasn't doing a very good job of it.

The sound wasn't a generator and it wasn't people talking.

When he stood, he knew it was at some distance a river, and as he walked toward it and saw clearly the mortifying fissure through which such a vast river ran, the geology of the entire plateau settled in his mind as an entity, a huge primitive place that few men had seen. He went to the edge of the sandstone gorge and looked down. In the deep gloom he could see the electric white gashes where the water boiled over the boulders. Here the sound was terrific, magnified, real. It sucked the air away and drew you toward it. Key measured up the river, estimating the vertical canyon at fifteen hundred feet. He couldn't sense the width. Below him as his dizziness abated he saw a shadow sweep and then an osprey rose into his face, a small cutthroat trout in one talon. Across the chasm the first sunlight clipped the western echelon of ruined mountains and cones of the badland volcanoes at the edge of the world, and they were gray and red and gold in the moment. Two low spires of smoke smudged the sky far away; it would be early in the year for such fires.

Key heard a sharp painful sigh and turned to see a figure moving on the ranch road, a thin man whose shadow in the new sun cut a hundred yards toward the canyon. It was the kid, Ronnie. He was walking away in the barren place and then Arthur Key saw the man begin to run in the cold, a stride purposeful and beautiful at once. Key folded his arms and watched until the shadow streamed slowly south and disappeared.

Darwin Gallegos, still in his sleeping bag, had watched the young man move to the gate and run away. He'd already seen the big man, Arthur, move to the canyon edge. The sun was up now, but it was not warmer, and the frost filled every shadow and coated the glass of the two vehicles. He crawled out of his sleeping bag and laced up his boots and put on his jacket. He was unfolding the metal stove table and opening the stove when the big man, Arthur Key, came back from his tour.

"Where'd Ronnie go?"

Darwin was a little sick now that he realized he'd made a mistake by hiring these two. He'd been desperate—it had been late in the day and the country was full of men who couldn't work, wouldn't work, and they were hard to get rid of. Just driving back to Pocatello would cost him more than a day. He'd been tired and he was fooled by the big man's size, he knew now. Darwin lit the propane and set the coffeepot on the burner while he pulled the heavy cast-iron frying pan from the cookbox. In forty years at the ranch he'd hired maybe six bad apples, and now for the first time on his own he'd started with an error.

"How well do you know the boy?"

"Three days. He joined a cement crew as we were finishing the storage unit foundations in Pocatello. He was day labor and worked all day long, though he is not a cement man."

"I think he's run off."

"He's run before, he told me. He's had reasons. But he may be all right."

When Ronnie had opened his eyes, he'd seen the big man, Art, walk over past the trucks, his breath torn balloons trailing behind. It was cold. It was headache cold. Ronnie was still wearing his Levi's, and he felt his old ragged Nikes there halfway down by his belly. Beside him in the sage he could see the top of the head of the guy who had hired them yesterday in Pocatello, Darwin Something. Oh, Christ, it was cold in the gray world. Ronnie put his head back in the sleeping bag and covered it up. He hated this. When he was cold like this, and he'd proved it to himself, he'd rather be in jail. A year ago he'd waited as long as he could bear it in the jail work release in Rockford, but he'd walked away in late April and walked back two days later, too cold to think. He still did not move and worked his shoes on and then eased himself out into the frosty new day. By now he remembered the truck ride in the snow, the trouble and arriving here.

Without a sound, the way he had moved so many times in his life, he stood and stepped away through the sandy soil, past the big white truck which had brought them to the place, past the other equipment. He was out of here the way he had fled a dozen weird jobs. Two dozen. There would be something and he would be away. Art, the big man, had been decent, but this was all wrong. He nearly ran into the barbed-wire fence but found the gate and the stupid dirt two-track ranch road and he trotted out onto it and he stopped. North there was nothing but the world, the low dark hills and not a light. South was the steel sky and a distant horizon. There was frost on the fence posts and the edges of all the sagebrush. This was a wild place. He looked up and down the road, and then Ronnie Panelli, sick at not seeing a bus stop or an alley or a parking lot, some vehicle to hide in, turned south and started to run.

Darwin laid rashers of bacon into the huge black frying pan. He was cooking breakfast on his old camp stove, the dish towel over his shoulder. He would have liked to have had the tent up and a table constructed, but he hadn't known he'd hire anybody in Pocatello. Now, goddamn it, he'd feed them and take them back.

Yesterday had felt like luck. The whole day had run smoothly, one—two—three. The utility poles had been already separated at the lumberyard and ready to load, and he'd had no difficulty in locating and packing all the hardware, couplings, and wire, as well as the bright new posthole auger. He'd gassed up and driven by the old Grange near the railroad station just on the off chance that it might be open. He'd seen Key and Panelli smoking cigarettes on the stone steps, and the sight of Key, his size, his obvious strength, so soon after

Darwin Gallegos himself had worried the ten half-ton poles onto the truck made Darwin feel lucky and he'd stopped and spoken to them.

When he'd approached and stood above them, Key had extended his pack of cigarettes, certain that this dark-faced stranger was out of work too and wanted to spend the sweet heart of the twilight there talking the way strange men talk to each other on the swept steps of the hiring hall. You meet somebody new, his history anything, a big unknown story that you know only the end of—something went wrong or stopped; he's sitting there too, eight or nine bucks in the whole world, maybe less, nothing now but the gathering darkness and finding a place to go.

Darwin had taken the cigarette and sat beside them. He could tell that they didn't know each other very well, had probably met that day, and that the younger one, the smaller one, had been in jail; his look went all over the place—he was pale and starved and jangled. But Darwin had known some men who had been in jail who had worked out just right, and for years you could count on them. The strong one was even larger up close, his biceps defined even through the blue long-sleeved denim workshirt. As Key lit the smoke for him, Darwin asked back, "Ever do any carpentry?"

The answer came slowly. "Yes, sir, I have. There's some of that work in this town. We're about to frame some storage sheds. Day labor." The large man's eyes were gray and clear. He wasn't in trouble, Darwin thought, but there was damage of some kind.

"Ever do any construction drawing?"

The man looked at Darwin, his eyes full of a knowing confidence. Then they narrowed and he laughed. The man nudged the kid. "Well," he said, "you're looking at two prime architects."

"What's the pay?" the young man said. "I can do it. What's

the pay?" His dark curly hair shined in the early evening light. He looked like Sinatra at nineteen. "Is it a day a time, like this shit?"

"I only need one man," Darwin said.

"Then there you go, Ronnie," the big man said. He looked at Darwin and lifted the younger man by the forearm. "Good luck."

Darwin said, "Just a moment." He looked into the gray eyes again. "You can work from construction drawings?"

"Yes, sir, if they're sensible I can do that." Then, for the first time, the big man sat up and folded his arms, but it was clear that they were talking about more than his strength. "And I can do it well. I have experience." He nodded at Ronnie. "And I have a partner."

"I see that," Darwin said. "He looks like a good man too."

"What's the pay?" Ronnie said. "And when do we start?"

Over chicken-fried steaks and mashed potatoes in the Cliffside Cafe, they traded names and Darwin told them it would be ten, maybe twelve weeks at a hundred dollars a day, paid on Fridays, plus room and board. The kid, Ronnie, lit up to that, his forehead widening, but he was too canny to say anything. The other, Arthur Key, sopped up the gravy with his toast and nodded at Darwin. "Good enough," he said. "If the work is good."

It was the moment that the waitress was pouring second coffees, and they were about to order apple pie with ice cream, that Darwin wondered if this was a good idea. These two men had appeared and it was one-stop shopping. He knew not to hurry and he had hurried. He had thought he would be traveling back to Rio Difficulto alone with the materials and then on the next day to Twin Falls to hire a crew. He watched Arthur Key spoon some of the vanilla ice cream into his coffee, and Darwin made up his mind and reached for the check.

So then he had his two-man crew and they drove carefully

in the big truck back along the railroad tracks to the rooming house where Art and Ronnie retrieved their small traveling kits ending that chapter in each of their lives. It was full dark and the temperature had dropped hard. The three now picked up one more coffee each for Darwin and Arthur and a can of cola for Ronnie at the famous Double American Truckstop at the junction with 86, a highway they mounted and took west. In the cold May dark, as 86 became 84, they hit a rain which was rain for only a moment and then a light sleet that thickened. Darwin drove. The windshield closed and opened each beat and the tires stopped sucking at the pavement and now began a steady roaring splash.

"Idaho," Ronnie said. He sat between the two men in the cab of the big Ford flatbed. The heater emitted a faint hum. "What is this, winter? I hate this."

"Let's take him back," Arthur Key said. "I'm sure it's balmy in Pocatello."

The precipitation intensified, the sleet sharp and drier now as it tried for snow. Along the interstate, semis were parked, their flashers periodic in the white night, between them occasionally a passenger car lodged, waiting out the weather. As they passed north of Burley, they crossed into the coming snow, the storm coming down along the Aleutians and crossing west through Oregon, all snow for a thousand miles and here already six inches on the roadway. The sky was an uninterrupted cascade. The men were silent in the truck. Here there was no traffic and Darwin slowed as he squinted for the road markers.

Even going only fifty they left the highway. Darwin went by the book. When he felt the front end lift and he knew he had lost it, he didn't brake, and as they floated gradually sideways, he steered into the skid. It didn't help. Ronnie tensed, stabbing his feet into the floor, and Arthur Key braced himself, his arms along the frame. At forty they began shearing the road markers, the huge Ford and its fifteen-ton cargo cutting the metal posts off as if clipping weeds, each one making a simple snap and disappearing. Darwin was eyes ahead, looking for what they would really hit, breathless, knowing the fifty-five-foot utility poles would come through the cab like the very weight of the world, but nothing appeared, and at twenty the vehicle suddenly dropped and swerved back onto its aligned path, throwing the men together against Arthur Key as the Ford nosed through a wire stock fence with a hard rocking dip and up onto what Darwin took to be, under the fresh snow, an access road parallel to the interstate.

"Shit! Shit! Shit!" Ronnie said, climbing over Arthur and dropping to the ground. "Shit, shit, just shit! This damn Idaho!" He was wet in a second, covered by the soft petals of snow still descending, an impenetrable blanket through the quiet night. Darwin and Arthur looked at the thin young man, hugging his arms and blowing hissing curses into the snow.

What ensued in the dark snowy field ten miles northwest of Burley, Idaho, was that Arthur Key and Darwin immediately looked to see that their load had not shifted, which it had not. The whole time the snow unabated settled on their uncovered heads and shoulders, as Arthur checked the six chain hitches. Ronnie Panelli sat in the cab, cold and unhappy, his hands pressed between his knees, his pale face vaguely blue. When Darwin attempted to move the truck up the slight incline, they found it only slid. Arthur Key instructed Darwin to lower the pressure in the dual rear tires ten pounds each as he adjusted the front tires. "Try it again," Arthur said, disappearing to the rear.

"Stay clear of the back!" Darwin hollered. He started the engine, adjusted the rpms and began to ease out the clutch. He didn't want to spin the tires. It all held; as the engine whine rose, the truck did not move. Then as Darwin was certain he was about to lose the lock and slide, the truck bumped once strangely, and Darwin knew that Key had jostled the entire vehicle. It began to creep up the slope. He was quick to guide it along the lowest angle until he leveled out and sat idling on the frontage road.

It was a wonderful feeling having been forty seconds before destined to spend the night in the snowfield in the truck and hire a tow late tomorrow, losing all the luck he'd felt he'd had, and now he was made again, the night which had been so old a minute ago was nothing now but promise in the beautiful snow. He clapped Ronnie Panelli on the shoulder. "Here we go!"

The blue terror was gone from Ronnie's face, but he still looked miserable. He rolled with Darwin's push, keeping his hands between his knees. "Yeah," he said. "This is the life, all right. You're the Big Boss and he's the fucking giant . . ."

"Let's keep it on the road now," Arthur Key said, pulling himself up into the truck, bumping Panelli. "Stay under forty with the tires down like this." His hands were red and muddy, and his blue denim shirt hung soaking on the axis of his shoulders. Ronnie moved away from the wet man and adjusted the heater lever, an act that again had little luck making things happen. Darwin navigated the truck by means of the road markers, back along the frontage road, staying centered and finally mounting the interstate, and ten minutes later they again passed the point where they had skidded. Their tracks were gone, already covered by the snowfall, but they could see the absence suddenly of the markers along the highway and then the gap in the stock fence. "Yeah," Ronnie Panelli said. "We got it made. This is absolutely the highway to heaven. I can just tell."

Now in the brittle morning sunlight, Arthur Key held out his enamel mug and Darwin poured the first cup of coffee steaming from the old percolator pot. The air was sharp and clean in Arthur's head and he was hungry.

"There's cream for that in the orange cooler," Darwin told him. Arthur opened the large Igloo and smiled at the colorful array of provisions packed there like a puzzle. He poured some half-and-half into his coffee. Darwin had sawed thick pieces of sourdough bread and set them into the stove's wire toast rack and he was breaking eggs—four, five, six—into the sizzling bacon grease.

He paused and looked at Key.

"He'll be back," Arthur told him.

Darwin broke three more eggs which bubbled white immediately in the hot pan. He decided to speak. "You two want this job or should I just take you back to Pocatello?"

Arthur Key stood before his new boss. They watched the eggs stiffen. "We're here," he said. "Let's look it over. I don't want that drive again."

"Just let me know," Darwin said. "The roads are well dry by now."

Ronnie Panelli came back into view on the old ranch road a few minutes later, his shadow shorter with the sun higher now and his shoulders lower. He was shuffling slowly toward the camp, his hands in his pockets, even though every startled rabbit startled him, and he approached the two men without speaking.

He looked at the laden frying pan as it steamed and then looked from Arthur Key to Darwin. "What?" he said. "Good morning."

Just before noon the plans arrived. After breakfast, Ronnie Panelli had climbed into the closed cab of the big Ford and wrapped his sleeping bag around himself, the one Darwin had issued, and begun smoking cigarettes waiting for the sun to warm things up. The other two men walked the area and Darwin inventoried the materials for Arthur Key.

"It's not a house, then," Key said.

Darwin was noncommittal. He replaced the canvas and cinched it down. The sun was at things now, cutting the frost, and the brush stirred as creatures began taking a look. The purring of quail was general. He wanted to show his new man that all this stuff was A grade. As they walked out to the clay road that had brought them to the high plateau of the worksite, Darwin noted again Arthur Key's size and was pleased. He literally walked in his shadow. Darwin was still uneasy, but he wanted to keep this man; it would make the job go right.

"Where you from?" he said.

"California," Key answered. He said the word in a way that shut that door and Darwin knew it. He didn't care, really; you hired a crew and they came from somewhere. The trick was to line them up right and tight, let them adopt the job and keep them happy. This wasn't a permanent job or anything for the real ranch; this was just a rough summer. The clay ranch road was a quarter mile from the lip of the gorge. Arthur Key turned at the gate and eyed the prospect. "This private property?"

"Yes it is. It's all part of the ranch where I worked."

"And we're going to run a power line, but it's not a cabin."

They could see Panelli trying to extricate himself from the sleeping bag and climb out of the cab of the truck. He was having difficulty and ended up almost falling. They watched him kicking out of the bedroll though his curses couldn't reach them.

"We're going to set the poles. Idaho Power will run the line."

"There's some money here. Who's paying for this mystery project?"

"Lot of people. Don't worry about it. I'll get you anything you need for this job. We'll go over the plans and I'll get you anything you need." Key was smiling as if he'd heard this or something like it before. Darwin couldn't read him. "It's a nice place, right?"

"Beautiful," Key said. He started back. "We'll fix that."

Darwin gave Ronnie Panelli a pair of his steel-toed Red Wing work boots almost new and they fit, and so Arthur Key and Darwin got to watch Ronnie walk a big circle in those shoes. "Now you're making some footprints," Arthur said. "Though they'll be harder to run in."

Ronnie looked at him and kept walking, long strides. He hadn't had new shoes in over a year. Darwin gave Ronnie the job of erecting their quarters, a large white canvas elkhunter's lodge, room inside for four cots, a woodstove, and a small table. They selected a level site on one side of the area up against the sage and he began unpacking the tubular frame.

"See," Arthur Key said to Darwin. "Listen. He's not grumbling. He's a good worker. He's made the decision not to sleep under the truck tonight."

Darwin wasn't sure, but he was hoping.

"Is the stove here?" Ronnie Panelli called. He was on his knees sorting the parts. He liked this work. He liked that they'd left him alone to do it; he could figure out a tent.

"Yes, sir," Darwin answered. "We can unload the stove when you're ready."

"It's going to be toasty," Arthur told him. "Better than the Hilton."

"I've never been in a Hilton in my life."

Darwin started the Farmall tractor and backed up to the crated portable john. Arthur Key attached the chain to the upper portion and Darwin dragged it off thirty yards beyond the lodge. Key used a bar to disassemble the rough wooden crate and then rocked the small structure level in the sandy soil. The work and the snorting tractor and the sun on his arms pleased Arthur Key. The air temperature was almost fifty. Ronnie fought with the steel tubes and the cluster connectors for a while and then took what he had apart again and laid the pieces out in the dirt so he could tell the corners from the roof peaks, and then he started again at one end and snugged the frame together front to back.

Key drew a deep breath and looked out across the arc of the earth wrinkled and steaming in the distance. On the western horizon the blue sky was always ruined and working with ascending clouds, flumes and thin streams of gas. At night once or twice a week, they would see irregular tongues of flame, tiny, miles away in the mystery of the distance. Beneath their feet a hundred miles of magma would shift and the sunsets would be green and orange for a week.

Darwin parked the tractor and started to help draw the rippled canvas over the lodge frame, and in the second that Arthur Key exhaled, the memory of his crime chilled his heart again; he used the word *crime* when he thought of it—and he thought of it unbidden. He should have protected his brother and he had not. He had let his own selfishness blind him, and he used the word *selfishness* when he thought of it. And he knew he had been blind, because he had made an entire life of seeing until last March. He winced with the tide such memory delivered and he said his brother's name, *Gary.* He wanted it right in his face. The snow and the cold empty day and now the sun in the big fresh place had taken his guard down.

Darwin and Ronnie pulled at the reluctant canvas, heavy and stalled in its folds. It kept collapsing at their feet. "Just where are we then?" Ronnie said. "I know for a sure fact that there is nothing down that way. At all." He pointed south.

"That's Ranch Road G Seven," Darwin said, standing up and waving his hand the other way. He was breathing hard. "Seventeen miles north is Mercy."

"That's a town."

"Yes it is."

"Idaho, right? Still Idaho."

"Yes, we're still in Idaho and so is Mercy."

They had the canvas unfolded to its length and Darwin studied the frame which angled up to over eight feet at its apex. "Let me get the rope," he said and walked off toward the Ford. Skinny Ronnie Panelli stood amid the half ton of drapery like a character caught in the wrong myth. Arthur Key, smiling, came over.

"How do you like it so far?"

"Okay by me." Ronnie stepped heavily across the big pile of canvas. "Big place, nobody around, put up tents. I won't have to stand on the fucking street corner in the morning hoping to get hired. I'll take it."

Darwin came back with a heavy coil of rope and began to open it in loops on the ground. He was going to tie it to the lodge cover in three places and drag it all up and over with the Farmall.

"Here." Key stopped him. "Do this." He lifted a bundle of the canvas in the center and hoisted it above his head. "Pull your ends around each side." As the other two men did this, he moved into the tent frame, holding the canvas over his head. Seesawing it from Ronnie to Darwin they were able to work it up and over the rooftop and begin to pull it down the other side while Key lifted and fed the piled canvas to them. With the thing almost complete, there was a hitch that required Arthur Key to go inside the tent and shake the frame so that the seam along the roof beam fell into place. The canvas mated on the frame and settled. When Key came out, Darwin and Ronnie were backing through the sage to take in their accomplishment.

"How big is your crew?" Key asked him. The tent seemed huge.

"I don't know," Darwin said. "You tell me after you've seen the plans. This may be the crew."

"Where's that stove?" Ronnie Panelli said. He couldn't take his eyes off the tent. "This is fucking cool. We're making a camp here."

By the middle of the day, they had unloaded the crated woodstove and backed the tractor away as a dark cherry Chevrolet four-wheel-drive pickup turned in the gate and bounced toward them slowly along the rutted two-track. The vehicle was startling, as all approaches are in lonely places, and this was a beautiful truck with a double cab and dual wheels under the rear fenders which arched and sparkled like something fabulous. Key and Panelli watched the truck with a begrudged awe. They'd been on the river plateau half a day and they already knew how to look on this deep red truck as an intruder. The three men actually backed a step as it drove in. Then Darwin handed Ronnie the crowbar. The young man was already lined up with the generator and the circular saw; his instructions were to uncrate the stove and then cut all the stack of cratewood two-by-twos into stove lengths. The big pickup had wheeled in a circle and parked so that they could read the blocked and shadowed lettering on the door: BABCOCK ENGINEERING, TWIN FALLS.

Darwin went over to the truck, hesitating for a minute as a signal to Arthur Key to come along, but Key stayed behind. He and Ronnie watched a pale young man in an expensive plaid shirt and bright brown boots climb out of the cab and extract a roll of blueprints from the toolbox in the bed of the truck. He handed the plans to Darwin and they spoke for a moment, sighting an imaginary line to the river that the young man drew in the air with the blade of his hand. Then they spoke several minutes more, toeing the ground, and talking the way men do on the pitcher's mound in baseball games, making no eye contact whatsoever, looking past each other and tucking in their shirts with a finger, as if everything had been settled long ago in the big book that rested shut somewhere else far away, and Arthur Key noted this with interest, seeing that Darwin responded to the other man with too much deference, too stoic in the pressure of the orders being given.

"Nice vehicle," Ronnie Panelli said.

"You're a shoplifter," Key kidded him. "You wouldn't touch that truck."

They watched the man in the plaid shirt climb back into the Chevrolet and do an easy U-turn in the dirt, headed out.

"I wouldn't touch a truck like that because you can see it ten miles. They'd catch me for it."

"They caught you for shoplifting."

Ronnie's face, too thin for guile, looked hurt. "A few times. They caught me a few times. I took some cars. I'm not afraid of taking a car if I need it."

Darwin was walking their way with a long blueprint tube in his hand. Before he could reach them, Arthur Key turned to Ronnie Panelli and said, "You took your father's car the day you left. Everybody does it. It's not car theft; it's escape. I was just kidding. Don't be proud of thievery. Be happy we're out here. This is just right. Like you said—we're making camp. And, we're about to find out the big mystery." He said the last so that Darwin could hear and the older man responded by nodding and waving them on, to the tailgate of the little open jeep. "I can see we're going to need a proper table."

They unrolled the paper sheets and kicked four stones loose from the sandy soil to hold down the corners. Ronnie Panelli said, "Okay, so what is it?" He didn't understand the intensity with which the other two men stared at the plans. There was something going on. Arthur Key studied the smudged purple sheet with its intersecting lines long beyond Ronnie's ability to figure it.

"Can you do it?" Darwin asked Key. He was speaking quietly.

There were two of the large sheets; Key looked at both carefully. A minute passed, the minute between morning and afternoon. Panelli knew it was the strangest moment of the day. He wasn't used to silence this way, three men in the open. "Okay," he said at last. "So, let's do it. Let's build it."

"Just a minute, son," Darwin said, which was two wrong things at once, the call for patience and the word *son*.

Panelli danced away; he knew how to behave now, or thought he did. "Just a minute? Good. Come on, you two. We can do this. What is it? Hey, look at that tent. Are you listening? Hey, Conan the Engineer, what is the problem? Let's just—"

Key had him in both hands in less than a second and held him out like some sour varmint, one hand closing the collar of Panelli's shirt. "Call me that again," Arthur Key said. His tone was even. Darwin hadn't moved. "Go ahead. Use your little shoplifter's wit one more time." Panelli's workboots were just off the ground and it was clear to them all that Key could throw him over the jeep.

He knew enough to meet the larger man's eyes and say, as best he could, "No, I don't believe I will. Let me fucking go."

Key dropped him into the dirt, tossing him onto his side into the sage dust, and he was sorry for it in less than a second. Ronnie Panelli started to scramble up and then sat again, his elbows on his knees still as a statue avoiding both men's looks. Darwin looked at Arthur Key simply to give him again the next move. Key said to Ronnie Panelli, "Let's get up." Darwin turned back to the plans, adjusting the rock weights, business as usual. Panelli did not move. "Here. Come on, Ronnie," Key said. And though Key didn't step toward him, Panelli lifted his chin quickly, affronted. After a second, tears appeared in his eyes. "Oh, Christ," Key said. "Come on." Of course when he went to lift the young man, there was a struggle. Ronnie skittered away in the brush and then ran off a few paces. Key considered following and then just stood there, finally, dropping his chin and shaking his head. He turned and went back to the tailgate of the jeep where Darwin waited over the sheets of blueprint. There was an expectant look on Darwin's face, and Key met it with "Yeah, I can see what it is." He said it with disgust.

"Just a moment," Darwin said, and he went out to Ronnie in the bushes and led him over to the generator, the saw, the pile of rough crate boards. Key heard the generator kick up and begin to blather, then he heard the circular saw fire two or three brisk bursts. Darwin was showing Ronnie how to saw the white crate pine into stove lengths. Arthur Key rolled his shoulders and felt the tension there. Such a beautiful place. The blueprints ruffled in the breeze. He was thinking it over and he just didn't know. In his business in Los Angeles, he'd avoided such work, projects like this, stupidity and a lot of money meeting in some bad, temporary place. He watched Darwin take the saw back from the young man and turn him so he wouldn't cut himself or the cord and then hand it back. Key liked it here and he knew he needed to be here, but the job was wrong. It was fresh in the early afternoon and soon it would be late day and then the evening on this plateau. He scanned the western horizon as he would twenty times a day for the two months he would spend here and he saw the great folds of the floating ranges and the ancient cones among them in the white-blue sky. It was all sky here and never the same sky; he was standing in it. Now Ronnie had the circular saw in hand and the air was filled with the high ringing of the steel blade as it trilled through the lumber.

Darwin strode back to Arthur Key. "If he doesn't cut a finger off, we'll keep him," the older man said and smiled. "He hasn't worked very much." He pointed past Key to the plans. "Can you do it?"

"This is a shitty little job," Key said. He wanted his voice full of blame.

"It could be," Darwin said. "Let's walk here. Get away from the noise a little." Ronnie was in a rhythm now and there was a cut every few seconds. Darwin led them out toward the gorge.

"Who's your man in the pickup?"

"Just a consultant. An engineer."

"Not much of one. His little plans are wrong top to bottom. But it doesn't matter, does it? I mean, somebody's going to get killed out here." Key had raised his voice and pointed out over the river. "Right here. That's all this means."

Darwin kept his eyes on Key's, holding his gaze. Suddenly a small white-tailed hawk flared before them, rising from the canyon, so close Key could see the grain of the talons. They watched the hawk make a quick tour over where Ronnie Panelli worked at the pile of wood. "The saw scream made him think something was hurt up here. A rabbit or a fawn," Darwin said. The hawk disappeared into the sky.

"There's deer?"

"Antelope. Deer. Elk sometimes."

"You're going to ruin a pretty good place with this project of yours."

Darwin pushed the pack of cigarettes from his shirt pocket and shook one out to Key. They sat down on the broken rock shelf above the river and smoked.

"You can build it, can't you?" Darwin said. "You're my man."

"Anybody could build it. This piece of shit. I take it this is a one-use item."

"Those decisions have been made elsewhere."

"And you want to do it."

"I'm the foreman on a pretty good ninety-day job. The money's good and I need the money. One life ended. I'm doing this now. It's just my next thing." Here Darwin came up to Arthur, leveled his face before the larger man, and said with a forthright tone that could not be mistaken: "But, I want to do it right." Key liked the way Darwin spoke directly to him, and he had known since they met that he trusted this man, and he'd always been right about people in that regard. He had been ready to leave, to ask for a ride back to town, to any town really, to quit this rare place and commence again the nickel-and-dime days he'd been living for these terrible weeks; in fact, he could see himself once again sitting on the edge of a starched bed somewhere in a rented room the way he'd spent some afternoons since his flight from California and his wrong-doing, but now he saw he was in because he trusted this man. The river flashed in its ribbon far beneath them like some trick of light in the arch recess of the canyon. Across the plateau a short distance Ronnie pressed his steel circular saw into the screaming lumber. Arthur Key felt the decision turn in him and settle. He would just do it as a job, not get involved in anything else. As Darwin had said, the decisions were made elsewhere.

"We can do it," he said. He took Darwin's upper arm in his hand and squeezed it in a friendly gesture. "I was really hoping this would be a bridge. That would have been more than I could chew, but I was hoping."

Darwin nodded at him.

"But we're going to have to redo those plans. Will that work?"

"I'll get you anything you need."

The saw had stopped and the distant rush of the river rose up to them. They could see the pile of bright boards Ronnie Panelli had sawn. The young man himself was at the jeep now, leaning over the blueprints.

Arthur Key nodded at the truck and the trailer of material and equipment. "You've about got it all. We're going to want plywood, any grade, for those three-quarter-inch sheets of particleboard. We won't work with that stuff. And we may need some more cement. Let's make the boy some lunch and then dig those holes."

THEY WORKED INTO the early dark the first day, but the three men had equipment trouble, and they didn't drill any postholes. Darwin had stepped off the intervals and marked where to dig, but the tractor didn't cooperate. The day would prove like so many days at the campsite to be too small a thing for the plans they made. Too often even as the days lengthened through spring and into the high Idaho summer and the two-hour twilight, the irrevocable night would rise up between them in the middle of their workings, Key turning to Darwin for the level and not being able to see him there with the instrument ready. They fell into a pattern then without having to speak about it, retrieving their gear, lifting all the tools off the bare ground into the tractor shovel or laying them on the hood of the Farmall, and a listener would have heard only this certain clanking as the hammers and chisels and crowbars and screwdrivers were gathered against the night. "Nothing worse in the morning than finding a crescent wrench in the dirt," Key had told Ronnie Panelli the second or third day, when the young man finally understood what a crescent wrench was, the whole nomenclature of tools coming to him in daily increments, a lesson he resisted only for the moment before he saw that these tools were somehow his too, that he would get to wield them, be expected to, without assistance. He knew the language of only two things before this and one was the street and the other was golf, his life as a caddy. If the weather threatened, the men took the extra time to locate and place the tools in the large waterproof ammo chest by their tent. And so their days ended with this regard for their tools and the days began, as they squinted over coffee, in the exhilarating open air knowing where the shovel was, the chain, the awl.

On the first day, after a lunch of roast beef sandwiches on the sourdough rolls Darwin had brought from Pocatello, they'd fitted the tractor power takeoff assembly with the eight-foot auger, and already the light had lurched so that shadows were twice as long as things and the various wild birds began traversing the high sky. That first lunch had been odd, Darwin sawing the bread on his makeshift tailgate table with the butcher knife they would all learn to use, a tool big as a hacksaw, while Ronnie Panelli stood in front of the truck, well away from Arthur Key. And then the sandwiches themselves, each the size of a loaf, the largest sandwich Ronnie Panelli had ever had in his hands, were outsize for only a moment until the magnitude of the place registered once again; midafternoon in such a world required food this big. Panelli held his sandwich in both hands and tore at it still standing in front of the truck, keeping the vehicle between Key and himself, while the other two men sat on a bale of two-by-sixes and talked.

The bread was fresh and rough. Darwin watched Arthur eat. "Good?" he said. Arthur Key nodded, and Darwin went ahead. "Listen, do you want this job?" He pointed north where the sky was ripped with flags of rained-out cloud fragments stark in the blue day. "If you want, we can eat and just take you back to Pocatello."

Key, glad for the sun on his face, the warmth, looked up, chewing. He shook his head. "I don't want that drive again."

Darwin set his sandwich on the cutting board and twisted open the big jar of pickles offering it to Arthur Key. "Just let me know," he said. "We can pump up those tires and that snow will be long gone."

After a minute, Arthur Key said, "It is a good sandwich, certainly good enough for who it's for." He held it up. "A little wine wouldn't hurt."

"A good red wine?" Darwin said.

"Any red wine. White wine is not for drinking. White wine is something to do with your hands."

The older man laughed. They both talked through their chewing.

"There's water here," Darwin called to Ronnie Panelli. He meant the five-gallon cistern that now sat near the tent. When there was no answer, Darwin added, "You don't have to stand out there and eat. There's room on the bench." Panelli didn't turn. The sun at just after one o'clock on the plateau was flat and, if a person stood still out of the light chill wind, warm. It was actually sixty degrees and would be twenty-five by midnight. These were the days that the ancient rock worked against itself, pressing and shrinking away, the red sandstone binding and yielding, calving a boulder into the vast gorge every century, even though they stood ready—rows of hundred-ton rocks—all along the ruined, steadfast lip of the canyon.

Darwin ate. He eyed Arthur Key. He was trying to say something and have it lead to the next thing, the thing he didn't know. He considered and then retreated. Finally, he tried, "But drinking isn't it for you. That's not why we have you here."

Key looked up from his eating as if he was as comfortable with this agenda as with any. His look showed that other men had tried for his secrets. "No," Arthur Key said. "It isn't. I'm just traveling."

"Well, no matter," Darwin said. It was early in the season and he still wanted his power poles and his job done right more than he wanted to know about this large man who leaned against the jeep tailgate beside him. "We've got some work out here in the country, bit by bit. Today, water and the power poles, and in a night or two we'll have our wine."

But they didn't even unload the poles until almost noon the next day with all that lay before them in preparation. First, a while later, there was the sweet moment when Ronnie Panelli came around the corner of the Ford, walking slowly back toward the two men with his hand on the fender, his expression different now after eating, already his chemistry changed twenty-four hours after leaving Pocatello, a town where he had spent a bad month and not had a square meal. Arthur Key, himself now different too having settled into this brief life on the plateau, this job, and not being chafed by a single second guess, said across to the younger man, "What then, you eat the whole damn thing?" And in a flash Panelli's face took it as accusation, as it had taken everything said to it for years and years and years, ten years at least of his twenty, but then something happened that had never happened to him before because he took it in as accusation and it changed to something that showed on his face as pride, really what is called a shit-eating grin rose despite his galled determination to hate Key forever for having thrown him down this morning. There was a half second when Darwin watched and then without deciding to, he led them into the laughter which rang there.

"You're goddamn right, I ate it," Panelli said. "I came back here looking for another."

"You deserve it," Key told him. "Look at that house." They turned to take in the large white tent, the only edifice in the round world.

"I know," Panelli said. "Look at that wood; somebody cut that up." Unhidden in his voice were the first naked notes of pride, joyous and sobering. "That saw is wild."

But assembling the auger took the rest of the light. It was eight feet in length, one piece, two hundred pounds of stainless steel, new. Key couldn't remember seeing a new one before, and the shiny curved blade reminded him of the money behind such a project. The bit on the new tool was a wrong fit in the old tractor's drive, and the men wrestled with it past the golden smoky sunset. The tractor and the auger had been manufactured fifty years apart in different countries and Arthur Key had to re-rig the takeoff acceptor. It all would have taken another day had Darwin not had Key to stand and steady the huge device while he and Ronnie crawled up the power takeoff mechanism to hold it in line so they could secure it with Arthur's homemade cotter bolt. Arthur, with his arm around the steel auger like a lover, tapped the bolt through the upper brace with a small sledgehammer, each tap a smart steel snap. He told Ronnie, who by now was greasy to his elbows, "Sometimes engineering comes down to using a bigger hammer."

In the early dark, Darwin climbed into the Farmall seat and started the tractor. When he engaged the auxiliary switch and the takeoff clutch and the auger began to twirl, Ronnie Panelli called into the twilight already thick with bats and swallows risen from the canyon wall, "All right!"

It had been a day. They gathered their scattered tools, the pliers and the monkey wrench and all of the hammers and the oil can, and putting them away, the men retreated to the tent. They took another minute with the hissing gas lantern looking for discarded bolts and steel lock washers. They could feel on their shoulders and bare heads the unmeasured chill descending as if in netted sheets from space as darkness filled and doubled. There were still the army surplus cots to erect by flashlight. They had a brief discussion about the stove, the sum of which was that Ronnie wanted to take the hour it would require to install the stove tonight; his wood lay in a pile like a rich promise. While they reasoned, Darwin's old lantern glared and blinked from where it hung on the tent tether. But the older men prevailed by promising to do it in the morning and then by climbing in their bedrolls and being quiet, which left no argument but sleep.

The fourth day on the plateau at Rio Difficulto after drilling all ten of the foundation holes for the utility poles at forty-yard intervals from the ranch road to the encampment and grinding an inch off the leading edge of their new auger in the sand and clay and red sandstone, Darwin, Arthur Key and Ronnie Panelli put their tools away early in the afternoon and quit the site, headed for Mercy all three in the front of the old jeep, which made a cramped twenty-mile ride with Key's size and Panelli's injury.

Behind them six of the long brown posts stood loose in the ground, like the beginnings of a crazy fence for giants. They drove without speaking because there was nothing to say. Darwin had warned them that the doctor wouldn't be in Mercy, that he'd have to come out from Twin Falls, but there were a couple of EMTs and the clinic was well stocked with the kind of material they would need to remove the ragged pine splinter from Ronnie's shoulder.

Arthur Key didn't speak because he didn't want to say again, as he had when they set out on the clay road after every time they jostled, "Are you okay?" and have Ronnie lie in his strange voice, "Yeah."

And Ronnie Panelli didn't speak because his head kept going milky, and he thought he was going to die. The dirty foot-long spear of wood was right there, protruding from the top of his shoulder, both front and back, taking all his thoughts away, as he leaned forward, his head in his hands.

The sixth pole had slipped. The three men had drilled all the holes and cleaned them to seven feet, Ronnie on his belly in the dirt with the shovel as if he owned each one. Using the lift bucket on the Farmall tractor, they'd chained and hoisted the treated telephone poles one by one and levered them each into a socket. They were solid fits in the rigid earth and Darwin was pleased about how little cement they'd have to mix later. Art had rolled and muscled so many of the wooden timbers through the day, kicking the round poles over the chain, that Ronnie had also started acting like they weren't a thousand pounds. When the sixth pole rose to forty-five degrees, Ronnie had shouldered under it the way he'd seen Arthur do all day and then the heavy post stopped, suddenly biting into the side of the earthen hole and catching Ronnie. When it broke free, it took him to the ground like an insult, the big sliver nailing him there.

Now the jeep rode smoothly over the dirt-packed road. Deeply, quietly, in a room of his mind that he had closed and secured so well, once and for all, he had thought, Arthur Key was thinking it all over: the big things in his life, the things he could see from this distance, were certainly his fault, and he was trying to figure if this too was of his making. They had cut Ronnie's shirt off right after the pole had slipped and pinned him just long enough to gouge him this way, and Key could see the exit wound and the sharp bloody edges of the section of wood. It was high in the shoulder, but it looked serious. Darwin looked over at him and the look said simply that: This could be serious.

In half an hour they crossed the abandoned rail trestle which had carried tons of potatoes to the west coast during World War II, now clogged with the ebullient weeds of spring which sprang from every crack in the earth, and the little truck rose onto the paved section of G 17 known as Main Street in Mercy, Idaho, passing the green-garden lawn of the Mormon church and slowing through the patchwork of Mercy—even the unpainted ramshackle assemblage of Main Street sending Arthur Key a note of warning; he hadn't realized how much the remote encampment met his atavistic need for clear days free of anything at all like civilization. This old town seemed a hundred layers of ten thousand decisions, only a few of them even interesting.

Darwin began talking as soon as the town of Mercy came into view, looking like a cowlick at the alluvial edge of a vast farming plain, bordered along one side by the beginnings of the Mertz mountain range and the other by the river gorge.

He told them that with the exception of the scattering of homes that surrounded the little town, there were only two structures in Mercy still functioning as what they were originally erected: the pink brick L.D.S. ward house surrounded by its stunning green lawn, which exhibited a lush healthiness that ran counter to so much of the local landscaping; and the one-story flagstone medical and dental clinic at the other end of Main Street.

Everything else along the street had had at least two incarnations and now he cited them, talking because he could, because he wanted to flatten his own heartbeat, come out of the near panic. He liked this kid and he wanted Ronnie to be all right. He wanted him to be all right, and he was uncertain of everything. "The Sunrise Cafe," he said, pointing to the yellow sun painted on the window peeking over a giant cup of coffee. "It was the old drygoods. Here's Schindler's, which is our hardware. You'll be in there sometime certainly. It's in what was the old Trail Bank building." Darwin drove and pointed and talked as if he had an audience. "That First Security Bank was originally a hotel, the building was maybe the first in Mercy, and still the tallest with three stories. It's had maybe twenty names, and was The Little Sky when we moved to the ranch forty years ago. There's Gem Arts and Crafts where you can get stuff to make a scrapbook, like that, and it is in the lobby of the old Gem theater. There used to be a sign clear over the street, 'The Gem,' a big green arch which was nothing but a hazard. It finally got torn down by somebody towing a combine through town, oh, ten years ago."

Darwin saw Arthur Key looking across at him astonished at the speech and maybe worried, he couldn't tell, but he could not stop himself from talking. "And that's the video store in the old Mercy Restaurant which had been originally established by two families that dropped off from the Oregon Trail. And there, the Bradshaw Auto Parts in the defunct Liberty Bar, which closed in 1967 after two men were shot over a silver hatband or a hat, one; and the Antlers, the best place to eat in town still, which was once Baum Jewelry. One of the guys from the ranch is now the cook. When old man Baum ran his store, I bought my own wife a ruby pin there; it was something, a ship or a robin, some jewelry." He turned right into Arthur Key's gaze and said, "And the clinic. We are here. Everything is going to be all right."

Arriving in the gravel parking lot in front of the clinic, they pulled up aside one other car, a white Oldsmobile big as a boat. Panelli's eyes were glass, his face a luminous gray. He was conscious, but let Arthur Key carry him into the clinic. His wound was a classic radical puncture wound; there had been little bleeding, the wood dagger and stanch, friend and enemy at once.

Darwin had to get the receptionist to open the medical side of the clinic. They had interrupted her studies. Her desk was spread with the dozen pamphlets and worksheets for her real estate correspondence course. Key looked at her—a woman in a brown sweater who was probably thirty-two years old—from the distance from which he witnessed all the useless commerce of the world and he felt the dark open under him as she stood and came around the dreadful display of written material on the counter, her eyes on Ronnie's ashen face. Arthur Key hated this woman with unutterable force for that second and he clenched his jaw and held it. He hated her and he hated that he had become a man who looked at useless behavior as a capital crime. He wanted to clear her desk with his forearm, tear the entire installation from the room and hurl it through the dirty front window into the street. Key's vision dimmed and then he focused again on the room and followed the woman and Darwin down the hall to an examination room. Ronnie Panelli was now unconscious, his face a gray monochrome. The woman said something to Darwin and left the room.

"No way," Arthur Key said to Darwin, indicating the examination table. "I'll just hold him."

Before they could say anything else, a diminutive man in medical whites slipped into the room and opened one of Ronnie's eyes with a thumb. The man pulled the blood pressure collar off the wall and handed it to Darwin. "Put it there," he told him, pointing to Panelli's upper right arm. Then, to Arthur Key, he said, "Are you okay, holding him?"

"Yes."

The man was moving quickly and Key appreciated that. He felt the pulse and applied the stethoscope. Then he checked under the chin and behind the ears. "I don't see it," the short man said. "What happened? Wasn't it an explosion?" His bright blond hair ran thin and precious across his pink scalp. "Are you mining?"

"Utility pole," Darwin said. "Fell. Slipped."

"Good," the man said, reappraising the awful splinter. He touched the sharp end of the thing. "A treated pole. He's going to taste creosote for a week or two if we can wake him up." He stepped to the door and said, "Linda, get Randy over here."

The female voice came back, "I already called."

"When Randy rides in, we'll get this sliver out of the boy and send him back into battle. Put him here," he said patting the table, "and we'll warm him up."

"You're not the doctor," Key said, carefully adjusting Ronnie on the high table.

Now the man was setting up an IV stand. "No, I'm not," he said. "I'm Bob Freeman." He handed Art a blanket. "Let's get him comfortable. There's no doctor in Mercy. I'm the dentist. He didn't hurt his mouth, did he?"

The dentist Bob Freeman turned out to be all right. He had keys to the cabinets and he was careful giving Ronnie the tetanus shot. After they'd treated Ronnie for shock, elevating his feet and inserting the intravenous tube, Bob took Darwin back to the waiting room to do paperwork. He never looked at Key, marveled at his size, strength, any of it, and Arthur felt the muscles through his neck relax a measure. He felt absolutely claimed by the tiny rooms of the clinic, the white acoustic ceiling only inches above his head. He stood still by sheer pressure of will, finally relaxing his jaw and letting his arms descend along his sides. Panelli lay sideways on the table, slack, his face now two muted shades of blue. A moment later Bob Freeman came back into the room and asked him to step outside.

"It's superficial," Freeman told him. They were sitting on the railroad ties that lined the clinic's small patch of dead lawn. "I'm pretty sure it's a simple puncture and that none of the muscles are involved." The smaller man sat with his elbows on his knees and gestured with one hand. "Got a smoke?"

"You don't smoke," Arthur Key told him.

"Who's going to know, you?" Freeman smiled.

Arthur Key shook out one of his cigarettes. "The Mormon dentist has a cigarette."

"Hey, seize the day," Freeman said, setting the end of the

cigarette against Key's match. "I've got other virtues. Where you guys working?"

"South of here on the river."

"At Diff's place? Are they really doing that?"

"We're putting in the power poles. It's going to happen. Who's Diff?"

"Curtis Diff. That's all his from the Vernal Cliffs to the river. He's cattle and potatoes and some mining and everything else, I guess, even this deal with you guys out there, which he is just doing to piss everybody up here off. The town doesn't care for that man. He's too rich and he's too happy. You'll hear about it or have some visitors, I'm sure. Remember, Knievel did it years ago, that mess?" Freeman pointed. "That was way north at the narrow gorge." A yellow Subaru wagon pulled into the gravel parking lot of the clinic and a kid in a blue windbreaker got out with two large tackle boxes. "Hey, Bob," the kid said. He had a thick run of freckles that disappeared into the tremendous strand of red hair that grew down his forehead like a challenge.

"Hey, Randy. We got something ugly now. You got a bolt cutter?"

"We're ready," he said.

Arthur Key liked these men immediately. The young EMT was already in the building.

"Come on. I'm sure he'll have something for us to do."

Inside, Darwin was holding Panelli in a modified sitting position while the EMT tenderly worked the piece of wood that protruded from his shoulder in a small, slow circle. "This is from a telephone pole," he said to Darwin.

"We were setting poles."

"Entered here," the EMT said, pointing to Panelli's back.

"Yes."

"Nothing else?" he asked Bob.

"Just the puncture. Maybe shock."

And that seemed to be all the young redheaded man needed to know. He knelt and opened the huge medical boxes, their trays unfolding in four tiers. He selected the bolt cutters from one and fit it against the spear where it emerged from Ronnie's upper shoulder. He adjusted the bite. He handed a package of gauze to Bob Freeman, along with two bottles of disinfectant. "We've had our tetanus shot today," Randy said.

"Yes, we have," Bob said.

Randy lifted the bolt cutter again, placing the blades flush with Panelli's skin and closed the handles. There was a crunch as the wood was sheared away. Putting down the huge clippers, Randy grabbed the piece of wood from behind Panelli and pulled it. Nothing happened. Ronnie Panelli's head jostled. "Oh, shit," Randy said.

Arthur Key moved up and put his hand on Panelli's shoulder as if it were a gearshift knob and with the other hand he pulled the large splinter from Ronnie's flesh in one steady slow movement. Immediately Randy bent his eye to the wound, which then began to flush with blood.

"Clean?" Bob said.

"Clean enough," Randy said. "No muscles. He won't be able to lift this arm for a few days and he's going to be as blue as you get from here to here." Randy touched Panelli at the shoulder and the waist. "But he's still warm."

The dentist was now working at the wound front and back with gauze pads and disinfectant while Randy prepared two pressure bandages. Ronnie Panelli opened his eyes and closed them again. There was some pink below his chinbone.

Now with the boy on the table, Darwin moved back to the doorway. He could hear the hum of the fluorescent lights, and his heart was chugging. It was funny what shook you. Here he'd come back to the ranch, this world, for the money, but being in town opened it all again. When his wife Corina had died in January, he'd left this country for good and now he was back.

"You guys mining?" Randy said as he put away his gear and washed up.

"We're the crew putting power poles on Diff's ranch," Arthur Key said, looking at Darwin. "So he can raise hell with you guys."

"No problem," Randy said, already backing out. "Just don't drop any more and you'll all survive."

As the young EMT left, a girl of about ten or eleven appeared in the doorway wearing a dental bib. "Shauna," Bob Freeman said. "Good. We're all done here. Everybody's fine. We can get back in the chair now." He led her out, turning at the door. "You guys have fun out there. Call me if you chip a tooth."

Now Panelli's complexion had changed utterly, his face rosy and dark, and his eyes were open. He lay on his back. "It never hurt until now," he said to Darwin. "Now I can feel it."

"Good," Darwin said. "You're okay. Stay here and rest. Art and I are going to pick up a few things around town and we'll be back for you about six. Can you do that?"

Ronnie Panelli closed and opened his eyes a few times. "Yeah," he said. "I mean no. Don't leave me here. I'll go with you." He slid his right leg off the table, and when it fell, he lay back and closed his eyes. Darwin took Ronnie's foot and lifted his leg back onto the table and carefully untied his workboots. He put his hand on Ronnie's forehead and heard the boy's breathing as he slept.

It was outside that Arthur Key discovered he still had the sizable wooden splinter in his hand. He threw it into weeds beside the clinic.

"He's going to be all right," Darwin told him as they got in the jeep. "Let's get what we need, come back for him, have some supper in town, and get back to the site tonight."

"Fine by me," Key said.

Darwin turned back to town and drove toward the farmers' exchange. Darwin didn't know how to get to what was bothering the larger man; he was so obviously troubled. He'd seen other people hurt or had a hand in it, but now wasn't the time to speak about such things. There'd be time. "We had some injuries. There's always stuff on a ranch."

"What was the worst?" Arthur asked him.

"We had a man break his back," Darwin said. "He fell off a tractor. And we had a guy killed, but he was drunk coming back from town. I think the other guy was drunk too." He pulled the big truck parallel to the broken sidewalk, and the two men climbed down. They stepped up the steep curb on Main Street and went into the old bank building: Schindler's Mercantile.

The huge vaulted room was of some comfort, the broad neat aisles, the blond hardwood floor, the banks of new tools and parts, the balconies of nails and screws. Both Schindlers were at work today, the old man and his thirty-year-old son. The old man nodded at Darwin, and Arthur Key noted that the two knew each other. Their meeting was not loud or loaded with the high jocularity of men who see each other regularly through the work year, the way that he, Arthur, had known some of his jobbers in Los Angeles. He had always been in places like this, larger places really, warehouses of specific trades, huge auto parts sheds and plumbing supply depots and electrical houses where the aisles were wide enough for golf carts and where he was always greeted with the hale bravado of bullshit that workingmen exchanged. In Los Angeles County there were two hundred countermen at these places who knew his name. If he were to reappear tomorrow they would call out, "Oh, well, Key's back. Who said he fell in the well? How's it hanging, Arthur? And what are we up to today?" They'd seen his work in movies and would introduce him down the counter to the head of some contracting firm as the man who made the bridge fall down in that one film and balanced that semitrailer over a cliff in another. Entering those shops had been good, almost bracing, as his company started up and gained recognition.

Now he stood halfway back in the big sunny room full of general hardware, one hand on the huge spool of yellow nylon rope, pleased with its weave and manufacture, and he listened as the old hardware man Schindler and Darwin spoke quietly over the cash register. They seemed to him the picture of continuity and he imagined them for a second to be lifelong friends, something he would have wanted, but then he shook his head and saw it again: he was tired, stressed out from the deal with Ronnie, and his thoughts were nothing but some fatuous illusion.

He had a list in his pocket and he began assembling the items: wooden stakes; heavy twine; steel hinges; two hundred yards of the rope; a one-inch tempered steel drill bit; forty-yard-long dowels, diameter one inch; a basket of steel fittings; boxes of wood screws; bags of brads; a roof stapler and staples; five gallons of wood sealer; five gallons of white enamel; spray enamel, white, black, red; coarse-bristle paintbrushes; four paint rollers with extension handles; ten bags of posthole mix; five gallons of creosote; and a shopping cart of miscellaneous small tools, including chisels, a rasp and a fine Stanley wood plane.

In addition, he and Darwin ordered the lumber they needed, including twenty-four sheets of one-inch plywood, grade A, to be delivered in two days out of Boise. As the young Schindler packed Arthur Key's purchases into cartons, Darwin stood aside, assessing the equipment, smiling. Key saw the look and said, "Do it right the first time."

"I've got no problem with this," Darwin said. "Get what you want. They'll pay for it."

"I didn't see a transit," Key said to the young man.

"They're all out on jobs. We won't get one back until say August; they're monthly rentals."

"We're okay," Darwin said. "Do we need one?"

"Do you know the span?"

"Do we need to? We've got the drawings, what it says there."

Key turned to the older Schindler. "Who's here in the region? Surveyors? Isn't there a road crew?"

"They're paving up over the saddle to 71. They should be there all week."

Darwin said to Key, "I know where that is." He smiled at old Schindler and shook his hand. "I'm going to take my engineer here up there to borrow some equipment. We're doing this job right the first time."

"Diff will like that," Schindler said. "If it's going to be a mess, might as well be a royal mess. We'll get your lumber out by the first. Somebody will be there, won't they?"

"They will," Darwin said. "We live there now."

"Good news. Well, say hello to the old man from this old man."

"I'll do it," Darwin said.

"I'm glad you're back," Schindler said.

"I'm not back. I'm here for this project, but I'm not back."

It was twenty miles north to the saddle and they drove up behind the cluster of orange state vehicles just before five. The old road had been bladed into a sharp row of asphalt and dirt that dipped and rose two miles over the hill. There wasn't a man around. Idaho fell away from them in grassy dales to the purple edge of mountains on every side, and the sky was a thin wash of cumulous bright white in the angled sun. In the empty place Arthur felt the vacant rush of terror, the guilt he had known for what had happened in California. He was tired now and he'd spent what he didn't have getting through this day. He should have gone with Gary, his brother; he should have checked out the worksite; he should have stayed away from Alicia. He had gone where he couldn't see and there was only harm in it, and this loss of equilibrium.

Key had Darwin drive up beside the road grader and he could tell before putting his hand on the side that the machine was cold. "They quit early."

"It's a road crew." Behind Darwin the high plain of Idaho ran into the glimmering mirage of smoke and the mountains of Nevada south on the horizon. Over the rise, they found three men in gray parkas about to climb into separate state vans. Here there was a late-day breeze riding the contour of the broad bare hill and in the last sunlight it offered a general chill. The foreman was a young man named Clark LaRosa. He stepped toward them to shake hands, and Darwin was surprised to hear him call Art Key by name.

THREE

FIVE DAYS LATER, in a scattered cold wind that gusted all day, a dirty yellow road grader cut a first pass through the sage on the gray plateau of the new worksite, the ruined blade just grazing the primordial soil that had pressed there undisturbed since the gorge below was a storm-driven rivulet nosing its way south, hundreds of miles from the sea. The machine was old and used hard, rusted fully at every dent, the pale yellow state-guard paint oxidized everywhere else to a papery white. It too ran in fits, creeping and jerking, as the blade cut and pushed and then found only air for a second before the next bite of hillock or sage or the odd rock. The throaty roar of the vintage diesel was torn into sections like the black knots of exhaust and ripped away in the overcast bellows of the day. Ronnie Panelli drove the grader, sitting in the drafty cab and bouncing as the terrain dictated. He was paying attention. He'd bladed almost to the rocky canyon, inching the big wheels until he was ten feet from the edge and he could see the river glimmering in a string so far below, and then he'd set the blade as he'd been instructed by Arthur Key and powered forward, steering by the stakes they'd set in the dark early day. It was a quarter mile in a straight line to the farm road.

The wind was cold, no spring in it at all, no warm strand, and it gusted against the two men watching Panelli's work. Darwin and Arthur stood by the stacks of lumber, but there was no shelter. They could see Ronnie, chin up, craning to keep each stake in sight as he struggled with the oversize steering wheel. The young man had surprised them both by saying yes when Key asked if he wanted to drive it, blade the runway. The shoulder was sore, but Ronnie could raise his arm and there was color in his cheeks. His bouncing on the cracked leather seat played unevenly on the accelerator and the vehicle jerked and plunged as it shaved the sandy hillocks and tore at the clusters of sage.

Key watched, almost smiled, pleased that the kid was okay, and that the road grader, with a fresh oil change and the rusted radiator flushed, now ran without grinding or stalling. The state operator had lined Ronnie up yesterday afternoon: the clutch, the brake, the four gears and the blade angle and elevations. Now Darwin, keeping his hands both in his work jacket pockets, bumped Key with his elbow and nodded toward the tent. "Let's get a coffee," he said. "Ronnie will be all right."

The tent was warm, the stove pounding out heat, and Arthur Key threw his jacket on his cot and sat down beside it. The tent was tightly secured, though the sides bellied now, filling and falling with the steady late-winter wind. He pulled his notebook of drawings out of his kit box under the bed frame. Darwin swung the large blue enamel coffeepot over the two tin cups and poured. Arthur could see Darwin's face closed up; the day for some reason had claimed him. "My wife disliked the wind tremendously." Darwin, still in his coat, spoke quietly in a voice that Arthur had not heard before. "She grew up in a windy place in Sonora, summer and winter the air moved through their house, even with the doors closed. Her brothers as boys raced little paper boats along the floor. There were few trees in her town and those trees were bent always with the wind." Darwin put the coffeepot on the edge of the stove and sat on his cot. "At Diff's ranch in the early spring like this we'd have a full week of wind." He looked at Arthur and the larger man knew this was Darwin's news. "She'd get real quiet that week." Darwin set his cup carefully on the cooling deck of the stove and stepped from the tent. The canvas walls billowed and fell taut and then billowed. It was a comfort to hear the road grader laboring, the work nothing but six levels of engine noise. Arthur Key was not practiced at talking, except for the pragmatic discussions which had always steered and conducted his days. When to meet, what to bring, how to ready and where to start. The inventory and the schedule and the honest appraisal of what had been accomplished. But there was something about him now that needed another talk, needed it, and he knew it was not in his vocabulary. There had been times when he'd exchanged a glance with Darwin that, if it had held, would have led to the first sentence that Arthur Key had ever said. He wanted to tell his story to someone other than himself, and he could not.

The tent flap opened again, ripping with the day, and Darwin came back now with a shrug and his changed face, everything brought back to the moment. "This wind," he said. "Does the weather affect you, Arthur Key?"

Arthur Key had been preparing a sentence about Darwin's wife, a question, and it fled. He drank the milky coffee and said: "I like a good long day. Sometimes in Ohio, certain days in January and February could be short. I didn't care about the cold, but I was working for the city repairing vehicles, and I didn't care for it to get dark when I was halfway through something. Most of it was fieldwork, out on the street somewhere.

It'd be about noon and we'd see the lights in the houses going on. All that dark."

"Automotive repair," Darwin said.

"These were garbage trucks."

"A garbage truck is a complicated machine."

Key said, "I repaired their hydraulics."

"But now you've been in construction."

"That's right. We build things, structures and mechanical devices."

"The man yesterday said these things were in films."

Outside, the road grader thrummed and sighed, its roar muted in the wind. Arthur felt himself drawn again to the edge of what he wanted to talk about. "Most of the work is for the film companies. Somebody needs part of something in the picture, a fence or a dwelling. We never build a whole house."

"So you build one side."

"One side or a corner. Sometimes just a frame with a tile roof. Even with a barn it was only three sides. Wouldn't keep a horse in."

"Ohio," Darwin said.

"It's fine," Arthur said. "I grew up there. It was green and it was hilly where we lived. Not like this."

"There are hills in Idaho. Mountains, and plenty."

"Oh, I know."

"The main ranch is in a valley south of here. Our house was on a hill there." Darwin pointed downriver.

"How long did you live there?"

Now Darwin spoke again with a narrowed voice. "Fifty years."

"Your wife passed away. When was it?"

"January," Darwin said.

"And you left that place."

"I did. I have."

"I hope to get down there," Arthur Key said. "See it, meet your old boss."

The road crew had delivered the road grader yesterday afternoon, two men, one in a state vehicle, a white Ford 150, followed a while later by the high-riding grader as it crawled up the dusty farm road. They were through with their roadwork, and it would be parked until August. The man who knew Key was happy to loan it for a week. He had parked his truck and come over and talked about Diff's project, which was already half famous in the area. It was the state highway foreman, Clark LaRosa, and he had worked at the Santa Anita racetrack five years before when Arthur Key's company had done a project there. He and Key walked the length of the staked runway all the way from the gate to the lip of the great canyon. La Rosa's mustache was a gray plume, which jumped as he spoke.

"You guys are blading a road to nowhere," the man said. "Even when you finish building your monster ramp here, this is a road like nothing I've done." He had his hands in his pockets and he leaned and spit over the rock shelf. "It is strictly a one-way street." A few minutes later the big yellow machine lumbered into the yard, and the driver climbed down, a man in overalls that Clark introduced as Rudy. Rudy took a look at the material and equipment in the encampment and said, "Well, here's some stuff." Darwin furnished them each with a beer, and they stood around the raw wood table that Ronnie was building for the camp.

At the Santa Anita racetrack Arthur Key's company had constructed two horse barns that were to be blown over in the scene. Key remembered the project, of course, the light-duty hydraulic units he'd employed. "It was good stuff," Clark

LaRosa said to the other men standing around the table. Ronnie was mesmerized by the mustache; it made the man look judicial. "I mean these looked like old barns, the wood, the doors, the old paned windows. Walking by you'd think they were a hundred years old, but we'd seen them go up the week before."

"What'd they do?" Ronnie asked the man. "What were they for?"

Clark LaRosa put his beer on the plank tabletop, ran a finger along the bottom of his mustache and told the story using his hands. "It was a cool thing," he said. "I'm glad I saw it. The deal was for the storm to come through and these old barns, which were trouble anyway and were supposed to have been replaced by the wicked old track owners or something, were going to fall down, and horses were going to be injured, somebody's good horse in particular, I think."

"Whose horse was it?" Ronnie asked Key.

"Some horse," Key said. "Some boy's. No, it was a girl's horse."

"It was. There was a girl about twelve around there, braids and the like."

"So it fell on her horse?" Ronnie asked.

"Back up," Rudy said. "He made the thing to fall down? Clark, are we off the clock today?"

LaRosa nodded and Darwin handed Rudy another beer.

"Listen," the foreman continued. "They look like barns, old barns, we don't know. I'm keeping the track drained and dragged, and watching this through a couple of weeks. Then one day there's a major fuss. Twenty trucks and all the shit they can haul. Well, I've seen a movie company before, and we all go over, and these goddamn barns fall down like a house of cards." LaRosa lifted his hands to stop the story. "But they go over in slow motion while Mr. Key here walks the property, showing how it works to the bosses, the film guys. They can stop this at any time, and they do. It goes over halfway, stop. Another five feet, stop, like that until it's all on the ground in a ruin. Afterward"—here he lifted his forearm to the vertical— "they both go back up like a man standing up from a chair. Perfect: two barns again. It was something."

"They needed to get the horses out," Darwin said. He was smiling.

"That's right," Arthur said. "They film at different speeds. It's a trick."

"Some trick," LaRosa said. "They put it down and up twenty times in two days, and then they put some horses in there and let them run out while the thing went down, and later the girl came out and screamed for a while. I think they filmed the thing one night, I wasn't there. Then four days later, the whole program's packed up and gone, not a scrap of barnwood, not a nail. Bare ground. I'll never forget it."

"Was the girl okay?" Ronnie said. "Her horse?"

"You should do the same thing out here," LaRosa went on. "Make this deal so it unfolds piece by piece to the far side so somebody doesn't ride their motorbike into the little river. Thanks for the beer."

They shook hands. Rudy thanked them for the beer and climbed in the white state truck. Ronnie was already aboard the road grader, opening the door, sitting in the cab, working the elevation lever, the angle.

Now, in the billowing tent, Arthur opened his notebook on his lap and stared at his sketch of the ramp. He'd never drawn anything, even a portion of an entity, like it. He turned the book so Darwin could see the structure again. "We're going to cantilever it almost twenty feet." Arthur pointed to the substructure and where it anchored below in the cliff shelf. "We'll pour eight footings." He pointed them out in the overhead view. "And this upright frame will all be those eight-by-eights, or better, railroad ties. The cross members are four-by-eights." It was a beautiful drawing in three levels: the symmetrical square uprights, the grid frame for the platform, and the ramp deck itself reaching out over the void.

"How do we attach these?" Darwin pointed to the place underneath where the frame met the topdeck. "Does a man hang from a rope with one hand and a wrench? Is there some movie trick I don't see?"

"We'll figure that out," Arthur said. He was pleased that his new friend had pointed out the one problem in the schematic. "But until then, you should start working out. Practice hanging with one hand and driving home a carriage bolt with the other."

Key had not finished his sentence when the men felt an odd concussion. The tent rippled in the wind, but this shock ripped at the ground. Key thought immediately that it was the road grader's transmission tearing out. The two men pushed out into the raw day as the terrible noise exploded into the unmistakable scream of metal bending. There was a wrenching squawk like a bell gone wrong and then the grinding of the great old steel blade biting rock. It was a spectacular sight, the pale elongated machine run off the edge of the escarpment, rocking there in a weird balance, its front tires hanging into the ravine, the rear tires, motorbox, drivercab, and Ronnie Panelli tilted up, buoying almost a foot off the ground. The fulcrum here was the ruined blade, folded now under this new weight.

Art pushed Darwin toward their big flatbed, saying, "Get the truck." He ran to meet Ronnie, who now was out of the cab and seeing how to jump down. "Whoa, whoa," Key stopped him. "Wait a minute. Only jump if I say."

"My boot slipped on the brake pedal," Ronnie said.

"I know it did," Key said, climbing the rungs to stand by the young man. His added weight did not adjust the tilt. "I think it's pretty secure on that blade. And all the real weight is back here."

Darwin backed the big truck up to the block motorbox of the road grader and chained the come-along to the steel tow hook. He walked around to see the state of things. He yelled through the wind, "We can't drag it off of that. The blade's a stone-cold anchor."

With the two machines secured together, Key and Ronnie climbed down. The road grader sat nose down, wheels agoggle, but it had taken a hard high center which wasn't fragile in the least.

"Where's your camera, Ronnie?" Arthur Key said to the young man. "You'll want to show them this when you take your driving test."

"The pedals are slippery. My boots kept sliding off."

"The rubber covers for those pedals came off forty years ago. Don't worry about it," Key said, trying to shake the minor panic out of his throat. He stepped back a step and then another, measuring the problem. "We'll need to lever it up before we tow it back off that blade," he said. "You get hurt?"

"I thought I was going over," Ronnie said. "My foot slipped." He pulled at his pantleg and his right leg above the boot was barked four inches, bleeding. The wind ripped at his open jacket and he stood and after two tries zipped it shut.

"You hit your head?"

"No."

"Okay, we're good then. We're going to need two of those eight-by-eights and some two-by-fours as cross members. Let's clean up that leg a little and then get our hammers."

In the warm tent, out of the wind, Darwin knelt and swabbed Ronnie's shin with alcohol. "Okay?" he asked the boy.

Ronnie sat sober. "I'm okay."

"Hurt?"

"I'm fucking everything right up."

They heard Key call from outside: "Let's do this, boys."

They nailed a simple frame so the big timbers would stay parallel. They lodged the heavy wooden frame at forty-five degrees under the front of the machine, finally roping it in place. When the device was secure, Arthur Key looked at the entire plan: the truck, the chain, the road grader, the lever and the front wheels hung out in the windy canyon. "We're making up this tune as we go along."

The accident had cost them the day, and now they stopped and had a late lunch of rolled tortillas stuffed with cheddar cheese, shredded steak and the crisp green salsa that Darwin's wife had bottled. They ate it in the tent and went over the next part, when they would try to tow it all up over the blade and back onto its wheels. Key gestured to Darwin with his coffee cup. "I'll start it up and get it in neutral. When I signal, give her hell." Arthur turned to Ronnie, who hadn't eaten two bites and who sat on his cot looking cold and scolded as the tent caught the wind in pockets and the canvas bellied and fell. "You'll be on the back of the truck. If I come down and those wheels bite, snap the come-along free and you guys get out of the way."

Ronnie sat still. He'd put his plate on his bedding. "Ronnie," Arthur went on. "It was not your fault. I should have checked out those pedals. It wouldn't have been right for anybody. This machine should have been retired a long time ago." He got no response. "You scared?" He put his hand carefully on Ronnie's injured shoulder. "You did not go over the edge. We're in the warm tent drinking coffee. How's that shoulder? Come on, boy, this is the good part." Darwin did not show his smile. He stood and pushed out through the tent flap into the gray windy day.

Outside ten minutes later, Key checked the two jerry-rigged wooden timbers propped under the front of the trapped machine. He knew he was guessing at the angle. If it was too acute, the whole thing would act as a brake, stop the tow and possibly propel the old machine farther over the gorge. If it was too wide, it could simply slip and something he couldn't see would happen. He hated not being able to see it all. He hated operations where the cause-effect wasn't 99 percent. He'd broken in every crew and every crew member with that mantra: 99 percent certainty and also all of the possibilities in the last 1 percent. That was why he refused to be involved in active car stunts, fires or explosions. He'd worked one job where two cars pass in a one-car alley, and he had seen the producer wave off the variables and hope for the best. Arthur wanted to know the weight of the vehicles, establish their center of gravity, and if not, use chains or wire, but it was hurry and hope in the end and a crash that stopped work for a week. He hated not knowing.

In the cab of the worn road grader, Arthur swung the door open and secured the latch. The clutch and the brake pedals were small shiny steel ovals, the gas pedal was gone, just a rod. He marveled darkly that he had been willing to let Ronnie even handle this thing. It had been good for Key to have the boy, lining him up, teaching him this and that these days. It kept Key away from looking in or back, but now it had led him to this mistake. He pulled out the choke and adjusted the throttle. When he pushed the cracked starter button, the huge machine trembled and assumed a rheumy roar that shook it all and he could feel the back end floating around, but it started and coughed and the black smoke once again fled in the sharp wind. He adjusted the rpms and wrangled the old bent gearshift into neutral. He could see Darwin in the cab of the flatbed waiting. The truck was running and Ronnie stood on the bed with one hand on the cab watching it all.

Now Arthur Key pointed at Darwin and gave him the thumbs-up. The chain was taut. Darwin eased the clutch out and felt the weight pull at the rear of the truck, dragging it a full foot left, shaking Ronnie but not shaking him loose. Twelve feet of chain connected the vehicles. Then the flatbed truck found a purchase and they saw the grader come slowly back. The large wooden lever was binding, trenching in the clay, but the front wheels of the road machine began to rise. When the rear tires then came to earth, Key already had them in reverse and they pulled the timbers up to two o'clock, one, noon, where it all held for a strange second. Ronnie knelt and yanked the come-along open and it clattered into the sand as Darwin eased the truck forward, away, and up off the graded runway. Now Key punched it and the cocked frame of his machine lifted up, the front wheels now six feet off the ground and then backward and down, the wooden levers rolling back through eleven, ten, nine, and finally falling to the roadway where they were run over by the road grader, now on four wheels again, bouncing for a moment and then on four wheels for good, the blade hung down bent up almost double.

FOUR

DARWIN COULD COOK a breakfast fry like no one Arthur had ever seen. He was quick and quiet and before a person had his boots tied right, the sound and smell of bacon was in the morning air and then the skillet eggs with onions and ham, sometimes with the sharp cheddar he bought in the village in a big brick, and the thick fried bread, close to burned the way Darwin had learned the other two men liked it. Every day he fried a small pan of hash brown potatoes, lacing them with salsa from a mason jar he kept in the cooler. Ronnie didn't like the burned bread at first, and then when he tried the extra piece the first week, he took over as the king of burned bread, claiming to have invented it, holding out for the darkest piece, black and smoking under a stripe of the tub butter. There was coffee all morning and all day and into the night. They cooked on the tent stove until the days warmed a little and then the three-burner camp stove on its foldable legs in the open air. Beside the thing hung the two cook towels and on a hook, the big spatula.

"Can you weld?" Key asked Ronnie when he came out of

the tent. Ronnie had become an expert at many things in his short time on the plateau. He emerged from the tent like an expert and he eyed the sky every day first thing, wandering off with his bootlaces untied all the way to the fenceline before he stood and urinated like an expert. All the while he measured the sky, and by the time he'd turned and strode back to the campsite, he was ready to tell them what the weather would really be.

Today when he came back, he said, "I could probably weld. It's a torch, right?"

"What's the weather, Ronnie?" Darwin asked. He raised the spatula and made two passes over the three plates with both frying pans and breakfast was served.

"That wind has quit, at least," he said. "I think we're in for a gorgeous spring day here in the world," he said. "Chilly tonight, but we can get something done today."

"Today, we're going backward just a touch," Arthur told him.

Ronnie dunked his bread into the big mug of milky coffee. "How's that?"

"We're going to weld those bent blade struts, so that Idaho can go on with her roadwork." Key pointed his burned bread at where the old yellow road grader reclined in the bright sage like the rusted skeleton of a creature as primitive and forgotten as the isolated plateau. The big blade lay to one side.

"I cannot weld that," Ronnie said. "That's got to be the biggest thing I ever broke."

"Never in a car crash, racing away in one of your stolen Mustangs?"

"Never stole a car and never crashed one."

The sun cleared the first banks of eastern haze and shot the shadows of the men in antic relief out over the river canyon, printing their faces brightly in the day.

"Your past as an outlaw is less colorful every day. The leg-end is absolutely drying up," Key told him.

"It never once was colorful."

"Well, that sounds like the attitude of a person ready to learn to weld."

An hour later they had loaded the grader blade on the flatbed and chained it down for the trip to the machine shop at Diff's ranch. To load it, they had pulled one end in the bucket of their little tractor, and Key had braced the other as it ascended, his arms flexed. When it was up and almost clear on the truck bed, it had bound up. "Get away a minute," Arthur Key had in-structed Darwin, who had been helping him. "In case it goes down." Key had then shoved it up clear and the old steel sheet had clattered heavily onto the truck platform.

"Chain it down, Ronnie," Arthur told him. Darwin tore a flat piece out of a grocery bag and drew them a map with a carpenter pencil. Finally, Art asked him, "You're not coming?"

"Absolutely not. I left that place," Darwin told him. "You won't need me. The old man will be there or Roman will be in the shop or thereabouts."

The drive was a bit of a treat, up in the high truck, and Arthur Key handed the rough map to Ronnie, who was ex-cited to get out, see some new country. Ronnie opened and closed his fists, admiring his new calluses. "What is the deal with that guy?" he said. They bumped through the narrow gateway onto the ranch road, turning south. "He's locked up tighter than you, big man." Ronnie glanced to see if Arthur was offended. "Admit it, right? So weird. So fucking stiff. 'Ab-solutely not. I left that place.' Christ."

Arthur Key looked at the young man.

"You're not weird. I'm not saying you're weird. But you

guys." Ronnie put his elbow in the open window and felt his bicep with his left hand.

"His wife died."

Ronnie looked across at Arthur. "Well, I'm sorry for that, and I know that I don't really know what it means. What did it do, change every fucking thing?"

Arthur Key spread the torn brown map on the truck seat with his hand and saw the ranch turnoff was twelve miles. "Yes," he said. "It probably does."

After a minute, Ronnie said, "There's a lot of lifting." The truck drove the well-worn farm road and Ronnie could see the low billow of dust generated from the dual rear tires in their wake.

"There is," Key said. "You'll get big and strong and you won't be able to hide in the small places."

"Listen, you can let all that shit go. I know what you think of me."

"What do I think of you?"

"You don't care for reckless punks."

"That's true," Arthur Key said. He drove with his left wrist on the top of the steering wheel. "We'll see if that has anything to do with you."

"You were always big, like that—those muscles?"

Key looked at the young man. "Yeah, from when I was a kid."

"You married?"

"No, I'm not."

"Oh, the way you say that. The end. You guys are something." The day and the daylight and the wilderness here, the low brown hills, whose ravines were clogged with long triangles of the deep green piñon pine, made it possible for such talk.

"We are, are we?"

"Oh, fuck," Ronnie said. "What were you doing when you were my age?"

"I'm not sure I was your age. When I was nineteen I was repairing garbage trucks."

"In where? Dayton, did you say?"

The road dropped through a dry streambed and rose again to confront ten cows standing in the open road. Key slowed and eased up to the animals, who gave the truck no regard.

"What are they, wild?"

"Just get out and clap your hands."

"I'm not getting out. Honk the horn."

"Ronnie, move those cows."

The cattle did not step left or right.

"Go."

Ronnie opened his door and the nearest beast turned away. By the time Ronnie clapped his hands and came to the front of the vehicle, the small group had started and were walking along the farm track. Seeing them go, Ronnie followed behind calling, "Hey, let's go. Get out of the fucking way!" and slapping his hand along the side of his leg, and having some success he began to hurry them. They would not leave the road. Arthur Key watched the boy until the last cow hearing the slap too near turned back annoyed and stopped. Ronnie halted and made seven or eight little running steps backward, keeping his face on the animal and his hands out before him. The cow turned and they all slowly walked. Key switched off the truck and rubbed his eyes. The air was full of pine and mesquite here, and Arthur Key was not surprised that even now watching this kid with his first cows, his own heart hurt afresh.

He could get through this day; his past was his blindspot. The year he was twelve he had risen to six-three, and his shoulders had grown broader than his father's by the time he entered seventh grade in Dayton, Ohio. By high school he'd learned to speak last, tolerant of the kinds of introductions and commentary he received. He was the person that people felt they could come up to and put their hands on his shoulders. He played football because his father hoped he would, and he played extremely well, although with restraint. He'd never had a temper and those who tried to test him in this regard were met with diffidence and silence. His father worked for the city's many-faceted maintenance department, and he secured Arthur Key a job in the motor pool garage, where Art became a kind of apprentice mechanic, eventually being transferred up to a team that repaired garbage trucks. He had a head for math, trigonometry and calculus, and these things linked with his workings in the huge leverages of the damaged city vehicles made him a brilliant street engineer; that became his phrase to describe himself through high school. He was in his second semester at Auburn when his father died in an accident with an elevator.

Arthur dropped out and came home to help his mother square things up while his brother, Gary, graduated from high school. Every two weeks he had to find Gary at some kegger or other before the police came, and Arthur warned and scared his brother's buddies. He went back to the city maintenance sheds, and in the year he was there, he saw and invented a better compressor design for the trash haulers, one less likely to fail. In all of his workings, with his hands and his head, he began to see engineering as a kind of balance. Things wanted to balance; you could use lack of balance for energy of all types. It was a strange epiphany to have looking into the shelf compactor of a greasy garbage truck, but he saw a kind of universal field application which would fuel his future career.

Dayton wore on Arthur Key. His mother was well and only fifty years old, so when Gary matriculated at Antioch, headed for a major in communications, whatever that was, Arthur Key headed west. He had promised his mother to look after Gary, and he had. He had pulled the boy out of the wrong crowd and overseen his homework, and now that Gary had college, Arthur wanted more daylight. He was twenty years old.

In Denver, he took a great job with a bleacher company, Stadium Services, which set up temporary bleacher seating at festivals, fairs, parades, road races and civic functions. He worked with a crew of five other men on two trucks. He loved being outdoors in the larger weather, and he instantly went to the head of the class, selecting the setup sites, directing the overview before diving into the various duties of erecting the seats. Some of this work was on hard gradients or in remote places, and he was called on because he could see what each site required. They did seating installations throughout the West; some were weeklong jobs setting up a dozen units along a bicycle race and then moving them every other day along the mountain route. Some were two-day rodeos or bridge dedications. Arthur Key planned each job top to bottom, then plunged into the physical setup with a kind of joy actually—something right done well.

He lived in a single trailer in a park at the edge of Littleton by choice, paying his rent with maintenance work and banking his money away, five and then ten thousand dollars. The second June he was fired. He got into a famous fight with one of the firm's honchos while assembling three thousand seats in a semicircle on a windy plateau just outside the gates of the Air Force Academy. Key had arrived at the last second to take over, and the first thing he did after seeing the deluxe chair-backed aluminum bleachers was order the crew to disassemble what they'd done and double-brace the entire structure along the back frame. The cantilever was too much if the upper deck happened to be full while the lower shelves emptied—which was the case many times at events. His order meant that the crew would still be bolting the last section when the event began. The manager, a guy named Laird, was still on-site, hanging out in fact to meet the vice president. Laird blew up and stopped the work short. The crew looked up. Half the braces were in place. He told Arthur Key that he was fired and to get out. The larger man stepped to his boss and said quietly, "You're making a serious mistake. The balance in these last sections is not right." He looked along the bright line of seats as the dignitaries and their wives stepped up the assembly. His only inclination, and it rushed him like a blow, was to turn and go to his car. He hated chance and he hated accidents. He studied them: every mezzanine that collapsed in a hotel, all the failed domes and arches and roof spans of sports arenas and airplane hangars and department stores laden with snow, and construction site calamities, even some earthquake damage and overloaded ferryboats. It was rarely material failure; it was design and construction failure.

Arthur Key picked up his extended ratchet and crawled back under the seating and recommenced affixing the two-inch bolts. Two men joined him and they ignored the manager as he pointed at them to stop and yelled for them to stop and ordered them to and told them they were all fired and again to stop. It took half an hour for them to finish. They did not double-bolt any of the fittings as they planned, but Key knew one would suffice—if they had them all and not every other one.

Eight months later he was in Venice, California, doing bodywork and minor mechanical work for UPS when he heard of a job with a scaffolding company which subcontracted to Paramount. It wasn't long with that outfit before his ideas on-site were part of the program. He started being borrowed around informally, and he saw it for what it was: his chance. With his tools and a panel van, he began specialty work subsubcontracting one-of-a-kind jobs: creating and troubleshooting tricky setups. On his second job, he ran into one of the guys from

Colorado who told him that all the bolts in the back deck were bent ninety degrees the next day. Without the bolts, the whole thing would have gone over. He said the manager, Laird, had been canned on the spot. He said that during teardown they'd had to cut the bent bolts with a torch.

Ronnie was gone now, nothing in the ringing daylight except the hills, the trees, the truck and the dusty road ahead. Arthur grabbed a rag and cleaned the layered dirt from the cracked windshield, standing on the running board. He started the truck and crept in first gear along the tracked dirt road a quarter mile to where it bent following the gradual vale and then to the second turn and the third when he finally found Ronnie still driving the cattle, which were now in a single file, straight up the road. Arthur could hear the boy calling to his charges as he came up behind. Ronnie looked at Art and smiled, his shoulders saying, what is wrong here? Ronnie got in the truck. "Don't say it," he said.

When the truck came up behind now, the last cow stepped into the sage and suddenly they all did, scattering slowly to both sides.

"Seriously," Ronnie said. "Are they lost?"

At the turnoff for the ranch known as Rio Difficulto there was no huge log arch, but a small woodburned sign on a fencepost: DIFF. Arthur Key smiled: if this was the big ranch in a film, the gate would have been four tons and varnished. Two miles later the road, which wound in a generous serpentine between the humped brown hills, crossed an amber creek on a timber bridge which did not groan when they drove over. Key could see game trails zigzagging up the inclines. The valley became studded with old poplars and the men drove into the shade for the first time in the late morning. The creek now was beside them. "Smells good here," Ronnie said as the road opened into the ranch yard.

"Mr. Diff's estate," Arthur Key said. He had expected a big place, but this was more than a simple ranch site. The three-story main house was as big a log building as Key had ever seen. It sat on a fine red stone foundation and was circled by a wide covered porch.

"It's a town," Ronnie said. "Where are we now?"

"Darwin lived here."

Well behind the mainhouse on the southern hillside were three other log residences, each with a double garage. Clothes hung on a line behind one of these homes. Across the dooryard from the main house was a classic red barn, newly painted, halfway down. The aluminum extension ladder leaned up under the two-story eave. Arthur Key slowed his truck and two dogs came around the house, both big black Labs, one with a gray muzzle. He drove past the barn to a row of pale gray metal outbuildings and stopped finally in front of the cement apron of one with the large bay door open. Ronnie was taking the place in: the basketball court between two huge poplars on the far side, the three kids hauling at the tire swing under the trees, near where the narrow stream ran, the corral beyond that and the six horses there, and at the end of the lane, the little brownstone building whose roof was generally collapsed. Next to it was a large garden plot in full leaf. Arthur could see the bladed gravel runway beyond that and a windsock drooping on its pole.

As soon as Ronnie had stepped down, the two dogs found him from the back and he climbed up again into the vehicle. Then they drifted smoothly around the truck and each put a nose into one of Arthur Key's palms as he bent to greet them. Key admired the way the ranch was set in the shallow valley, protected by the grassy sage slopes but affording plenty of light. A hundred years ago somebody had stood here and made some good decisions.

The big dogs were affectionate. He could see they were father and son. Ronnie came down and watched Key handle and talk to the animals. "These are good guys," Key told Ronnie.

"I can see that."

"Come on over. Your troubles with dogs are long gone. You're not going to steal anything, are you?"

"Shut up."

Ronnie was approaching, tentatively, stopping short and holding his hands on his shoulders as either of the black dogs turned to him. Finally the animals saw they had him and worked their noses along his legs while he stood frozen before them. Arthur Key watched a man with a hammer emerge from beside the little stone building at the top of the ranch yard. He'd been parsing a pile of charred timber there, and his overalls were blasted with soot.

"Greetings!" he said.

"What are you digging for?" Arthur asked him.

The man's smile was magnified and he said with pleasure, "Today, it's the Lord's work. I'm peeling the old steel truss braces off the burned chapel roof."

"You're going to use them again?" Key asked. "They aren't cooked?"

"These are old World War One pieces, heavy gauge, probably the first steel braces ever used." He held up a blackened steel piece. "They go a pound each."

"Was it lightning?"

"It was."

The man patted his legs and the dogs relented, leaving Ronnie a statue, and they came around and lay under the truck. "Idaho gets more lightning than anyplace I know of," Ronnie said. "It's a place that wants to strike you dead. The sky won't quit."

The man set his hammer and the burned rafter brace on the flatbed truck and said, "Now you broke something." He peered under the bent supports of the grader blade. "And it looks like a bona fide antique. What'd you hit?"

Key stepped over and snapped open both come-alongs. He grabbed the big blade in one hand and pulled it around so they were looking at the bent attachment bars. "Can we cut here and brace this with some angle iron?"

"That's exactly what we'll do." The man smiled at Key. "You all are Darwin's guys, aren't you?"

"We are," Key said. "And you are Mr. Roman Griffith."

Griffith shook his hand. "And happy about it." He reached for Ronnie's hand. "Howdy, son. Those dogs won't bite you. And there'll be no lightning today. Can you weld?"

Using a rolling engine crane, they unloaded the broken metal part and laid it on the painted cement floor in the roomy repair shed. The place was impressive, and Key took it in: the tool cabinets, the bins of parts, the small paint booth. Roman Griffith was set up to do some work.

"Darwin wouldn't come over, would he?" Roman Griffith said.

"He's got a day," Key told the man.

"Let's cut these absolutely off and make something up," Griffith said, tapping the ruined steel tubes. "It's simple and it'll work." He went to the wall and wheeled over the cart with the cutting torch apparatus. He sparked the torch and knelt above the bent blade supports. The flame bloomed and then he touched it down to a blue blade and applied it to the old steel. In a moment the cut was established and he ran the torch around the perimeter of the first upright. When it clattered to the floor, he stood and handed the live torch to Ronnie. "Is this the man?" he said.

"He's ready," Key said. "It is a torch after all, Ronnie. At least to start."

Ronnie knelt and hesitated. Arthur Key took his hand and guided the torch to the second support. When the metal glowed and the cut began, Key stood and said, "Keep it straight. Go slow." Ronnie was rapt in the work, cautious, and he took his time following the melting line. After a minute, he stood and lifted the welding hood he'd been given.

"You better finish," he told Roman. "So we don't have to do it twice."

"You're on it," Griffith said. "Cut that last side."

Ronnie applied the torch again and reopened the cut. The bar fell away neatly a moment later. When he stood this time, he said, "We're welding."

"We're cutting," Griffith said, thrusting the hot bars into a metal bucket of water. "We'll weld by and by."

Key was at the bin of scrap metal, sorting through the odd bits, rebar and tubing. Griffith joined him, and they found four heavy angle bars and brought them over. "We're making a four-star strut for this one-star grader," Key said.

"Ain't that the way with government work," Griffith said. He quickly laid the bars on the cement and struck a tack with the torch at the top and the bottom, making a tube. Pouring water over the spot welds, he picked up the tube and placed it against the fitting on the blade where it measured just right. He tacked the other bar together.

"Run a bead right down this seam," Griffith told him. "When the rod starts to melt, keep moving slowly, pushing back the bead every inch. Like this." Griffith snapped his own hood forward and knelt to the work. The bead melted into the seam like putty. In a minute, the welder stood up and lifted open his hood. "It don't have to be perfect. It just has to be strong enough to blade the nasty roads of Idaho for another fifty years."

"Don't touch any of it, even with those gloves, Ronnie," Key told his friend.

Ronnie knelt and stabbed at the starting place until Arthur Key finally braced his arms and brought the welding rod into the flame.

"Can you see it now?" Key said.

"I'm good," Ronnie said back, muffled through the welding hood. And he was good, if slow. The bead wandered but he filled the gap steadily until one side was closed and ready. Using a pair of vise grips, Roman Griffith picked up the hot metal piece and turned it over so Ronnie could start on the second joint.

"Run that joint," Roman told him. "And then go ahead and weld that second unit right here." He pointed to the other angle irons. "Use the clamps. If you get in trouble throw this bucket of water on the whole deal. We'll be back in twenty minutes."

Roman stood and he and Arthur Key watched the young man reassume a stance over the metalwork and begin to weld. Ronnie was slow and sure, bumping back the bead as it filled the crevice.

Griffith nodded at Key and led him out of the work shed into the brimming Idaho sunlight. "You guys are having fun over there with Diff's project. That kid's a fast study."

"We're all right. It's something to do this summer."

Griffith caught that remark and appraised the larger man. "Oh, and you didn't have anything going on?" He led Key around the metal building to an old golfcart, which they boarded.

"I was free," Key told him.

"Nobody's free," Griffith said. "I've got ten things doing and I'm a peon."

Key wasn't up to it. He wasn't going to fence and fend with this good craftsman. "Darwin was a friend of yours."

"Was. Is." The low open vehicle wheeled through the ranch dooryard and Griffith conducted it up a gravel two-track past one ranchhouse and then past another where the road ended in a cul-de-sac. "My friend Darwin lived in that last house and this patch here was his wife's garden. It's still his house if he wants it." Griffith pulled himself out onto the ground. "Come on." He led Key up a narrow deer trail through the flourishing bunchgrass to a hillock overlooking the ranch in general. There was a short black iron fence around the grave. "This is her."

Key could read the stone: CORINA GALLEGOS 1933–2000.

"It happened in a goddamn minute. She cooked us all, twenty-six folks, a New Year's brunch—Diff had flown in all this stuff from La Paz, swordfish and fresh tuna and big old crabs—and Corina made a jumbalaya or some such, good good stuff, and she laughed in the faces of those of us who were pale and hungover, god it was the last one of a hundred good times here. That's the kind of outfit this is. For that party there was six airplanes. Diff is a generous guy. Then here's what happened."

Roman Griffith leaned on the iron fence that marked the grave. "A week after the party Corina's mother died in Albuquerque and Diff dropped it all and flew her down there in his twin-engine plane. He uses a pilot most times, a guy from Burley, but he flew her himself. He knows what to do. The old woman had been eighty-eight. It was on the way back, right out here, that they came into the wind." Roman leaned back and pointed out to the runway. "It was a warm day in January, no snow. The wind came across and wanted to put the plane on a wing, and they bumped and she hit her head on the side of the glass and Diff looked like he'd broke his nose, but it was just blood. She was all, no problem, no problem, and then didn't feel good two days, headache and dizzy, and finally Darwin decided to drive her to the doctor in Twin, and she died in the car, some brain injury. We went up there right away. I drove because Diff was a wildman, but Darwin was stone by then and would not come back to this place.

"She was a woman like no other and the heart of this goddamn place, the mother of this good ranch. Darwin wasn't going to stay. Diff argued with him, got drunk and made hell and
back out of one night. They had some words, and Darwin said
some hard words about God in heaven, like that, hard news it
was, just shit and shit and fuckall and Diff was drunk and
screaming. But no way. He still wants Darwin back." Griffith
looked at Key. "We all do. There's a hole here and everybody
knows it. He was a fine foreman. But no. He come down and
shook my hand and said nothing. Winter. He went up to Idaho
Falls to see his boy, and then this spring Diff came up with this
bullshit on the mesa, though I heard he's making one ton of
money from the movie people, or television, one. Diff is doing
this to try to get his best friend back, but I don't see how that
works."

Arthur Key had not been to a graveside since standing near
his brother's and he had found his balance on both feet, his
hands clasped together in front. It was a beautiful gravesite
with the black iron fence and the grasses on the sloping hills.
The ranch yard below was like a drawing by a child, roomy
and elemental.

"Did you weld this grate?"

"I did."

"I appreciate your bringing me up here."

Roman led Key back to the golfcart. "You've been down
there awhile now. I know for a fact that Darwin is a friend of
yours. Every man is. I thought you'd like to know about him.
He's making a mistake to go up to Idaho Falls, but I guess he's
got to."

They drove back down the easy road now, and Arthur Key
looked at Darwin's house, the porch overlooking the ranch,
the weathervane on the chimney a blue heron in flight. When
they reached the dooryard, Ronnie had already laid out the
blade and the new supports for the final welding. He'd used

sisal rope to snug it all taut while he ran a bead. There was a loop of burned rope on the floor nearby and splashes of water covered the cement. The two black dogs now lay inside the doorway in the shade watching him. "It's a smart cookie," Griffith said. The two men watched Ronnie as he knelt and moved with confidence over the last two steel fixtures.

"When you finish blading your big important road," Griffith told Key, pointing to the damaged stone building at the head of the ranch yard, "come back out here and help me paint this barn and put a new roof on that old chapel."

THE MEN SPENT TIME every day at the cliff's edge, alone
and sometimes together, looking into the sky, a great
deal of which seemed there to be below them. There
wasn't a clean precipice but a short step down and then another out onto the flat top of the sandstone column that served
as a corner for this portion of the ancient tableland. It was the
size of a room and would be where the men would erect the
motorcycle ramp at the plateau on the ranch Rio Difficulto.
The red stone was scarred freshly where Ronnie had backed
the old road grader. At the edge of this pocked stone, out of
which tiny sage and miscellaneous tenacious brush grew, there
was a shambling rocky declivity at eighty degrees for another
hundred yards and then a clear line straight down to the river.
In the morning, the gorge was in shadow, purple, black and
scarlet, and the unlimited air from the sandy shelf seemed
pulled into the yawning open space. All afternoon as the deep
cliffside fell under the direct sun and baked, the draft shifted
and pooled out of the canyon in thermal plumes, lifting the

hair of whoever sat on that last rock and drank his coffee or pulled the burrs from his socks.

It was on this red stone bench that Darwin found Arthur Key every breaking morning. They fell into a pattern in their days wherein after dinner in the twilight, while Key and Panelli located and secured the tools, the older man would set up the coffee in their large enamel pot and place it on the propane stove out on the cookbench. There was at that time in the day always the washkettle on the stove, the water warm enough to be ladled into the men's washcloths, and they washed their faces this way and scrubbed behind their ears with pleasure before going to bed. In the tent lodge, they undressed in the dark and climbed into their sleeping bags on the cots. They did not talk beyond a question or two about the next day's labors or what day it was exactly, the number and the name, though Wednesday was the same as Thursday in such a place.

Panelli slept first, his breath marching away smoothly, though he dreamed and twisted in the nights, and more than once in their season on the plateau, Key stepped from his cot and took Ronnie's shoulder until the young man shuddered still and slept again. Darwin was silent on his cot, and Arthur Key could feel the pressure for a while as if his friend wanted to speak, let the things unsettled take words, and even without the discussions Key sensed Darwin's grief and his anger over his lost wife. Darwin had used them to create a steely edge in himself which he wore like a new thing, something not quite the right size, too small and too big at the same time. Key was never sure if Darwin slept or not, though he hoped he did. There were nights when he knew the other man went barefoot out of the tent at the hour of two or three, and Arthur Key never followed him. He hoped Darwin's mind was not full of unbidden moments that just appeared in ragged intervals but never became a story, just flashes that flared until he could see them and try by force to close down. Key lay in the lodge tent on his cot and rode through his mistakes every night.

A few minutes after five every morning, Arthur Key carried his boots and his lined jacket into the cold new day and turned on the propane stove. While the coffee rose to percolate, he sat on another of the many milk crates and shook his shoes and socks, and he put on his footgear. The men were wearing their socks two and three days in a row, and he had gone over footcare with Panelli. They left the foot powder on a shelf under the stove. In the cold, with a blue line along the eastern mountains and the dark sky still brimming with the tilted starwheels, Key tried to keep his mind empty.

He couldn't do it, and he was disappointed in his will. He could not prevent the same mental loop from beginning. It wasn't memory and it wasn't logic. It was a sickening series of gray moments and faces, many of them his brother and his sister-in-law, Alicia, and before he had poured his coffee from the steaming pot in the dark and tossed in a tablespoon of powdered creamer, he was affected, sick. There were times when he thought, I should just make a list and burn it to see if that would work.

He would have written his last conversation with his brother, and that he did not go with Gary and pull him from harm, and he would have written down the whole afternoon as it broke. He remembered Dayton making the calls at midnight twenty years ago, waking people until he found out where the party was, and he remembered having traveled there, apartments, and once on a golf course, places he was not welcome, and goddamn fighting with Gary, who was drunk and shining, even lifting him up like an animal and carting him home while Gary's coterie of friends watched and made disparaging remarks, though not ever very loud. Key knew that he'd been a better man then, but it was no help.

And he knew he would have written the night he met Alicia, years ago, when he hauled Gary, drunk and fighting him, from the blue twilight of a wedding reception. The party was breaking up and Gary spun and shouted, No, Art, I'm okay, these people are my people. He had the neck of a bottle of champagne in his hand and there were grass stains already on the knees of his seersucker trousers. Arthur pried the bottle from his brother's hand and it was as if it had been holding him up for he collapsed and vomited on the parquet dance floor. Arthur carried him to the car and felt someone beside him, the girl, and when he laid Gary in the backseat she got in the front. She was the only young woman with glasses at the event. I'm Alicia, she said. Later, after he'd put Gary to bed and come back down in his mother's house, Arthur Key found Alicia in the kitchen having tea with his mother. Arthur made the same excuses for Gary; he does love a party. He looked at Alicia and said, "We both love him."

She was young but what she said sounded weary: "We both drive him home."

Arthur drove her back to her car at the country club and she came around to his window in the dark. She said, "Will he get better do you think?"

He knew what she was asking, but he said, "He'll be better by noon." Her touch on his arm at that moment stayed with him. He was alone and determined and he wanted to find a way out of Ohio.

But he made no list, just let it all live in him. He stood with the heaviness and walked in his work boots over to the rocky apron of the mesa.

He wanted a way to abandon his thoughts, even for a few days, enough for a deep breath, but he was aware that he could not. They arose and he was no better for them. They arose every day. He was glad to move, to walk, but they arose every day. At times when the labor was demanding and continual, as when they dug the many footings for the bleachers, his thoughts disappeared and the work was everything.

When Gary and his wife Alicia had come to Southern California, Arthur knew it wasn't great news. Gary had folded many tents, staying with one public relations company for almost four years; that was his record. He was what? Too young. He knew how to measure his drinking so it seemed charmed to his acquaintances. He was an incredibly personal guy whose charisma would last for a year and by then most times he had earned a place in the group. What he was great at was prepared public speaking, a talking head on filmstrips and the like. He'd go to the top of the class on his popularity, and then Gary would coast for a year and then he would founder. He loved the new jobs. If it was new, he could do it and when it fell to the details, the day-to-day, the troubles would start. Arthur had taken many of the phone calls. Gary, he was jocular and acerbic, laughing at the assholes he was working with or whom he had just quit. He had a dramatic gift and laughed through the stories, describing the faces and offering what he said and what they said in return, and then what he said as the parting shot.

Gary and Alicia took an apartment in Santa Monica, and Arthur got Gary lined up as a sales representative with one of the hardware suppliers he knew. Alicia found a slot teaching theater at a private dayschool. They all spent a lot of time together, and at first Arthur tried honestly to get them to reconsider the move. Los Angeles was expensive and no place really to start a family. But it was another new stage for Gary. He bought a small white Chrysler convertible and started making calls. He and Alicia would come by and Gary would always say, "We've got to get you a woman."

Arthur Key was furiously busy running two crews. His company, Good Measure, did all kinds of field projects for the film studios, but he had become the expert on extreme vehicle positioning, and because his safety record was exactly 100 percent, the contracts he took on were all big tickets. Executives knew they could save a hundred thousand dollars in emergency insurance by using Key, and he prospered. He drew the line at crashes, explosions and fires. "You can burn it up when I'm done," he was famous for saying. "I'll make it look like it's about to fall or that it has fallen, but no fires during our contract. Not even a small one while my men are on the site."

He had begun his career in Los Angeles as a freelance grip, and by the end of the second week, he had work for months. Art was a man who could immediately assess the problem, inventory the materials and line men up. In a world of laborers who stood back chewing their gum, he was a standout. Soon opportunities for independent projects came his way. For months he built parts of things that appeared in the frame, and his ability to conceive of what the frame was surprised the directors and producers. He bought the little warehouse he was leasing in South Venice, near the waterfront, and he tore out the walls in the second floor which had been a warren of plasterboard offices, one of which he'd lived in for a year. There he made himself a loft with windows on three sides. The great pleasure in this was making a roomy workspace along one bank of windows, and he was at those drawing tables and computers late into the night.

His days in Los Angeles were dear days, the mornings he went to the current worksite, whatever film it might be, and met with his foreman Harry Burdett and his four-person field team, offering help if they needed it. Twice a week, he had lunch with producers, either at their studios or out in town,

and he listened to their hopes to put a yacht in an office building for a comedy or have two houses move closer together,
yard by yard, in a thriller. Then he spent the afternoon at his
favorite thing: back in the shop he built the devices of his own
design, and he felt only blessed by having great bins of levers
and pulleys and rope and chains, and an entire wall of utility
goods of all sorts, including hinges and springs and hardwood
dowels and steel rods. Some days he welded with his crew or
built frames from lumber. He employed nine people in all, including two women (one the best welder he'd ever met), and
he liked moving among the craftsmen and watching things
come together. They tested everything before it went out in the
red Good Measure trucks.

Alicia and Gary came down to Arthur Key's loft two and
then three nights a week, carting a take-out dinner and bottles
of wine, and Arthur felt obligated to spend time with them.
Gary wanted to get into film, and he saw Arthur as the way.
He started showing up on job sites, and at first Art would walk
him through the plan, how they were going to hang the tractor
trailer over a bridge, where they would run the chains and
hide the counterweights. Gary's head was always scanning the
areas for the actors or stuntmen or director. He got to know
Arthur's foremen and talked his way close to the action even
when Arthur wasn't there.

The difference between the two brothers was marked. Gary
was ebullient, personable. He immediately upon arriving in
California started wearing open-throated silk shirts with a small
silver chain. He wore linen trousers and expensive loafers.
He looked the part. Arthur was quiet. He wore chambray work
shirts even after hours and ankle-high workboots with khakis.
He spoke, if he spoke, second. He did not go to parties.

His brother, frankly, made him nervous. When Alicia and
Gary would bring a woman with them to his place, a friend of
a friend, somebody for Arthur to meet, it was terrible. The

women would come because Gary would have talked them into it, and Arthur told him to stop it. He explained that he had his work and that next fall he'd meet a woman, certainly, or next spring, and he'd take company. He folded his hands together over his plate and said, "Women are everywhere. I've seen them. You'll be the first to meet her." He was trying to be jocular but it came out like a homily. The night he made that little speech, Alicia had come back from the car for something she'd forgotten though there was nothing, and she came straight to Arthur, pushing him into his kitchen, where she took his elbows and she said, "Don't you do that." Then with her face serious and close, she said the rest: "I want to be that woman."

He shook it off, but a few months later Arthur steered a weeklong project to the little theater at Alicia's school, supplying a dozen huge corny flats for scenes in a film that took place in a high school theater. These figures were all monstrous animal silhouettes, a ten-foot duck, a car-size alligator, a camel, and as Arthur was installing them in the fly, Alicia came down and asked if the theater could keep them when the shoot was finished.

"It would be a nice donation, just the materials," she said.

Arthur was helping one of his crew adjust the chain clips to the support on the huge rabbit. He stopped and looked at her, a blond-haired woman in Clark Kent glasses and a maroon cardigan in the air-conditioned theater. He pointed to the director, who was halfway back in the auditorium. "See that man right there." She started to go, and he added, "Tell him it's okay by me."

The director was pleased not to have them hauled back to his property lot. They were already budgeted out. The following weekend, Arthur met Alicia at the school, and working alone, he rehung the flats in the spaces where she wanted them. "It's going to be a hell of a play when you finally use these," he said, walking around the colorful figures where they lay on the stage. He separated and hooked the chains in pairs to the steel grommets in the animals. "This duck is going to stop the show."

Early in the afternoon, he'd lifted each creature into the fly, except a sitting bear which now filled the back of the stage like King Kong, his head cocked as if listening to something. Arthur Key climbed down the ladder and found he was alone in the dark theater. Then he heard the side door open and Alicia came in with two white paper bags. He hadn't realized she'd been gone. They sat on the stage apron and ate croissant sandwiches and potato salad on paper plates. She'd brought a thermos of milky coffee and they drank that out of the same red plastic cup. This was the first time they'd been alone and Arthur felt at sea, undermined, lit. Lunch with a pretty woman. He didn't notice she was nervous, because he was nervous.

Two weeks later, she took him to a late thank-you lunch, though he told her it wasn't necessary. It wasn't like him to have a lunch that wasn't business. They were at the Dockside in Venice alone on the terrace in an imperceptible light rain, a mist. He liked that she preferred being out along the rail like this instead of inside the café, out of the weather. He liked the way she dressed in her long-sleeved white blouses and silk vests, her shirtwaist dresses, her glasses. She had become the soft edge of his long days. He hadn't touched her. Below them in the gray day, a big crew was trying to film a commercial on the front of one of the yachts. It was slow going. A girl came out in a black bikini and lay on the huge white deck while they worked the lights left to right, then a grip brought her a blanket, and everybody waited while they did the lights again one, two, three. They could see a man in a white dinner jacket inside the cabin on a cell phone.

"What do you think they're advertising?" he asked Alicia.

"It's not the boat and it's not the bikini," she said. "That guy's got some serious hair cream, but so far, the only thing I would buy is that blanket."

He smiled. The girl on the boat lay still as a mummy, clearly unhappy. "It does look good."

Alicia was looking at him now, and very quietly she put down her fork and stood and so he stood, a question still on his face. Their Caesar salads were only just begun. Arthur Key dropped some money on the table and followed her around the wet decking to the half-empty parking lot of the Dockside. He knew that every step was over the line, north of north. At his truck he helped her with her door, but she stepped back and they kissed for the first time. Arthur Key was aware of himself as sharply as he had ever been, his body in a truck. He had felt his affection for the young woman blooming for the year he'd known her. He liked her delicate voice and her precise diction and the way she paused sometimes before she spoke. They drove to the apartment where she lived with Gary on a hillside with a wide view of the trees and rooftops as they trailed away toward UCLA and downtown. They didn't speak. She was flushed, and he flooded with gratitude when she got out of the truck and shut the door carefully. The rain was light and even and as she looked at him through the window, he saw the water gather on her face. Then she walked around the truck and he lowered his window so she could put her hand on his arm, just that, before she turned and went inside.

I T TOOK ALL OF A MORNING to reassemble the Idaho state road grader, and Ronnie and Arthur Key struggled in the cool shade under the rough machine, dragging the blade with its new supports in the dirt. Ronnie held the two big wrenches while Arthur angled the blade up, aligning the braces. When he saw that their improvised repair would fit perfectly, Arthur hooted once sharply, and Darwin looked over at the two men from where he was putting the kitchen galley away. In the high-contrast light with the vast world beyond them across the canyon, they looked like two men in the belly of an insect. He saw Ronnie hand Arthur the big steel crescent wrench.

When they crawled out, Arthur climbed aboard and started the rumbling vehicle and fed the fuel down until it ran without fighting. The black diesel exhaust rose and then stood in plumes visible for minutes, an inky staccato punctuation in the blue sky. Ronnie and Darwin could see him manipulating the blade up and down and then angling it left and right, forward and back.

Then the grader roared and rolled back through the campsite out to where Arthur parked it by the barbed-wire fence.

Darwin had poured some more coffee for the three of them and set the cups uneasily on the tailgate of the jeep, amid the dried overlapping maps of spilled coffee there. "Ronnie," he said. "Let's build a table, shall we?"

Drinking the coffee, they talked about the project. Ronnie wanted to go get the lumber and start nailing things together. Darwin asked him what his plan was, and Arthur Key drew a couple of sketches.

"It's a table," Ronnie said. "I've got it covered. I know what to do. You guys go ahead and start that camera platform." He grabbed the circular saw from the toolbox, pointed at Arthur and added, "Safety first."

The table took all day. Ronnie had cut six six-foot planks for the top in twenty minutes and then, after walking around the parts for half an hour, went to Arthur and asked a few questions. Art lined him up with the pine one-by-two connecting braces and a design for the legs, two sturdy X's which would require forty-five-degree cuts and a connecting bolt. Late in the day, with the solid tabletop upside down on the earth and the legs starting to take shape, Ronnie got a little proud of it and he walked around the assembly with the power drill and a pocket full of a hundred drywall screws. Just before Darwin quit the small platform that he and Arthur were building on the canyon rim and walked across the campsite to cook, Ronnie put his drill in the box and went back and lifted the edge of his wooden creation into the evening air, tipping it right side up onto its legs. He was brushing the dirt off when Arthur came across the yard. They carried it over near the tent and set it down and then moved it again, right between the tent and Darwin's cookstation. Ronnie boosted himself up and sat on it, swinging his workboots in the last light.

Later that night when they'd sat down to eat Darwin's elk stew, Arthur accused him of trying to make a monument.

"You want me to make a table that's going to spill the soup?" Ronnie answered.

Arthur watched the younger man eat for a moment and then said, "This is a hell of a first table for a carpenter like yourself."

"It's a stable table," Darwin said. "We could use it to work on an engine if we founder."

"It is a damn good table," Key said, fingering the indentations where Ronnie has used three screws at each joint. "Are there any screws left?"

They ate in the spring twilight, their bowls steaming into the air. Finally Arthur Key said that night, "It is your first table and a fine job. I'm going to put my elbows on it." And he did. "You'll be a while before you out-table this deal."

A moment later, wiping his bowl with a section of the rye bread that Darwin supplied, Ronnie said without looking up, "I could paint it tomorrow if you guys wanted me to."

The troughs for the footings were shallow and the cement pads themselves would be the size of stepping-stones. Arthur Key measured and cut a piece of forty-foot sisal rope, and he and Ronnie used it as the leg of a compass to walk out and mark the quarter-mile line along which the aluminum seating would be erected. Ronnie had a backpack of pine stakes and he knelt and drove one in the northeast corner of each footing, the way Arthur had shown him. There would be eighty footings. The two men worked and walked out through the sage, not talking; Arthur stood on the east and then the west corner of each set, so Ronnie could double-check each stake. The sky was a patterned field of cumulus headed east, and when one blocked the sun, the air grew cold and Ronnie felt the chills along his upper arms. When the sun was unobstructed, Ronnie could feel it burning his neck.

From the campsite, Darwin blew the Acme Thunderer whistle, and Arthur stood and waved. It was lunch and Ronnie gathered the roll of flagging. On the way back to camp, the two men flagged each stake with a short fluorescent tape, so they could find them in a week when they did the cement work. Carrying their coiled rope and gear, the men approached the sky blue table. They sat on upended milk crates and Darwin turned from the stove stand and slid tin plates of grilled ham and cheese sandwiches down to each. There was a tub of pasta salad and a bowl of red apples and hard-boiled eggs already on the new table. The two coats of enamel were just dry to the touch and the display appeared the subject of a gaudy still life.

"Looks good," Ronnie said.

"There's coffee," Darwin told them.

Key got up to retrieve his cup. "Diff is coming at three?"

"That's what he said."

Ronnie looked up.

"It's okay, Ronnie," Art told him. "He's not a cop."

"I'm not afraid of cops. I don't get what we're fucking doing."

"He's taking us down to the river. You want to get down to the river, don't you? We're going fishing with the landlord. He wants to show off his ranch, the rest of it. I expect he wants to meet us and see his old friend Darwin."

"So much more of God's country. It doesn't stop," Ronnie said.

Darwin had a funny look on his face, a shadow Key had seen before. "This isn't," the older man said.

Arthur Key knew instantly it was the spot. He had known that the older man was wounded, and he'd thought it had been wear and tear, disappointment. Now it fell into place. Key knew also not to say anything further about it. He picked up his second sandwich and one of the eggs and stirred his coffee.

"Can you balance an egg on end, Ronnie?" Arthur asked.

"Is this one of your engineering challenges?"

Arthur stood the egg and it rolled. He held it still and it rolled again. He handed it to Ronnie. Ronnie set the egg, holding it five seconds. It rolled. "Not here."

Darwin stepped up and took the egg. "It's an old joke," he said, tapping the egg so it cracked and stood.

"No, it's a new one. Let me show you something about your beautiful table." He took another egg and set it up and then slid it over to the dimple where paint had almost filled one of the screw holes, standing it there.

"Two geniuses at work," Ronnie said. He stood the other two eggs in indentations on the tabletop. "Now we do need a camera."

"You ever been fishing?" Arthur Key asked Ronnie.

"Golf balls."

Darwin looked at him.

"A business opportunity," Key said, and Ronnie nodded.

"A buck apiece."

"In Chicago?"

"Near there," he said. He stood and picked up an apple. "I told you I worked as a caddy. Are we taking a break until our little trip?"

"Are you a good golfer?" Darwin asked him.

"I played a lot of golf," Ronnie said.

"Did you ever play golf?" Darwin asked Key.

"I've seen it played," Arthur Key said. He had stood up and was heading for the tent. "My brother," he started. He had thought he would say the entire sentence, "My brother liked golf," and he had the words arranged in his head, ready, but he now could not go on. Of all things, he never thought he'd crash over a sentence with the word *golf* in it. He walked into the tent. They had tied back the flaps to air in the spring weather. He retrieved his notebook of drawings from his suitcase along with his pencils and he came back to the blue table.

"You've got a brother who is a golfer?" Darwin persisted.

Arthur Key sat and opened his oversize notebook. In it he had drawings of each component of the project on the plateau, but he had not drawn the ramp yet. These were freehand sketches, simple and out of scale, with the accurate measurements inserted: the approach, the long line of bleachers. He turned to a page showing the gap of the canyon. There was no number for the yardage between the two arrows.

"We need that transit."

"What's that?" Ronnie said. He had gone over to the lumber bale and sat in the shade there, his legs straight out on the ground, eating his apple.

Darwin lifted his crate and moved around to look at the drawing with Key. "How close do we need to know?"

"Is there a hurry, Darwin? Is there a bonus for doing this wrong?" He didn't care about speaking sharply. "I need to know to an inch. I need to know how much the people who are going to do this hideous thing weigh. I have an idea about their motorcycles, but I want to know the rest."

"It's two hundred and sixty yards across," Ronnie said. He was taking a bite and then studying his apple carefully. "A two-iron with the wind."

"And you know that because?"

"Art," Ronnie said, lifting his hand out to the river. "I looked. I look across the thing every day. It's right over there, a short par four."

"Diff said it was about four hundred yards," Darwin said. "Does that help?"

"Look," Key said, turning his notebook to a blank page. "Let's get a transit. It's the difference between some kids breaking all their bones in the sage or falling half a mile. We're ahead of schedule, right? We won't get this seating for a month. When I know the gap, we can build the ramp in two weeks, I think."

Darwin had risen and was pouring himself another cup. He raised the enameled pot in a gesture to Arthur Key and Key nodded. "Whatever you want, Art," Darwin said. "It's going well. We can wait." The clouds made a monstrous map of the sky, and they continued to fold and cover and cool the high desert world every twenty minutes. "We can get over to the other side and shoot back, if you want."

"If there's time, I'd like that." Key turned to Ronnie, who now was carefully going around the scant core of his apple. "You can't use that golf stuff out here. This isn't the Winnetka Country Club; this is the West. It looks like you can just jump over something, so clear and so close. You can't jump over it. There's a ton of air you're not considering. You'll see when we're down in there today."

"Whatever," Ronnie said, struggling back up and throwing his apple core toward the farm road. He walked over past their portable john and stood out in the sage with his back to them, pissing.

"He'll get used to pissing out in the world, and find himself unable to go east again," Art said to Darwin. "A genuine cowboy." They watched Ronnie hitch his shoulders as he adjusted his pants. He spit dramatically.

"And where are you from?" Darwin said. "If you'd like to really say."

"I'll let you know," Art said. He was now running his hand along the bevel that Ronnie had cut in each end of the table with the belt sander, a nice touch. "And you can tell me why this isn't God's country anymore."

Two hours later, they heard a vehicle approaching and saw the train of dust it raised rolling south. It was Curtis Diff's big silver Suburban. He wheeled through the narrow gate without slowing and pulled into the workyard and stopped. Ronnie stood from where he knelt cutting five-gallon buckets into sleeves with the jigsaw, the way that Arthur had lined him up: eight inches off the top, another section eight inches lower and then finally cutting off the bottom. At his feet were a dozen of these white hoops in a pile. Darwin had watched them work together. Key had run the heavy yellow extension cord from the chugging generator, and he used the power drill on each pail, punching three quarter-inch starter holes for the stubby blade of the jigsaw. It was clear from the way Ronnie leaned in and watched the larger man work that he wanted to get it right. They formed the picture of a lesson with Ronnie leaning to see the way Arthur made the cuts. When he started sawing the circumference of the first white plastic bucket, Ronnie held the edge in his left hand with the confidence of a pro. There were moments like this that Darwin liked this project. These plastic circles would be forms for the bleacher footings.

"Jesus," Diff said, stepping out of the truck and taking in the stacks of lumber and equipment. "We got a little city going here. There hasn't been this much new lumber in Fendall County since they built the whorehouse in Mercy. No wonder everybody's pissed off at us." He was a tall man in a plaid western shirt with scalloped pockets, and he left the truck door open and took long strides along the graded approach to the rampsite until he stood on the lip of the precipice. "Whoa mama!" he yelled. "Better them than me."

By this time Darwin and Arthur Key had come up from where they had been hauling lumber to the camera platform position. Diff seized Darwin's hand and reeled him in to a hug. "Qué pasa, my friend?" he said. "Sorry it's been so long. You knew I took Lynn to Europe, right? Jesus, what a trip. They got more churches than the Mormons, but they seriously need an electrician!" He laughed but then held Darwin by the shoulders and looked into his face. "How are you? Okay?"

"We're good," Darwin said, moving past the personal question. "We've got some expert help here." He pointed at Arthur Key.

"You're Art Key," Diff said. "I know about your work. What are you, on vacation?"

"I am," Key said, stepping up and shaking the older man's hand. Curtis Diff was seventy years old that summer with red cheeks and long wavy gray hair combed straight back.

"Where's the heavy equipment operator?"

Darwin introduced Ronnie whose shirt was coated with plastic crumbs. "We're making some forms for the footings."

"You're doing more than that. This is the whole shiterie." He pointed to the line of bare telephone poles. "When do you get electricity?"

"Today or tomorrow," Darwin said. "Phone too."

"Sonofabitch, this is something." Diff turned again to face the abyss. "What's that platform?" He nodded at the area Key had staked a hundred yards farther along the rim.

"That's the camera station."

"Of course it is. No sense in losing an expensive two-wheeler without taking pictures." He shook his head. "I brought you out a case of wine and a transit." He brushed at the front of Ronnie's shirt. "Let's go fishing, shall we? I can see if I stay out here, you'll put me to work. It's French wine. We plundered that place."

They drove twenty miles south on the ranch road in the Suburban, through the sage plain and then along through a series of domed hills where pines grew in shadowlike formations on the side of each. The road became a powdered two-track smooth and sinuous winding through the scattered cattle who didn't lift a head to watch the men pass.

"These are yours too," Arthur Key said to Curtis Diff. Darwin had arranged that Key sit in the front for the ride. He did not want to be quizzed about his well-being, and Key could furnish all the updates on their work on the plateau.

"They must be," Diff said. His place, the ranch called Rio Difficulto, was ninety square miles: open range mostly with three rivers and some timber, which had been amassed through his family via their work with the railroad and by supplying potatoes during both world wars. He had pointed out the various landmarks on the drive, where the road turned east for his homestead, as he called it, the string of cabins which had been his grandfather's summer place, now abandoned, the roads heading off toward the mines, the hot springs, the fall hunting. They passed a camp of three tents and four white vans which Diff explained was a group from the university studying the ospreys.

Diff had immediately noted that it was Darwin's wife Corina who had, forty years before, named the place. She and Darwin had come to work for him, and she'd become the financial manager and sometimes cook for Diff while Darwin was ranch foreman. "She overheard me explaining something on the phone with the governor or the bishop or the town manager up in Mercy, yet again one more argument, like this deal here up at the plateau with you guys, and when I hung up she was shaking her head and she said it." Diff looked up and nodded at Darwin in the rearview mirror. "Rio Difficulto. Christ, I was as mad as you get, and when I understood what she had said there at the desk, I had to laugh. She nailed me to the door with that one. Rio Difficulto. She was a good woman."

Arthur had turned to Darwin in the backseat. "And she died this winter?"

"January," Diff said.

"That's when you moved to Idaho Falls."

"My son's up there." Darwin's expression did not change.

"He's a good man," Diff said with enthusiasm. "Got his own little company. I'd like to get him down here. I was lucky to get Darwin back for this ramp. Everybody doesn't have to goddamn move away."

Diff drove too fast it seemed at first, cruising along the smooth, winding two-track, and then it became apparent he knew the roads very well, being his. The road rose out of the hills onto a barren plain of sandy badlands, and Diff pointed out the clusters of antelope in the distance on each side. Finally, he turned off through a gate in the single-strand fence and assumed a smaller road, ragweed and speargrass tall in the center. "Gentlemen, now we'll go down to Diff's Landing." He turned to Ronnie in the backseat. "Don't worry, young man. I'll keep it on the road. This is a track my grandfather carved with nine bona fide Chinese heroes in the year 1899. It took all summer."

Above them now, the sky had stopped and the clouds were backing up like bricks. The gray day was kind on the eyes and the clarity of the grass and the rock walls emerged.

The road such as it was followed a dry creek bed for a mile until the drainage deepened, and the vehicle dropped into a channeled ravine, crisscrossing the sandy creek bed every hundred yards, dipping and swinging in descent. This wash grew in magnitude, a broad arroyo choked with huge boulders and ancient cottonwoods, and finally Diff slowed the Suburban and stopped in the sandy wash under one of the gigantic trees. Before them now in the looming distance was a strange striated red wall. "I always piss here," Diff said, getting out. "So it isn't scared out of me in this next section. I recommend it." The men climbed out of the car in a kind of wonder under the magnified and illusory rock wall which seemed to be very close but was not. A moment later they gathered in front of the dusty car. "Which way would you go?" he asked Ronnie. "Right or left?" Ronnie walked out another fifty yards to the fall mark, where the sandy basin fell into the river gorge, a spillage of a thousand twenty-ton stones which descended, as far as he could see to the blue river. He also could see that the weedy track had been cut both north and south. The other men walked up.

"You choose one," Diff said, "and we'll try her. One of these goes only two hundred yards and gets cliffed out. Then these hardheaded road builders came back and started the other way and success was theirs. They were good and had learned road making on the railroad. Go ahead. Choose."

"It was all hand tools," Arthur Key said to no one.

"Every man on that crew got a hundred dollars and a train ticket to Oakland. They had a party at the bottom. Granddad brought a team and a buckboard down the road and they roasted a pig. All summer, he'd been taking their recipes. Ask Darwin. Rio Difficulto has the finest Chinese cuisine in the West."

"I know," Arthur Key said.

"The river is not right there, is it?" Ronnie pointed straight down to the water.

"It looks like it, doesn't it?" Diff said. "No. That water is almost a quarter mile below the line of those rocks."

Back in the car, Ronnie closed his door and saw Darwin lift his left thumb. He said, "I've already driven over the edge once, Mr. Diff. I'm going to ask you to take us down the right way, but just to make sure, take a left at the cliff."

Diff laughed. "Let's try it. We're a little bigger than a buckboard, but hey, we have got to go fishing!"

At the bend the road changed from sand to a flinty ledge of rocks, each one, Key realized, broken by hand. The trail as it was cut in the steep cliffside was exactly one vehicle wide. The men had all the windows open and Key and Ronnie, on the passenger side of the vehicle, could see only down. The mountainside was the length of an arm from Darwin's window as Diff dropped them section by section down the old cut. Fully half the time, the only thing visible over the hood was the river, a distant blue illusion. "Is this something?" Diff said. "There were days when they didn't go five feet."

"They moved a lot of material," Key said.

"It's like one of your movies," Diff said.

"It's like they make the movies look," Key said. "This is much better." The drop below his elbow was four hundred feet.

"What's the better part?" Ronnie said, and Diff laughed again.

The Suburban dropped and lurched a tire at a time. "Does anybody want to walk?" Diff said.

"How does that work?" Ronnie said. "Darwin can't open his door and I'd drop straight down onto those white rocks."

"Limestone," Diff said. He was having fun.

"When was the last time you drove down here?" Arthur asked him.

"I come down every year, once a year, need to or not. In a goddamn ranch full of weird little places, this landing is a place there haven't been twenty people since that party with the Chinamen." He pulled the wheel, correcting under the loose shale. "Now, Mr. Key, what is it that finds you in lost Idaho working with the best ranch manager in the West?"

"I can tell you without lying that I needed a break," Arthur told him. "I wanted to get away for a while and think it all over."

"The big picture?"

"That's right." Key pointed quickly. "Watch it there." They had inched around a rocky cornice, and a juniper trunk had fallen across their path like a twisted gate. Diff stopped the car.

Key opened his door and looked down the cliffside. He could now see the river, razor blue in the red rocks. By holding his doorframe and then grabbing the lip of the fender and grille, he was able to edge to the front of the car.

"I've got a chainsaw," Diff called.

"We may need it," Art said, bending to the trunk.

"We won't need it," Ronnie said. They watched the big man lift the fallen tree to his belt level and then walk it forward until the broken roots snapped and gravel showered onto the ledge road. Arthur dropped the deadwood, stepped over it, hoisted it again, walked it to the road ledge and let it tumble down the cliff.

The big car squirmed down, down, along the mountainside. "It's like driving on piles of pennies," Diff said. "But don't worry. Darwin knows I've been down this drunk, in the dark, and once I had to back all the way up to the top. And Mr. Key," Diff said, taking his eyes away from the sweeping panorama and facing the big man across the seat, "we've mainly hired people who needed to be away from someplace else, and I'm just saying welcome."

"What's that?" Ronnie said. "Up on the other side."

Diff leaned forward and looked. "Those are sheep, bighorns."

"I can see two rams," Art said.

Diff pointed as the car continued sliding down the trail. "There's a ewe lying just above them. See her?"

"I do. How many are there?"

"My dad started with fourteen pairs in about 1960. We had eighty something two years ago."

"Eighty-seven," Darwin said.

"What do they do?" Ronnie asked.

"That's it right there," Diff said. "They stand in the rocks. We point them out to greenhorns. They're just using the habitat. They lived here a hundred years ago, they say."

Now Diff stopped fully at a sharp corner in the descent. Darwin squeezed out of his door and found his way forward as Diff began the crazy turn. "Real tight. Tighter," Darwin was saying. "Whoa. Back a bit," and Diff reversed two feet. "Now tight again." In this manner, they maneuvered the car through the last straightaway onto the river bottom.

"Welcome to Shanghai Landing," Diff said. "A recreational paradise." He pulled the car up beside the red stone pillars of an open ramada. The flat roof was constructed of long dead-wood poles. The canyon wall across the river rose straight up, a deep red in the afternoon shadow, and the escarpment they'd driven down loomed behind them like a shut door. From below like this, the cut of the road was barely visible, making it seem that they'd just landed in this strange rocky room. "Let's fish!" It was then that they could hear the river talking, though the roar was gone, just the water running over rock.

Diff opened the back of the car and the men unloaded all his coolers and gearboxes. In the ramada was a stone table, cobbled together crudely and around it six stout stumps, a per-manent picnic.

"Who's the mason?" Art asked, piecing together the flyrod that Darwin had handed him.

"I'm not union, but this table is almost fifty-five years old, not counting repairs."

"You did the spring wall too?" Key pointed to a pool against the mountain, ringed with the same red stones ce-mented together to form a brimming pool. "Is that steam?"

"Hot spring, Art. I tell you guys. This is the place to come if you're courting. We got the fish, the picnic, and the hot tub, but it doesn't matter." Diff showed his teeth in his laughter. "By the time you reach the bottom, you're in love."

The river came through this park winding in a perfect S and the sand and willows and twenty gigantic cottonwoods were half in the shade. The air rode down the river fragrant with water and willows. Darwin and Arthur walked down across a gravel bar and began to cast into a blue eddy below the riffle. The trout struck immediately and at the same time both men reeled struggling fish to the riverbank. Darwin knelt and removed the fly from his fish, showing the cutthroat to Arthur before setting it back in the stream. Then he did the same with Arthur's fish, also a twelve-inch trout.

"They've been waiting for us," Arthur said.

"There's always fish here," Darwin told him. "You can practice keeping it away from them."

"Diff wants you back at the ranch."

Darwin eyed Arthur Key, surprised that he would say something obvious.

"He knows I couldn't stay."

"Was Diff this easy to work for or is he showing off today?"

"It's not his problem. He's a decent man." Darwin moved off along the gravel bar airing his line back and forth, lazily. The conversation was concluded.

Upstream, Diff worked with Ronnie Panelli, showing him how the open-faced reel operated. They had a clothespin on the end of the line, casting that into the channel. Diff would take the pole every other cast and speak about touch and setting the hook, and the young man would then try two or three times. They saw Darwin step up and take another fish, his rod bent as he played the fish in. Finally, Diff showed Ronnie the tawny fly. "This is the ticket, right here." He had the tiny fly on the flat of his thumb and he tied it deftly to the filmy leader, whispering as he did: "Over, over, over, through and back." He snipped the extra leader with his clippers and handed the line to Ronnie. They walked a worn path through a clump of willows to a corner on the river and Diff showed him where to try for, under the cutbank below them.

Ronnie was a little sharp with his back cast, yanking it, but his cast billowed and ran in a true line across the swelling eddy, like a seam, and the fly popped lightly onto the surface where the shadow of the earthen bank cut into the water. The fish struck instantly, coming out of the water in a twist, and then Ronnie was beyond his training. The pole jerked and he jerked it back, surprised it had come to life. He pulled and reeled. Diff came over from his own pole, but too late for Ronnie's line, which was run up into a fabulous hairball now.

"I got one," Ronnie said. His reel stalled, choked by the backlash. Diff showed him how to pull the line through the eyelets. But the fish undid those efforts.

"You're going to have to work him for a while. Keep the tension even. I think you've caught the better part of supper on there. But don't touch that reel anymore."

Five minutes later there was a pool of the yellow floating line at Ronnie's feet and he took the net from Diff and scooped his big fish from the river. "We're keeping him," Diff said, quickly squaring the fish on his knee and tapping him smartly behind the cranium. "He's a beauty." He held the trout up. "See these dots? He's a cutthroat." He placed him in the wicker creel. "Now come on over here and we'll see to that reel."

Darwin and Arthur were out of sight in the downstream canyon. Ronnie sat on a flat rock working on the snarled line. The sky had closed now and become a luminescent charcoal ceiling scalloped with glowing seams. Diff showed him how to tease out the line tenderly, a few loops at a time. Diff was fishing from a fallen log, waving his line in the air and casting sweetly in the positions of the clock: ten, eleven, twelve, one, two, three, each time quickly taking a trout, then across the riffle, and kneeling to release it. After the sixth or seventh, Ronnie called, "Is that the same fish?"

"Nobody's that dumb," Diff called back, laughing.

Ronnie picked at the widening tangle of line as he looked up. He could feel the air thicker now, like the mottled dark cloud cover. He traced this gleaming ceiling north to south in the narrow corridor of rock. "I am," he said aloud. "I'm that dumb." Above them the sky seemed to tighten. For no reason, Ronnie remembered being under a bed in a condominium he'd been burglarizing, some new place. Half the units weren't even occupied yet. He'd heard a noise like a door and he had dropped onto his fingertips on the new hardwood floor and slid under the bed. It wasn't even dusty there yet. It was one of the strange times, because he gave himself over from fear to a kind of vacant wonder, staring at the gauzy liner of the box springs four inches from his nose. He wondered about the making of the thing, and he almost went to sleep. He wondered, filled with wonder that he was in such a place, that this was who he had become; the wonder was a kind of vertigo and he never again in his life as a thief shook it fully off. He listened from under the new bed and he lost track of time. Later he slid out still heavier than when he had gone there, and he lifted a small glass box full of pierced earrings, which he couldn't even give away at the golf course. Everyone knew he was a thief by then and lowballed him mercilessly.

Now the sky was stitched in bulbous dark plates which mesmerized Ronnie, pulling him somewhere, he felt. He knew the air was pushing down the canyon, drawing off the top of the river, an avalanche of air, the breeze doubling as the weather closed.

Diff had continued to take fish; he released the last and came over. "Get it?"

"Close." The nasty tangle was a loose ball now. Diff helped Ronnie and it opened nicely and fell apart. They pulled it all out and Diff held the tension while Ronnie steadily turned it back onto the reel. "You are good to go," the man told him. "Let's catch and keep some before this storm plays hell."

It didn't rain for an hour. The air washed down the canyon in long trains, gusting in swirls, all of it full of wet rock and cedar and the dusky smell of willows. Ronnie followed Diff upstream, room by room, on the river's edge, parking sharply when the older man did and concentrating on the work before him. Having fouled the reel once, he was careful with his thumbs and stopped the line both forward and back. There were fish everywhere, and Ronnie became adept at taking a knee in the stream and releasing the bright trout. Once, when he had waded in and felt the pressure on his knees, he understood this was the river again and again, all night and all day and the hours between night and day; how could it keep on and who was watching it? He fished. When the first rain came in a ripping wall, he had lost track of how many he had taken.

By the time Darwin and Arthur Key filed up the river trail, Diff and Ronnie had erected a ten-foot canvas cover over the ramada's skeletal roof. Diff had a camp box of hors d'oeuvres laid open, a vintage thing with compartments with cheese and crackers and smoked oysters and tiny carrots with dip. At one end of the stone table, he'd set up his two-burner propane and he was sautéing two large trout in a black iron pan. There was a bottle of gin and two limes. There were bottles of red wine and a bottle of white on ice. Ronnie raised his bottle of Pacifico and pointed. "I caught those two."

The rain was light but general, popping softly against the canvas. The gray world now smelled of mesquite and wet stone. Key's stringer held ten trout. They'd been gutted already, and he put them in the proper cooler. "Grab a glass," Diff told the men. "We're having cocktails on the veranda."

At dinner, Diff showed Ronnie how to pull the skeleton from the trout. They had a wooden tub of creamy Caesar salad and sourdough bread with their fish, sitting around the old stone table. "This was the first thing I did when I came back from the navy in 1945," Diff told them, placing his hand on the tabletop. "I lived down here alone for a month and built this, and repaired the spring wall, and ate fish until I felt like I was not either on a boat or in the Philippines. In October, I walked up that road and went to work for my pa." He pointed at Ronnie and said, "I was your age."

He looked at Darwin and added, "It was clearly the right

thing to do. I've told Darwin here that he should just come on back and work with us, like he's done all his goddamn life, but no. After forty years now, he's got to live in town."

"If it keeps raining, *I'll* walk up that road," Ronnie said.

"Time for a change," Darwin said to the table.

Arthur watched the exchange as he tore off another crust of bread and filled his mouth with wine. It was a remarkable place to him. The storm which was still building felt like a treasure in the vast rocky arena rich with sage and wet limestone and living wood. There were three more trout on the platter, browned skins gleaming with olive oil. Diff stood and slid one onto Ronnie's plate and Darwin's and Arthur's. "Eat up," he said. "We have a long tradition of eating with our fingers this far from the world." He pulled a fillet from the fish on his plate and dropped it into his mouth.

"It's a feast," Arthur noted. Darwin had moved to the perimeter of the shelter and was facing the upstream wind.

"Every day's a feast on the Rio Difficulto," Curtis Diff said. A moment later he filled his glass with wine and stood up. The rain had now doubled and snapped steadily against their canvas cover. He pulled his boots off and then his pants, folding them with his shirt. In a second he was naked. He put his boots back on, and his bare white ass disappeared into the dark rain. "There's towels in the car. Don't come over barefoot or without a drink."

"A hot tub?" Ronnie asked. He was still picking at his fish. "How dirty am I?" He went to the car and undressed, walking back to the table in a towel and his shoes to grab a fresh beer.

"Sounds good to me," Arthur said. "He's a character."

In the hot spring, the rain fell through the steam. The spring issued from the bottom of the cliff face and collected in a stone pool which had been augmented by a porous rock wall, cemented and now grown with moss and which leaked throughout. The men were silent in the strange place. Key could feel the warm water at the nicks in his hands and forearms. He knew that Darwin wasn't coming over. Ronnie kept submerging. The world around them was black, the rain dark, and the steaming water ebony.

"When I'm in here, I wish I still smoked cigars," Diff said.

"We're smoking just fine."

"It feels a long way from home, though, doesn't it, Mr. Key?" They were just dim faces in the steam.

"It does," Arthur said. "But that's why we came, right, sir?"

"I don't know." He was quiet, then pointed at Ronnie. "We came to wash the soot off this young heavy equipment operator. I thought you guys might need a break and Darwin would want to see it all again."

"I did. It's good." They could see Darwin's profile in the dinner shelter, drinking his wine.

Suddenly Key turned and the old man's face was almost against his. Arthur could see his eyes, the pale blue wash in the small light. Curtis Diff spoke quietly, ashes in his voice. "It was my fault, you know, with his wife. We didn't have warning of the wind shear, but I should have circled once; I always do it. In the crosswind I could barely hold, and we nearly lost it all. We caught on one wheel, and she hit her head just the way you can't do twice. And here we've got the rest."

Ronnie's eyes were two points of white above the dark water. It was quiet now in the deep canyon, the river a wind whisper under everything. The older man stood and sat on the wall with his white back steaming while he pulled his boots on. "Take your time," he told them. "There's no hurry in the rain. We'll get the gear and go up when you're ready." The two remaining men had washed between their toes by now and as Diff walked away they rinsed and rerinsed their hair.

"Fuck all," Ronnie said. The young man worked the towel modestly as he stood, then sat on the rock wall. His hair was back in a slick sheath down his neck. "My mother liked my hair. But I'd like to get a haircut tomorrow." He swung his leg over and out of the hot water. The rain pinched him and he ran in his shoes to the car, complaining in uhs and ohs.

Diff had Arthur drive up the ruined road. "Don't worry about it. You may scrape on the one corner, but a car wants to stay on the road." Ronnie sat in the back and covered his eyes.

"I don't know why you do that," Arthur told him. "I can't see anything either." The windshield was a speckled sheet, the wipers revealing only the powerful headlight beams crashing against the rocks on the far wall of the canyon. There was some slippage, the rear end shifting over the wet gravel. At the sharp corner, Key kept the accelerator down, and he pivoted around the tight spot without scraping the cliff. When they lifted into the upper arroyo, the sandy road had become a stream, but easily passable. At the gate to the ranch road, Key made the turn and Diff said, "Until next year."

Ronnie fell asleep in that last half hour, the road smooth mud, the rain a covering friction. Key checked Darwin's stony eyes in the mirror, but there was no story there, through all the rising rainy country of Diff's ranch. He knew that Diff had hoped the trip would soften Darwin. They were good men with the death of the woman between them now; the death of Corina, Key saw, was like a murder to Darwin, God's accident, the one that stops everyone. Arthur Key slowed and wheeled the heavy vehicle into the ramp encampment. Rain was upon everything in the tidy area. "Who lives here?" he said.

"I appreciate that, Arthur," Diff said. They'd opened the doors but sat inside. "Roman said you'd been over and looked at the roof on our old chapel. It would be a good three-day job when you're done here. I'll double what you're getting paid." Darwin got out and opened the rear doors. His silence goaded the old man. "Goddamn it, man; it's not a big job."

"I'm not going over there, Diff." Darwin had lifted a cooler from the back.

Diff jumped out into the rain, mad as if he'd been mad all day. "Goddamn it, man. People die." He walked around and confronted Darwin. They were both wet in a moment. "She was an extraordinary woman and we all miss her, but you're being a goddamned fool." Diff was raging. "Goddamn, Darwin, your boy doesn't want you over there in Idaho Falls meddling in his goddamned business. He knows what to do, just like you did. You've got a good place here, good work, god damn your goddamn bonehead." Diff had to stop. Key and Ronnie Panelli had gathered their gear and also stood in the rain.

"Oh, don't listen to me. Finish the goddamn ramp for these California clowns and do whatever in hell you are going to do. God knows I'm cashing their checks." He went to the Suburban and started it up. Then the men heard it shut down. Diff stepped out and came back to the blue table beaded with the rain. They were all four quiet in the wet night. "Good night, everybody." He rolled his hand at Ronnie. "You did real good for a first day with a fly. We'll try to do it again."

I N THE FRESH MORNING, Ronnie Panelli stood on the sandy earth and leaned arms and shoulders into the driver's side floor of the cab of the big white flatbed truck. He was stirring the two-element epoxy on a paper plate the way Arthur Key had shown him from where he stood on the passenger side. Key reached and held the two new rubber pedal sleeves so Ronnie could coat the underside of each with the powerful glue. "Press it there," Art told the boy, pointing at the clutch. "And the brake now." Ronnie fitted the pads onto the metal armatures.

"Do I push?"

"No. It's perfect. That will set like steel in ten minutes and then you can drive all over the county."

"I'm just going to town."

"And it is a wonderful town," Arthur Key said. He'd been kidding Ronnie a little all morning. They had woken to the sky a perfect trick, a magnified color well beyond cobalt. Tangible and tender, the air and the earth after the rain seemed minted, some rare promise in the leverage of the early sunshine. Rags

of mist stood twisting in the atmosphere. When the truck repair was finished, Arthur and Darwin were driving today up
to Idaho Falls in the old jeep to see Darwin's son. He was having the one-year anniversary of his little construction business;
he'd paid off the backhoe and they were going to celebrate.
Darwin also wanted his old chainsaw, which had a safety bar
and didn't torque as much as the new saws. They'd need it for
the ramp frame, and Ronnie was going to do a lot of that
cutting.

Ronnie had begged off, and none of them spoke of it, but
they all knew why, and Arthur had been nicking at it all morning. "That town is just full of beautiful women. Let's see. There's
that woman who works at the bank and that other one . . ."

They had already given him a list for the hardware: carriage bolts, two large chisels, a wrench set, and they told him
to pick up the ordered twenty ten-foot railroad ties from the
lumberyard. They had a good chainsaw, and Arthur had determined to fabricate the understructure of the ramp with these
timbers, setting and notching them to support the overcanyon
cantilever.

"I'll get the gear."

Arthur tested the edges of the new pedal pads and found
them solid. "And stop and see that nurse. Her mother runs the
Antlers."

The sky was ice blue, magnifying the perimeter of the
world after all the rain. Darwin had come up in his traveling
clothes, a long-sleeved white shirt and a tan leather vest. "Traci
is a nice girl. Her mother told me she'll be visiting our worksite soon."

Ronnie looked stricken. He stood away from the truck, gathering the tubes of epoxy, and went to the tent. Arthur closed
the passenger door and came around and closed the driver side
door. "Things are looking up. New pedals for the brake and

the clutch," he called to closing tent flaps. "Are you ready, Darwin? Let's go see your boy."

As soon as they had driven off, Ronnie pulled his shirt off and washed his face and combed his hair and put on one of the blue work shirts Darwin had given him. He tucked this shirt into his jeans, oiled his boots and drove the flatbed truck to Mercy. The new pedal grips were a help.

In town, he went to the First Idaho Bank and deposited his check. He got another money order for his mother and he walked next door to the post office and mailed that. As a return address, he just put his initials so she would open the letter. He wanted to say something in each of these mailings to let her know this was a job and not something he was doing wrong, but he could not. The first time he'd mailed her money, he stood at the table in the post office window and he printed out a little letter, but even as he was writing it, he felt it was an excuse. He would not have called it pride, but he was too proud to explain himself. She'd get the money and that was all he could do.

Across the street in the Antlers, he waited until Marion was finished taking an order at the bar. When she saw him, she came around and they stood just outside the back entry.

"Traci home?" Ronnie said.

"You know she's home," Marion said. There was a grin playing under her words. "She said you two were going camping."

"We're going out to the river gorge, yeah."

Marion stepped up and put a finger in one of Ronnie's belt loops. "You be careful. Things are going just fine, and it is a real good time for you to be real careful. Traci isn't just anybody."

"I know that, ma'am," Ronnie said.

"I don't know why I like you, but don't you ruin that." She let go of him and held his eyes for a second for emphasis. "I'll see you both back here by noon."

"Yes, you will," he said.

Marion went by him and picked four mugs off the bar and laid them in the soapy sink. Ronnie slipped out past the cook station to the back door. As he turned from setting the screen door closed, someone took his arm and spun him around and jolted him with two square fists in the chest so suddenly he was on his ass in the dirt. "Where's your bodyguards, you little shit?"

Ronnie didn't want to get this shirt dirty. He looked up at the kid standing above him. "You going to kick me now?" he said.

"Where are your friends?" It was a guy Ronnie recognized, a young guy with a tight haircut in an untucked flannel shirt, yellow and black, with no sleeves. He had the biceps you get from lifting.

Ronnie stood up.

"Where are your friends?"

The kid punched Ronnie again in the chest, looking around after he had done it.

"I want you to stop hitting me," Ronnie said. This was a new era for him, and every time he spoke now, he was surprised. He was surprised to have gumption, one of his mother's words, one she'd used against him, saying he didn't have any. He was surprised to speak and by what he said, and he was surprised he didn't scramble up and run. He'd been hit, but he'd never fought. He'd run out of his shirt twice, leaving it, or most of it, in a guy's fist when he'd been caught in a carport, under a Mercedes, his pockets full of dresser cash.

"That is not going to happen," the young man said now, stepping again after Ronnie Panelli.

The back door slapped and Marion stood there in her apron. "Darren."

"I know what I'm doing here," Darren told the woman.

"You are going to get yourself arrested again."

"That would take a phone call."

Ronnie stood and brushed himself off. "I'll fight him," he said. "But I want to take this off first." He unbuttoned his blue shirt deliberately and hung it on the rearview mirror of the cook's rusty Datsun, parked against the building. His scar was a red carbuncle on his shoulder. He now turned and faced Darren, his hands at his sides, unmoving.

"You're skinny as a rat."

"Let's just fight," Ronnie said quietly.

Darren had backed a step and folded his arms. "You are such an asshole," the boy said.

Marion had returned to the back door with the white phone receiver in her hand, which she held out for Darren to see.

"You are so full of it, Marion. This little rat is going to screw you and Traci over, big-time."

Ronnie stepped toward Darren and lifted his left hand out, fingers splayed, as if to measure the air. Darren backed sharply.

"You get, Darren. Just go. Or," Marion said, waving the telephone, "we can see if Jim wants to hear your opinions."

Darren swore and started to leave. He pointed a finger at Ronnie. "I'll find you. You touch Traci, and I'll smell it on her and I'll find you."

Ronnie put his arm down and surprised himself again by saying quietly, "I'm right here." It was so good to say what he meant; he'd never had that before. He was going to take a step toward the young man when Darren dropped his shoulders and backed away, walking among the vehicles parked at odd angles in the weeds of the parking lot and around the corner of the building. Ronnie retrieved his shirt and buttoned it up.

Marion was still at the door. "You got any food?"

"Yes, ma'am. We're going to cook some chicken in olive oil, and I've got the makings for breakfast."

"Coffee?"

"We've got coffee."

"Traci likes milk in her coffee."

"Thank you," he said. "I know. I've got some half-and-half."

Marion put her head down as if thinking it over and finally lifted it and said, "Well, get going. You guys be careful."

"It's okay," Ronnie said to Marion, waving his hand to dismiss the matter. "I'll see you tomorrow. Thanks. Really, thanks."

At the hardware store, Ronnie picked up a small case of carriage bolts and the large set of socket wrenches and the rest of their gear, and then he backed the big flatbed truck out into the lumberyard behind the old wooden hardware store. Mr. Schindler, the owner, met him by the two big stacks of railroad ties and guided him to the ten-footers.

"It's no surprise to me that Diff is making his own railroad now," Schindler said as he pulled on his gloves and hoisted the end of one of the long ties. Ronnie lifted his end and they started sliding the timbers onto the truck.

"These are going to be the ramp frame," Ronnie told the older man. "They're treated and stronger." Ronnie didn't care for wisecracks about the project on the mesa.

"Well, I imagine it will be just strong enough."

They laid the railroad ties onto the truck and Ronnie signed the paperwork. Then he threw his weight into it and chained the load with extra care, clamping the two come-alongs as tight as he could get them.

"That load won't get away."

Ronnie turned and it was Traci, leaning against the front of his truck, her arms folded, her face smiling and her brown hair lifting a little in the breeze. He was shucking his gloves and she said, "What are you going to do, shake my hand?" She hugged him, one arm over his shoulder and the other under his arm.

"Where'd you come from?" he said.

"I was born in Paris, Idaho, if you want to know, but more recently I walked from my house and down that alley, so we wouldn't have to have all of the spectators in town see your truck at my house."

"Your boyfriend already met me behind the Antlers."

She had let him go now, all but an elbow in her hand, and she said, "You look good to me."

He couldn't hold his face up to such a comment, but he averted his eyes and said, "I appreciate that." He pulled open the driver's door. "Hop in."

"Did he say anything? Darren?" She threw her canvas kit into the cab and climbed up on the big bench seat.

"Just that he's not done with me. That guy does not like me."

"Forget him." She slid over to her door and then all the way back against Ronnie where he leaned to start the vehicle. "Just forget him." Her words were good to hear, but there was something else, something hurt and bitter in them.

"There's a Paris, Idaho?"

"You need to get out more. Where'd you come from?" She laughed and suddenly ducked her head down and put it on the leg of his jeans.

"What are you doing?"

"Just drive. I'll stay down here, right here until we get to the turnoff, and no one except my mother will know where I am. Drive. Put it in gear and drive."

In that manner, they drove up the back alley behind the

bank and the little clinic and then onto Main Street in Mercy, the scattering of cars and folks walking there, and then out past the elementary school marquee announcing school starting September 4 and the town fields of alfalfa and onto the two-lane county road five miles to Diff's ranch road and then nine miles on that clay path to the worksite on the river gorge. She lay down the entire way, looking up into his face, interrupting their conversation from time to time to count the birds as they crossed in the windshield above her.

The feeling Ronnie got when they turned onto the ranch road was delicious, this freedom of being with a girl he liked, going out to a place he felt stronger about every day. He loved driving the old truck and was aware of her eyes on his arm as he shifted the big floor gearshift, and he was aware of her head on his thigh as he clutched and then pedaled the gas through the many changes.

His career with women was not a career. He had never had a girlfriend. There had been a girl at the country club whose name had been Vicky Lattimore and who was only a slut. She'd been brought to the caddies' clubhouse by some of the older caddies, though she was just Ronnie's age and had been in some of his junior high classes. She was unafraid to do sexual things to the boys there in front of other boys, and several times he took a turn sitting on the long bench behind the small building, a bench riddled and splintered from where golfers forever had bent over and tied on their golf spikes. He knew that she was a slut and it was a word that everyone used, but he also knew that she had power over him, and there were days when he'd finish caddying a round or sometimes two and he would be back there alone, cleaning clubs, and he would catch himself hoping she was around. He didn't like the way he felt when she was there, but there was nothing he could do about it. Eventually, a month before that last summer was over, the pro heard about her visits, and came down and fired four kids, including Ronnie. It was that day, three years ago, that he went in the back door of the main clubhouse and picked through three wallets, taking over four hundred dollars and a Platinum American Express card. The only good thing about that had been that he'd been sixteen and so it was juvie for four months. In classes there, he'd been taught the Constitution and the Bill of Rights as well as the Ten Commandments and how to balance a checkbook and what compound interest was. The information was so arcane that he made a quiet decision about further school right there. When he got out, his mother wept and wept, overjoyed to have her boy back, but he knew he was not back. He was ashamed of what he had done, but he did not know what the feeling was. He knew he had disappointed his mother, but he took the pain he felt to be simply who he was. And he started stealing things, because as he'd been told in juvie: he was a thief. It was the first thing he'd ever been called, and he took their word for it.

As they proceeded in the truck, Traci would assess where they were. "These are the power lines running along the town fields. Way off south you can see the abandoned farmstead. It is called the Olsens' but they lived there five families back. It's a party house sometimes in the spring; the week before high school graduates, you can lose your virginity there without hardly trying."

"Did you?"

"We just met and that's a personal question. But, no."

When a bird would cross the sky, Traci still laying on Ronnie's leg would say what it was, each time reciting the whole list as it grew: nine sparrows on the wire, two ravens, a hawk, a raven, a hawk, one seagull, two little birds, two little birds, a red-tail.

"Was that guy your boyfriend?"

"Darren was my boyfriend last year."

"Your mother doesn't like him."

"Forget Darren. We're forgetting Darren."

Ronnie Panelli could not forget Darren. "A year is a long time."

After a moment, Traci said, "A year is a long time."

Ronnie slowed and shifted down for the left turn.

Traci said, "Now you're turning onto Diff's ranch, the dirt road and we are now going south."

"Was he not good to you?"

"Forget him. I've forgotten him."

"Did something happen?"

"Nine sparrows on the wire, two ravens, a hawk, a raven, a hawk, one lost seagull . . ."

Ronnie stopped the truck sharply and slid quickly out of the door onto the running board, looking at the sky in every direction. "There is no bird here. You can stop that."

Traci's head was now back fully on the truck seat, and she looked at him upside down.

"What happened with Darren? Tell me. Did he make you do things?"

"It was a year," she said. "We did things."

They were stopped in the open sage plain; only the far mountains ringed them, marking the world. He came back into the cab and lifted her head onto his leg. Now her eyes were shut.

"It didn't seem like he was making me. I was almost eighteen; that's old. I didn't know about it. I thought we were supposed to do stuff and for a while I thought I liked it."

Ronnie sat still in the idling truck.

"You can drive," she said. "It will make it easier."

So he eased the flatbed into gear and edged forward on the dirt road.

"He wanted me to drop out of school and move out to his place with him and his dad. He's learning engines and thought he could get a job with the state or the railroad. My mom wouldn't let me go out with him at the end, and he'd come to our place and he'd lock us in my room and make me . . . You want to know this?"

Ronnie drove slowly over the well-worn two-track.

"Do you know I've never been on a date?"

"He took you on dates."

"Never. When he could still take me, he took me to the quickest place and we did stuff in his car. He took me to keggers and made me do stuff in the car while he sat and waved to his buddies. I didn't know what to do." Traci sat up and wiped her eyes. She slid back against the passenger door, sitting legs crossed now facing him.

"In my locked room he made me take my clothes off and then he'd talk to my mother through the door, saying I was sure an eager beaver, other things, until she threw him out."

"She threw him out?"

"After I told her what it was, the next time she came home from the Antlers and found he'd locked us in there, she knocked with a pan, and then came through the door with a hammer. In our house."

Ronnie's jaw was tight, and he felt the taste for trouble, the old taste when he didn't care what happened. He wanted to go back to town and find the other young man. "When was the last time he touched you?"

"February. He came to the school and waited. When I went with my friends, he grabbed me, my arm. I told him not to touch me and after a minute he let go."

"What does he do now?"

"He comes by in his truck every night, parks in front of our house, across the street."

"Let's go back to town and settle this up," Ronnie said.

"Ronnie," Traci said, taking his wrist in her hand. "Forget

him. Look at this." She waved at the broad desolate world. "Let's have the day we came for. Forget him, please. I'm so sorry I knew him."

Ronnie Panelli was vexed and simmering in a place he had not been before. The day had changed, deepened, and he knew that much. His concern for this girl had changed also and he could not quite get his thinking around all of it.

"Two ospreys." She pointed to the big birds winging slowly, easily over where Ronnie knew the open canyon ran.

"And these guys," Ronnie said, indicating the flock of white seagulls crossing in a desultory gaggle. "So far from the ocean."

"They're Mormons," Traci said.

Ronnie slowed and maneuvered the big truck through the ranch gate on the worksite at the plateau sometimes called Rio Difficulto.

In an hour he had toured Traci around the campsite and they had huddled together on the broken rock ledge over the river canyon, the ancient river working its ancient duty. They sat on the sandstone over the shadowed vault in such a way that he understood he should put his arm around her. He had little control over the moment. The gorge had always claimed him, and now his sense that he was alone with this girl felt suddenly only heavy. He couldn't lift his arm. They could smell the water in the arid world. She leaned and touched his shoulder with her shoulder, but his ability to move and his ability to speak a word had been taken from him. He had thought he could handle this, but now he simply could not touch bottom and was swimming in the new hour. He cared too much now to screw this up, and it all seemed swirling. There were ten ways to ruin it, and he wanted none of them.

"Remember what a pain in the ass you were about oatmeal?" Traci said. She was talking about the two days he'd spent in her house after his shoulder injury. "You acted like you'd never had it."

"I didn't want you to go to any trouble."

"Oatmeal," she said again and turned in proximity to be kissed, but Ronnie did not act upon it.

"I'd been in Idaho three weeks, and I didn't know you."

"Ronnie," Traci said, her face now on his. "You knew me."

"I liked you, but I figured you'd think I was . . ."

"What? You were hurt."

"Yeah, hurt. I was just another injured guy. Your mother . . ."

"My mother let me talk to you. That woman let me talk to you. A boy! Think about it. I mean, a man."

The sound of the river came to them in ribbons, sometimes a hollow rush, and sometimes an echo. They watched from afar the tiny white dots drift across the blue-green water back and forth below them, rapacious ospreys plying the river, sometimes rising in eager circles through the anticlines to become winged shapes and then birds in the clear air immediately beside and then above them.

Ronnie had listened to her speaking from his lofty perch, and he had his knees and his elbows craned and folded. He looked at Traci, and it all came over him like the warm winds sometimes had this strange summer, where he'd be huddled with a chill, sweated through and picking up tools or odd bits as the sun shouldered the far mountains, and suddenly he'd feel his chest coat with the dry air and he'd smell the sand and feel his shirt inflate with the momentary heat of the earth.

He used the infusion to stand up. Not knowing what to say at all, and being as far from any natural impulse as he had ever been, he said, "Come on." He was thankful to have the next thing. "Let's go see about cooking."

Ronnie Panelli had been watching Darwin for a few weeks and understood the cause-effect of recipe work. He lit the propane stove to low. Traci saw his preparations: the bowl of chicken breasts in garlic and tarragon from the ice chest, and his brandishing the cast-iron frying pan, which he put on the burner.

"I'm going to cook this chicken in olive oil," he told her. She sat on a milk crate behind him. "They must make it out of olives." He was speaking, saying words, because of a new nervousness that had come upon him. "Somebody picks a bucket of olives and then they smash the olives and then put the oil in this bottle." He adjusted the flames on the stove and kept talking. "They use an olive oil funnel to pour the olive oil . . ." Now Traci stood quickly and hugged him from the back, her head on his shoulder. "Oh Ronnie."

He was stilled by the action and put the pan on the burner and his head hung on his chest for a moment. He had not kissed her, and now he knew he was going to. Her hands on his chest ran chills there. "No, really," he finally whispered, "it's a perfect funnel and they do not spill one drop." The plateau was yellow-gold now, the shadows thrown double by the last sun, which was closed between the razored horizon and a train of distant clouds. With his hands he took her hands and he moved around so her face was against his face.

A moment later he said, "You know I built this table."

They ate and talked and Ronnie did not tell her about his year as a thief, and it was odd to him: he wanted to. She told him that her town wasn't a place where you hoped for much, and she did not know what was going to happen to her, and she was amazed by that and fearful. Most girls married the locals, guys were wild for two or three years and rough, but then they settled down and life went on. Ronnie had let her go into the tent first and change and get into her sleeping bag. Later, she said quietly across to him: "I'm glad I came out here. The river sounds nice."

He whispered back from where he lay in Arthur's cot, "I

told you I wasn't going to try anything," but all he heard in return was her sleeping breath.

In the deep night with the temperature inside the worksite tent forty degrees, Ronnie Panelli opened his eyes. It took him half a minute in the sure dark to place himself, and he felt a smile rise on his face. His dreams now were fainter than even a month ago. Something had filled the hollow place where a kind of terror had burned briefly every time he woke up. Now he smelled the canvas shelter almost happy, and he heard a noise, a small concussion, and he listened hard until he heard it again. It was odd; he perceived it as a tap deep in the scar on his shoulder. Ronnie quietly turned his head toward the opposite cot where Traci slept. Her breath was an exhausted whisper. He could hear the river also, a white friction tonight, and he could hear his heartbeat as he swung his feet onto the floor and sat up. The sound came again. There was something else too, and he held his breath until he ascertained that across the site someone was walking back and forth. In the tick of a second he was awake, every part of him, the way he felt in the old days, last year, when he was breaking and entering, sometimes in the room with people sleeping while he opened their dresser drawers, his mouth always the shape of an O as he breathed shallowly, silently in and out.

His old two-iron was under his cot, but he left it and stepped barefoot to the lodge flap, and delicately pulling the heavy fabric open near the bottom, he knelt and peered out. The first thing he saw was the far field of stars like some trick of vertigo, pulling him off balance until the yard focused, and in the shimmering night Ronnie witnessed the two men hauling lumber to their truck. There was no moon. They were joined by their load, four two-by-sixes, and one of the men walked backward. At the truck, they paused, adjusted their grips and silently coordinated the last lift onto the stacked lumber there. They were being quiet, but not overly so, and Ronnie Panelli understood that they thought the plateau was abandoned. Darwin's jeep was gone. They might have seen it go through town. He looked at his watch, one-thirty. The big guy he remembered from the Antlers.

Ronnie dressed and found and tied on his old Nikes, shoes he hadn't worn in almost a month. Now he grabbed the two-iron and knelt by Traci's cot. In the small light she smiled at him sleepily, her face an unreasonable joy in his heart. "Was I snoring?" she whispered, and he put his finger against her lips.

"There are some guys here," he told her. "Do you know them?" He helped her out of the sleeping bag and they crept to the opening.

After a half minute, she came back and whispered against his ear, "It's Buster Jensen and his dad."

"From town?"

"From Concept. They ranch out there." Traci pointed at the older man. "LaDonna—from the bank, the teller—is his ex."

"What's his name?"

"Don. They call him Big Don."

"He just goes around pissed off."

"Yeah, he does," Traci whispered back.

"Okay," Ronnie pulled her back and they knelt together on the plank tent floor. "You just stay right here. I've got to run them off."

"What are you going to do?" His hands circled her wrists and she held his forearms.

"Don't worry. Stay right here. I'm going to ask them to leave." He started to rise and she tightened her grip, bumping his face with hers until the kiss took.

Outside now the cold air falling from space stilled him. He crouched in the shadow of the tent until the men pushed the lumber onto the truck, which was almost half loaded, and turned to walk back to the stack. Then he ran quietly across open ground swinging way wide and coming up in front of the intruders' vehicle, a GMC three-quarter-ton pickup. Two of Darwin's big toolboxes were on the hood along with Art's tool belt as well as his own and a short keg of screws and their drill motor. Both doors of the truck were open, and Ronnie slipped into the driver's side and lay on the seat on his back. The plastic dome light was broken, he saw, and there was a rifle of some kind hung on the back-window gun rack. The cab smelled powerfully of years of tobacco and fresh spilled beer. Now his heartbeat eclipsed all other sound until he heard the men approaching and a couple of sharp breaths before he felt the planks jostle the truck and slide into place. This was his prime game, hiding at close quarters, and his breathing stilled. He waited for a count of five, lifting the fingers before his face, and then he sat up and saw the backs of the men walking away. The world was ten shades of gray, but he could see everything plainly.

Ronnie pulled the truck keys from the ignition and stuffed them into his pocket. He extracted the rifle from the rack and took it with him again to the front of the truck. He made a broad quiet circle in the sage, keeping the truck and then the tent between himself and the men as they marched carrying the new boards. He worked back to the yawning gorge and the river's roar multiplied in the night. The tiny silver slip of the water below him flickered in its length indifferently. No matter what was about to happen here, it would continue through the aeons. He'd never thought this way before, and it made him uneasy. He was becoming someone else. He laid the rifle in the dirt and stepped toward the men.

"Boys!" he called and shined his big flashlight at them. They were back at the diminished stack of lumber, and they stopped sharp and turned to the light.

It was the worst moment, the surprise. Once it all began, he'd be fine, but now Ronnie was uncertain of everything. Nothing felt solid. He walked toward them anyway. "Listen," he continued. "You're going to want to put all this lumber back."

"Say what?" the older man said. "Who is that?"

Ronnie Panelli didn't know what to say, but he heard his voice: "Security." The word sounded like four broken pieces. "Take a minute and put it all back. Now."

"Lift that, goddamn it," the man said now to his companion. The two began to stack four boards for another trip.

"Stop it, Big Don," Ronnie said.

At his name, the man dropped his end and the boards splayed into the sandy soil of the mesa.

"Who the hell are you?"

"I'm the guy who works here and who knows who you are. I'm going to let you put it all back and go home."

Both men, still in the flashlight beam, stepped toward him.

"We thought this was some kind of surplus deal," Big Don said. "They said to help ourselves, to clear it out."

"You need to put it back."

"We'll take what we've got and go," Big Don said.

"Look, Buster. Tell the old man that he needs to help you stack all these boards back in the stack and set the tools in the lean-to."

The two men spoke briefly, quietly, and then they moved to their truck. Ronnie could just see them load everything on the hood onto the wood already in the bed, and he heard both doors shut. He turned off his light and moved across to the canyon rim exactly where the ramp would be built. He sat in the sage.

A truck door opened and he heard Buster say, "Where's the keys?"

Ronnie waited.

The other door opened and Big Don yelled, "Let's have those keys, my man, before I kick your ass."

Ronnie waited until the older man swore a moment later, and then he answered them. "I've got your keys." He could see them searching for him. "I've got your rifle." Now they were talking again. Buster opened his door again and checked inside. He saw Big Don go behind the vehicle and begin to pull the bright new two-by-sixes and throw them onto the ground.

"Stack them where they were, and I'll give you your keys." Buster stood to one side, waiting to see what his father was going to do. Big Don folded his arms and dropped his head to his chest.

"I think you're the little asshole who was sniffing after Traci last week."

"Stack them and put the tools on top."

There was one more minute while the men searched through the cab of the truck, and then without a word, they began hauling the wood back to the supply stack. When they turned after the second trip back to the truck, Ronnie circled low through the sage way behind all the materials, taking his time and finally striking the dirt road a hundred yards from the gate. He continued for the next twenty minutes, moving as their backs were to him, until he was able to gain the front of their truck again, crouch there and place the keys on the front driver side tire. The truck bumped softly as he knelt in the dirt and he could hear Big Don and Buster breathing as they worked. As he let go of the keys, he realized it was the first time he had ever put something back. It was thrilling to steal things, to take a wallet from a pair of pants on a chair while you watched and listened for any movement in the strange house, but he knew now, kneeling by the front of the truck, that he had hated it. Even the thrill, he saw, was part of how sad it all was. He hated it. It was like a cage, always, in the cage and then gone. There was no upside. You put yourself into trouble and then got out, back to zero, never ahead. Now he shook his head at the thought: he had hated it.

He backed away from the truck again in his larger circle, staying low. When he reached the canyon rim again, he could see the truck was empty and he heard the tools jostling and the noise of them being placed on the mass of wood.

Big Don walked back to the truck and got in the driver's seat. Buster stood behind the truck, waiting. "Okay," he called. "Okay, let's have the keys."

"On the tire," Ronnie called. He saw the young man move around the vehicle, checking, and then hand them to his father through the window. The truck started and the sharp red disks of taillights lit the area.

"The rifle," Big Don yelled.

"It will be in the Antlers in a week."

"You asshole," Big Don said into the dark. Ronnie smiled where he sat in the brush. And then he heard the truck drop into gear and bump out of the yard. It slowed through the gate and then hit it hard on the gravel road north to Mercy. He could hear it well after the lights disappeared, and he listened for two minutes after that as he went and chained the gate, locking it this time. He was scared now for the first time and his heart was at him sickeningly.

"All clear," he called to the tent.

Traci stepped out of the tent, and he shined the flashlight in his own face for a beat and then at the ground so she could come to him and climb in his arm. "They put it all back," she said. "I saw them."

Ronnie crouched and let his heart beat. It was true; they had put it all back.

"I thought you were going to shoot the gun."

"So did they," Ronnie answered.

They walked over to the gorge and after a little search with the light he found the rifle. When he retrieved it, he saw that she was standing looking into the canyon.

"I've never been here at night," she said. He stood with her, his arm now around her in the chill. The river shivered in the rocky dark and light rolled in a narrow cord. "My god."

"That river doesn't care what happens," Ronnie said.

"Yes it does," Traci said. Her head was against his chest. "That river cares about us."

"What are you talking about?" Ronnie again felt dislocated and strange with the woman against him and the rifle in the crook of his other arm.

"That river knows about you and it knows about me." She was speaking quietly. "It knows we're up here. It knows about me, that I'm back in the world. It knows that you came to get me in town and that we're up here alone and your friends won't be back until noon tomorrow." Traci moved in front of Ronnie, her hands on his hips. He could see her face. "That river knows about us." She stood on her toes and kissed him, a kiss that lasted long enough that Ronnie Panelli lost track.

The two young people went back toward the tent, the air cold as they moved through it, and now the sound of the river faint and in the tent fainter.

EIGHT

WHEN ARTHUR KEY DROVE the camp jeep into the out-
skirts of Idaho Falls, Darwin sat up in the passenger seat and put his hand on Arthur's shoulder.
Arthur had been talking all day, and his story was complete,
the parts he could say. The touch startled him and he said,
"What?" They could see the farm lane ahead in the afternoon
shadow was crowded with pickup trucks. "That's his place,
isn't it?" Arthur slowed. Pickup trucks of all kinds lined the
long dirt road up toward the house, which was in fact a yurt.

"Keep going," Darwin said.

"Okay," Arthur said. "And why is that? We've had a bit of a
drive not to park this thing and have a beer with your son."

"Just drive," Darwin said. "We can get a saw in town."

"We want to get your saw," Arthur said. He pulled over in
the turnout by the one-lane bridge over a narrow surplus
canal. He turned and looked back at where the barbecue haze
drifted up in Roberto's dooryard. They could smell it. Darwin
stepped out of the jeep and stretched by joining his hands behind his back.

"I'm not sure," he said. He looked at Arthur Key. "I'm not."

"We're here," Key said. "Let's just step into it and see what happens. It's your family."

Darwin walked to the edge of the swollen waterway and stood arms folded. The man alone against the canal and the hedgerows beyond in the late day was the loneliest thing Arthur had ever seen. Then Darwin put his head down and stood. Arthur regretted telling Darwin his story, the shitty history anyway. The voices from the party came in threads and the birds now were moving in the sky. He should have gone over to the man, but he sat in the jeep like a coarse bag of stones. After a minute, Darwin dropped his arms and turned and then small-stepped over and climbed into the vehicle.

"I'll take that as a let's go see." Arthur hauled the vehicle around and entered Roberto's lane. The trucks parked along the ditch were all festooned with mud, weeks on end, and full of equipment, ladders and pumpers and gas containers and dogs. It was a long corridor of work. The dogs stood two legs on the truck sides as Arthur and Darwin crept in the jeep toward the dooryard. "They started without us," Arthur said. Smoke lay tiered above the dozens of men and women at the open-air celebration. Darwin pointed and Arthur drove forward. "I guess we should have parked at the turnoff."

"No," Darwin said. "Give the keys to this guy." A strong young man about forty with a jet-black crewcut came up and said, "Perfect right here, Dad. We've got a valet for you." Roberto pulled Darwin from the passenger seat into an embrace, and a teenage girl in Levi's and a Utah sweatshirt came to the driver's side and waited for Key to climb out. "I'm Cory," she told the big man. "I'll take it from here." She smiled getting in. "I'm not going to steal my grandpa's jeep. The beer's right over there, follow my dad."

In the early twilight Darwin and Arthur Key stood in the large yard of Darwin's son's place five miles south of Idaho

Falls, drinking cold beer from cans. They stepped foot to foot like men happy to be on the ground after the long road trip. Roberto had filled the yellow scoopbucket of his newly paid off John Deere frontloader with cases of cold beer under mounds of ice, and the freshly washed machine sat in a web of glowing Christmas lights to one side of the party. Three men worked a steaming pit across the yard; they were roasting a goat. Arthur Key had met Roberto's wife, Yvonne, and their daughter, Cory, a sophomore at the University of Utah, who had parked the jeep when the men arrived. Yvonne had been back to Darwin twice asking if he wanted a chair. There was a three-table buffet near the back door with one platform of pans of enchiladas and a make-your-own-taco spread, as well as great piles of potato salad and fried chicken and pea salad and platters of shrimp and cheeses and pickles and olives in dishes and a tub of coleslaw. There were two salmon and a bushel of breads. There was a three-tier cake with a little tractor on the top and there was an avalanche of brownies and seven pies, all of them missing a piece or two.

"Shall I get you a plate, Darwin?" Yvonne asked her father-in-law.

"Get this man a plate," Darwin told her. "You can see he's starving."

"Don't mind him," Arthur told the woman. "He's cranky because I talked his ear off in the car."

The beer was good in Arthur's throat; he'd been talking most of the day in the open jeep as Darwin motored them north at fifty miles an hour on the unrepaired springtime two-lanes. Arthur had started his story when they crossed the river bridge on the other side of Mercy, and he began it with the sentence "My brother came to Los Angeles and wanted to be in the film business, and I should have stopped him, but I made some mistakes and I did not stop him."

"You want to tell me this story?" Darwin asked.

"I'm going to say some of it," Arthur told him.

"Something happened to him."

"I was part of it and I should have prevented it. He was killed."

"I'm sorry about that," Darwin said. He had known there was someone dead in the story. Except for the business of driving, their stoppings for gasoline and a plate lunch at a truck-stop, their commentary on the features of Idaho and the places Darwin had been or done this or that, Arthur Key's story occupied the drive. The military vehicle had been sprung years ago and rode like it was built of rocks. Each word in Key's story had to be punched into the noisy jeep cabspace, and he was careful with each.

He had decided to tell Darwin before they set out and he did not know the reason for his decision. Early in the trip he had told the other man, "This will change your opinion of me," and Darwin had looked at him in the drafty jeep and replied, "Don't get your hopes up." In the roar of the wind and road, Arthur spoke in measured sentences and didn't hurry.

After starting, he stopped and sat quietly for a mile and then two, his hands between his knees. He went around it all in his head and knew he could only start at the end, which he did.

Arthur Key had stayed in California until the funeral was over, the short graveside service in Westwood on a sharp sunny day, laden lightly with the smog, almost sweet, and then, after he had watched the mourners depart, the three film stars first in their town cars, and then the stuntman Damon Sloan in his, and then the two dozen others stepping awkwardly in the spring grass toward their own vehicles, he went once more to his brother's grave. He was walking by taking each step and each step was expensive. It had been an entirely physical presence, the emotion that had possessed him since he had received the news. Even before he was sure of the terrible story, the pressure of his grief had begun in him, and he could tell that he could not stop or control it, simply stand under it as it mounted. He had no leverage.

The night of the first day, he had spoken to himself alone in his dark loft, surprised to be speaking in a whisper: it is what it is, he said. You have this now. It had taken every muscle he had to clear his worktables and organize the coming projects into the blue crates he and the crew used for each new job. He breathed noisily and steadily as if running slowly, and he used the breathing to gather each of his drawings and to order and file them and to print an order for each folder. After five hours of such work, the seven blue boxes were stacked by the stairs. Outside the window, California was dark. His worktables, beautiful long parsons' tables, had been made for him by Harry and his crew the year he'd moved into the loft. The top of each table was a door from a renovation at UCLA, and they still bore their names in five-inch black letters burnished into the heavy oak: MEN, UTILITIES, WOMEN, LAUNDRY. Arthur Key read the words for the first time in four years; the tables had never been clear before. He stood still into the night, unable then to move. He had no name for it, for he was sure it wasn't only the powerful guilt, something he'd never been bruised by in his life to the age of forty-two, but he knew he could not breathe deeply or stand fully up or turn his head or open his arms.

Now he looked at the grave of his brother. He wanted to say one word, Goodbye, and he could not get his mouth to open. He could not move his fingertips. After fifteen minutes, his friend and foreman Harry Burdett came over.

"You okay, Art?" Harry came around in front of Key and took his elbow. "You ready?"

"Do you have all the keys?" Arthur asked him. He had asked Harry this four times in the last two days. Saying it now with Harry's hand on him freed Arthur Key enough for him to turn and begin walking to the car.

They had talked about the rest. He had told Harry that he needed to go for a while, that he needed to go for a while. That's all I can say, Key told his friend. You handle *Housetime* and go forward from there. It will all be in the boxes. They had known each other for nine years, long enough. Harry didn't need more. He'd learned long ago to tell just by the way Key walked onto the set whether to move fast or slow. He knew what to do now.

Good Measure was exactly halfway through a complicated project, four scenes in a film called *Housetime* from Fox, in which they'd constructed the corners of two large houses. The houses had to rotate at moments of the protagonist's confusion. They were two-story clapboard houses with Georgian cornices, long paned windows on the second floor, and curtains in the windows. Standing at the edge of the Fox lot, the two odd pieces looked like the last remnants of an earthquake. Key had designed each with four railroad axles on large-gauge carousel tracking so they could roll in an arc of 120 degrees. His crew was used to him double-framing the undercarriages of all their projects, budgeting for it as the deals were made. On this project, Key had already overseen the construction of both frames. After they welded the steel armatures, he'd weight-tested it, and they were now building the platforms for the two faux fronts. Harry knew he could handle it all.

As they agreed, Harry drove Key to LAX and let him off at the curb. Key carried a small case. He was still in his suit. The two men did not talk, except for Harry to say when Key got out of the truck, "Take care." He did not know where his friend was going.

The interior of the airport building felt like a vacuum to him. Arthur Key chose his destination by how long he thought he could go without standing up. Standing seemed to help. When he sat, the feeling of being crushed and airless was over-powering. In the dark suit waiting in the ticket line, he looked exactly like what he was: a big man who had come freshly from a funeral. He looked stricken, but he could not, even try-ing, change his face. With his American Express he bought a first-class ticket to Portland. One hour and forty minutes: he could do that.

In the midafternoon in Idaho, Darwin pulled the jeep into the expansive parking lot of the Double American truck plaza and the men stepped stiffly from the vehicle. "Let's get a coffee," Darwin said, "and stay out of this goddamn jeep for an hour." It hadn't been all Arthur talking; Darwin had talked about the winters here, how the ranch hunkered down in the short days and how he and Roman repaired every vehicle in turn top to bottom, good work in the stove-warmed machine shed. Arthur told as far into his story as he could. He wanted to tell about Alicia, but he knew he could not say, "I was involved with his wife. I was with her on the day."

They had been in her bed when both of their cell phones began ringing. Hers was two bars of Chopin, and his was a four-note staccato bleat, not unlike a European siren. It was four in the afternoon and in the silver light in the ruined sheets, they had just turned and with her hands on his shoulders they had begun again. His mind was empty for the first time in his adult life, and he wasn't even sure where he was when the de-vices began to sound.

With Alicia, in his brother's bedroom, it was that strange. Moving again deeply and slowly, sweating, they were certainly not going to answer their phones. Alicia's eyes were closed and she bumped Key's forehead with hers softly and steadily. In her extremity she was crying. Key's hands pressed firmly into her lower back. The telephones rang for minutes, stopping and then starting again. Ten minutes. When Alicia opened her eyes, Arthur Key saw her look, which was only serious, and then her face was taken with fear. They separated somehow; Key did not remember that, except that before Alicia answered her phone, she pulled the sheet up over herself, and she said, "Yes?"

This scene came in circles for him sometime every day, and he could not deflect it. With Darwin over coffee at the Double American truckstop, it came at him again and again. The two men sat silently at the long Formica counter, glad to be in the swampy air-conditioning for half an hour.

Outside, Darwin handed Arthur the jeep key and told him it wasn't that far now. When Darwin climbed in the other side, he said, "I like Portland, but I know goddamn well that you didn't stay there."

"You ever sleep in your shoes?" Arthur Key asked Darwin.

"God no. Why would you?"

In Portland, Key had had no plan. He drifted through the gray airport afternoon with the crowd and filed out of the building, the world a deep overcast though it wouldn't be dark for two hours. Sometime later a guy in a green baseball cap asked the man in the dark suit if he wanted a cab. Without answering, Arthur climbed in the green and white taxi. Key didn't, couldn't answer any of the man's questions except to say, "Hotel." He was thereby taken to The Heathman Hotel downtown, disembarking as the lights were coming on up and down Broadway Street, the bars and the stores. He was aware of where he was now, and that he was in some kind of shock. His head was light. After checking in, he went up to his fifth-floor room, a small curtained room, dark and close, and he lay on the bed without even taking a glass of water. He lay down with his shoes on.

It was the maid, finally, who spoke to him. The DO NOT DISTURB sign had not moved for two days, and on the third, she used her key and stood in the darkened room before a man in a suit on the bed. She gasped, of course, thinking he was dead. The air was sour and the room still. Her half scream woke him from his grinding half dream, and he rolled his head to her. She left without closing the door. Arthur Key lay and watched the open door for an hour and then another hour. He had cramps in his arches that flickered steadily. In a state not sleep and not waking, he turned and put his feet on the floor. Bending his legs like that allowed the cramps to run up behind his knees and bite his quadriceps. This was a pain he could not ignore and he tried to stand. He could not. His mouth tasted intensely bitter. He sat up straight and gripped the edge of the bed. Finally, he pulled his shoes from his swollen feet and slumped to the floor to straighten his legs. He was lying like that when the door opened wide and the hall light spilled upon him along with the shadow of a woman in a business suit.

"Mr. Key," she said. "Mr. Key?"

Arthur Key closed his eyes. The woman was a mile above him, her shape ominous and bizarre. It was odd for him there and he went through a few phrases, but offered none. He was surprised that he could think, and his second thought was that if he didn't sit up, or do something, the hotel would probably call the police. He thought about sitting up. The woman was looking in his face.

"Should we call someone?" she asked. "Do you need some help?"

"Oh," he lied. "I'm drunk. I'm so sorry." Then he sat up and he felt the weight of the room in his head. "I'm just real drunk. This is embarrassing." He slurred the word *embarrassing* without even trying. "I'll be fine. I'll sleep this off and check out in the morning."

The woman stood up, her arms folded.

"I thought we should look in on you," she said, backing out.

"Thank you," he said. Talking was work. "I appreciate your kindness." Again, he slurred *appreciate,* and he saw the door close. He sat there a long time thinking that he would try now to rub his face with his hand.

In the same clothes on the streets at midnight, he walked down Salmon Street to Eleventh. There were men in suits in the parks, homeless men in suits, and so as he walked by, not shuffling, not staggering, just walking if slowly, he fit in. It was a wet night right on the edge of being cold. He'd always known the temperature and he said aloud to no one, "Forty-nine degrees."

He walked the five blocks on Eleventh to the bridge there, and he stepped forward on the walk lane out over the Willamette River in the broken dark of the city of Portland. He could catch a halo around the perimeter of his vision and he could feel a dull heartbeat in his elbows. His mouth was dry. Fragments of light glanced everywhere back off the river, and every lighted window upriver in the apartments and the convention center became a torn flame struggling in the water. The traffic was desultory; each car crossing the bridge felt like the last of the night. Hearing a noise he turned to see a group of joggers, ten men in white T-shirts headed his way on the walk path. They were singing something, which he then recognized as an old drinking song, and the phrase that was repeated every chorus was "Give it over, give it over, give it over, here take mine!" They were singing in a weird whisper and shaking the walkway just a little as they came by, their faces red, and a couple of the men nodded at him, and the last guy, wearing a pointed white nightcap, called back to him. "Dude. Don't jump. They fish you right out and it's jail. Totally humiliating. Go up to the pier, where they can't see you. That water is cold."

He wasn't going to jump. He was breathing the air, and then he had his cell phone in his hand and he dialed Alicia's number. He could hear people at her place, and she said hello twice before he said hello. "Arthur," she said sharply.

"I'm sorry," he said. The line was full of conversation, five or six voices in Alicia's place.

"Are you okay?" she said.

"I'm okay. I'm going to be gone, and I wanted you to know."

"Hold on, Arthur," she said, and he heard the noises diminish and a door shut. "There, I'm in the bedroom. Where are you?"

"I'm gone. I'll be away. Alicia. This is difficult." Key was speaking slowly, drawing each word from a dark part of his chest. "I couldn't stay and sort it out or whatever it would be." He lifted the phone from his ear and looked at it. "Forgive me." Then he struggled to say, "If there is anything you need, call Harry."

"Art. Don't. Everything's taken care of here. Don and Emile and a few friends are over. We had a roast and potatoes, the whole dinner."

"That sounds good."

"Are you out in the weather?"

"I'm walking around."

"Arthur," Alicia said.

"What?"

"Be kind to yourself. This wasn't your fault."

The phone dropped. Arthur Key did not know how it occurred, just that he watched the silver cell spin brightly into the waters of the night river. He stood up from leaning on the heavy iron rail. The bar was a five-inch pipe with seventy years of black enamel on it. He traced its length to the upright and admired the flange there and the facing bolts, all custom work from a foundry so long ago. An ironworks, for christsakes. Arthur Key put his hands in his suitcoat pockets and started to walk. His brain was empty for a minute and so he opened his dry lips and said to the sky, "Give it over, give it over." The tune was catchy, but he could not sing.

Arthur Key sat on the steps of St. Mary's Cathedral until dawn. He was surprised that he could sleep there, but he was out of the little wind and when he opened his eyes in the dark and saw the first silhouettes of the park and the tenements across the street, he was glad to be cold. The stone steps had chilled him where he reclined, and now too something else was happening: he was hungry. And he had to piss.

Behind the church in a crushed stone parking lot, he stood between the parish van and a white Lexus and combed his hair with both hands while he urinated, making the small steps of someone on a cell phone. He was wondering if he should speak aloud for a while but decided no. He felt the day pull at him, the way new days did, but he fought it easily by remembering the phone call, the grave, Alicia naked when she answered her cell.

At eight, the big church doors opened and Arthur Key followed six or seven women into the sanctuary. He watched them precede him up the center aisle, kneel and cross themselves. Without them, he could not have come forward. He was able to sit in the third pew from the back. The priest in the maroon distance was lighting candles and the entire dark room had the air of preparation about it, of housekeeping. Arthur Key was not Catholic, but he certainly believed in something.

All he could think now was to get out of town. He walked six blocks to the bus station, and it too seemed a kind of church to him, the penitents, the benches. The first bus was east: Pendleton, Boise, Pocatello.

NINE

ARTHUR KEY SLOWED the old flatbed truck to ten miles an hour and leaned to run his thumb across the scratched dial screen, cleaning a strip in the dust so he could check the odometer. "That's twenty-one miles," he said and he stopped the vehicle in the middle of the bladed sandy road. It was exactly noon. The sky was only white, bleached by a seamless high-altitude cloud cover, no shape in the elevated void in any direction, and the wind was steady and even as if it were a permanent feature of the desert around them, the sparse sage and periodic igneous cairns of porous red cinders. Ronnie slid out of the truck and climbed onto the bed and then onto the roof of the cab. Rabbits fled in every direction, stopping, returning, many seeking shelter under the truck itself. Key extended the binoculars out his window straight up with his left hand, and Ronnie knelt and took them from him. Darwin and Arthur again unrolled the USGS map of the quadrant. They'd given up trying to hold it open on the truck's hood in the wind.

"Straight east," Key called up to Ronnie. His arm pointed.

"Anything?" Arthur Key and Darwin sat in the cab listening to the young man's footsteps on the truck roof.

"It's weird," the young man said.

"Can you see the Pyramid?" They had named the bare pinnacle a mile east of their encampment the Pyramid. Ronnie had been on the roof of the cab four times already.

"There's about six."

Darwin unfolded his map another section and ran his pencil out the mining road they were on and made a dash. "Twenty-one miles. Stop it right here." They squinted at his pencil as he ran it east to the river. "It's over there about a mile. We're close. We needed a clear day. The sun's up there somewhere." It appeared to be everywhere. They heard two quick steps and heard Ronnie take a knee on the cab; he swore and the wind ripped the words away. His feet appeared in the rear window.

"Be careful, Ronnie," Art called. "You could fall down. Don't fall down."

The binoculars appeared in the window and Key took them. "Come on down. We're here." Arthur pulled the big truck two wheels off the road into the sandy loam, sending a dozen rabbits sprinting into the sage.

They packed up behind the truck. The sky was an amorphous glaring canopy, and the horizons were all tattered in such bright haze. Darwin had the transit head in his pack, and Arthur took the tripod and measuring stick. They each wore the cheap sunglasses they'd bought in Mercy on the way over. They each carried a quilted quart canteen. "Let's go see," Arthur said.

The soil was oddly like snow, packed but loose, blown in a speckled sheet for years without end, and each footstep made a three-inch-deep boot impression. They had to lift their feet, walking awkwardly in the bright windy day as rabbits were released in every direction, but it felt good to walk after the hot truck.

They had spent a half hour in the town of Mercy, and while Ronnie went to the bank with his paycheck, Arthur and Darwin drove over to the little brick clinic. They'd made Ronnie promise not to stop at the Antlers, saying they'd get dinner there later. Arthur carried the cooler full of trout into the medical building, ringing the hanging bell as he did. He set it on the receptionist's chair when the woman appeared, a white cloth medical mask across her face. "Here's some fish for the good doctor," Arthur said.

"I love trout," the dentist said, his face in the door. "How're everybody's teeth?"

"So far so good," Arthur said. "We're brushing morning and night."

Now, with the wind tearing at their backs, the three men walked toward the river gorge. "These aren't our rabbits," Ronnie said. The little creatures were everywhere, running from bush to bush. "These are longer. And check those black ears. We don't have any black ears."

He was right. These were some kind of jackrabbit with dark ears which lay flat when they darted through the sage. "Ten thousand years ago, the canyon got too deep for these guys to cross, and they were smarter than we are. They didn't want to get to the other side. This is a whole different population."

Darwin stopped and glassed the area before them. "I don't think it matters," he said. "Let's cut right a little. I hope we're not too far off. It's odd. We should be close."

Twenty minutes later, the terrain had not changed. They walked with the wind ripping and pushing at them. The high cloud sheet glowed, punishingly bright, and they squinted against it even with their plastic eyewear. It was as if the river had been pulled from the world. Then Darwin grabbed the back of Ronnie's pack, stopping him.

"What?"

Ahead, the world presented another illusion. The three men shielded their eyes and tried to fathom the strange distance which appeared to be both near and far, a telescoped panorama. Kicking forward, they saw the trick become apparent and the granular face of the far cliff came into view. The plain had appeared unbroken, sand and sage, the rocky chasm out of sight until they stepped to it. Darwin glassed the far side, but could discern nothing. "I wanted to see the tent, at least. Are we north or south?" He handed the field glasses to Arthur.

"Check it," Ronnie said. He had baby-stepped up to the edge and then come wheeling back. "It is a little different over here." Darwin went up and toed the demarcation between the sandy mesa and the yawning blue air of the canyon. The drop was a straight vertical line to the river, which looked blue and amber and about two hundred feet away when in fact it was almost a thousand.

"Get back a little," Ronnie said. He had backpedaled into the sage twenty feet. "This side is no good," he said. "It's all about to fall down."

"We're south another mile," Key said. He pointed. "I can see the tops of the electric poles, just barely."

"Darwin," Ronnie said. "Let's go." He had noticed the sand here was oddly clear of rabbit tracks. "How do they know not to run over the edge?"

"They just know."

Arthur Key walked up to the drop-off. "It is going to fall down," he said. "In about five thousand years. Come on. We better keep moving."

The three men walked south along the rim, Ronnie staying

farther from the canyon than Key and Darwin. "Did you tell Traci you're coming in for dinner?"

"I didn't see her."

"You went down to the Antlers."

"I didn't see Traci. I went to the bank."

"Then you went to the Antlers. What'd she say?"

"She didn't say anything because I didn't see her."

They were making their heavy steps in the thick sand.

Key continued. "Did she say she was looking forward to seeing you and your friends later and that she'd save the window booth for us?"

Ronnie marched in the bright wind.

"Did she say that she'd try to get off early so you guys could go back to her house and watch the television?"

"She didn't say anything because I didn't see her, you asshole."

"You went into the bank. Then you went to the Antlers, which was mostly empty and Traci was not there, which disappointed you because you bear real affection for that girl, and you stood there and Marion told you, because she remembers you from having you broken down in her house and for some reason that woman thinks the world of you." Key was speaking in short even bursts as the men did not mitigate their pace. "And she said that Traci was going to meet you later when you and your fine friends came in for their steak dinner, the wise older man and the strong handsome man, who doesn't speak very much."

Darwin walked and breathed this in. He'd been watching the flurries of dust his feet raised blow out over the chasm and spiral up and disappear, each step a ghost. Hearing Arthur Key play with Ronnie, hearing Arthur Key talk this way gave him a feeling he hadn't had for months, a kind of happiness that braced him in the day. "The wise man, who is dumb as a rock, is also quite handsome," he said.

"Oh for godsakes," Ronnie said. "Not you too."

"But what did the note say?" Arthur Key asked Ronnie.

"Shut up!" Ronnie called.

Key stopped in the sand and slumped his shoulders, shaking his head. "You did. You wrote her a note. That's good work. Notes are good."

"What note?"

"Did you give it to Marion?" He rubbed his chin. "No, she might have read it. You kept it, didn't you? Oh man."

"What note is this?" Darwin said again.

"The note in Ronnie's back pocket right now."

The young man was still walking, stabbing his steps into the soft ground.

"A note is the first signal of a civilized courtship. You"—he pointed ahead to Ronnie's back—"are a gentleman. Darwin, this is all getting good."

"Oh, it was good already."

"There's no note."

Key started walking again, nodding his head.

Soon they could see their worksite across the river canyon. The poles and the neat stacks of lumber and the tent were clear on the vast expanse. Again it was a different view and made their efforts small. Key was sobered by the panorama, and the vastness smothered his notions that the project might succeed. It was one thing, and a good thing, to secure a rail or build a step, but under the pressing sky and against this thousand-mile wind, and across the red and violet vacuum of the rocky chasm, every nail they'd pounded seemed a waste of time. The three men stood in the soft sand near the lip of rock in their sunglasses and looked across at their little jobsite. Ronnie used the binoculars for a moment and said, "Some blue table. Those guys have got one fine blue table." For the first time they could see the palisades and protrusions of the rock wall under their camp as the cliff stood, broken and crevassed, all the way down to the river. Key pointed out the two eagle nests about halfway down, the red rocks washed white beneath the aeries.

"If the wind blows like this during the big show on Labor Day, everybody's going to die. They can't afford even a breeze." Arthur was setting up the tripod, screwing tight the brass fittings. They all moved slowly now, step by step lining up with the markers on Ronnie's graded approach to the takeoff site across the canyon. When Art was satisfied, he secured the transit on the tripod in the sand. Darwin went south, stepping another hundred paces exactly, and stood the target stick in the ground, waiting. Key sighted straight through the open air where Ronnie had staked the base of the location of the ramp, focusing until he could see the plastic streamer twisting in the wind. Then he turned to Darwin and through the telescopic lens read the numbers off the stick, saying them aloud so Ronnie could write them down.

"Just how does this magic work?" Ronnie asked. "Does it say a number in there?"

Arthur looked at the boy and said, "Hold your hand straight out and hold up a finger." Ronnie did it. "Now close one eye. Open it. Close the other."

"And?"

"Now, if we knew how far apart your eyes are, we could find out where your finger was."

Arthur Key and Darwin changed places on the windy ledge. When Key was set again, he shot both alignments and Ronnie wrote them down. By the time Arthur Key and Ronnie rejoined him, Darwin had laid down the marker and again had the field glasses to his eyes.

"What have you got?" Key asked him.

Darwin handed him the glasses. "There's a truck."

"Is something going on?" Ronnie stepped over.

Key gave him the glasses and asked, "Do you know that guy? Who is the girl?"

Ronnie could see two figures walking around the camp. He recognized the young guy in a black T-shirt as the younger of the men who had come at night. The girl was about nineteen, and she wore a white tank top that left her belly bare above her cutoff jean shorts. Ronnie watched her pull open the flaps of their tent and go in.

"Hey," he said.

"What is it?" Darwin asked.

"The girl's in the tent," Key said. He held the transit lens to his right eye.

"The guy is one of the guys who tried to steal the lumber," Ronnie said. "His name is Buster."

"Sit down," Arthur Key said. "You too, Darwin. There's no sense now in having them see us."

The girl came out of the tent and opened the galley box. The young man was quickly sliding around a little, making sure that they were alone.

"It's a 'seventy-five Ford pickup, white with one blue door." He read the plate number to Darwin.

"This guy's on a mission," Arthur said, watching the boy on the graded runway, pulling the stakes up out of the ground one by one all the way to the precipice and then hurling the whole bundle over the edge. The pine sticks flickered against the red rock cliff face as they fell. The young man turned and looked toward the girl; she must have called him. Key could see her waving their bottle of George Dickel. She'd scattered the cooking gear on the ground.

"They're going to trash the place," Ronnie said.

Now the girl had pulled her shirt off and danced with her hands above her head, swinging the bottle. The guy came over and grabbed at her breasts, and she swatted his hand away. He took the bottle from her and drank. Now the girl was standing on the table dancing. "She's on the table," Ronnie reported.

"We can see it," Darwin said. The kid came to the table and reached up, pulling at her pants, which she finally helped him with and stepped out of. Her ass was the whitest thing in the white day, and there was a smudged blue karmic circle tattooed there where her pants would have hidden it. Ronnie still had the binoculars. Suddenly the girl jumped onto the guy's shoulders, his face lost in her, and they staggered back until he could set her down. Then she pulled him into the tent.

"Let's move back a little ways," Arthur Key said. "Behind the sage."

"No way," Ronnie Panelli said. "They're in the tent."

"Easy, Ronnie," Key said. "With this wind they can hear us."

"Good."

"No, I want this on them. Move back and watch." The three men retreated to the first substantial bank of brush and knelt there. It had been a minute. "Good," Key said. Now he went to the cliff edge again and clapped his hands three times, each a bass concussion, and he hollered once: a very deep "Hey!" He knelt out of sight. Five seconds later the boy appeared in the tent flap, tugging his pants on. He looked north and then out across the river and then north again. Now he was putting on his shirt and walking around the tent listening.

"He can't see us," Arthur said.

The girl came out struggling with her cutoffs and then snapping her sandals on one at a time. They both were looking north. The young man went to his truck, the wind pushing him. The girl went back into the tent and retrieved the whiskey.

"That's not the same truck from the other night," Ronnie said.

They saw the vehicle stop at the gate to the ranch road. The boy stood out on the ground again and the girl now helped hand him a rifle.

"Don't worry," Key said. "He can in no way see us."

The kid lifted the weapon and aimed and fired a shot and then another into the large canvas tent. Then he handed it back for the girl to put on the window rack.

"Goddamn it," Ronnie said.

"You didn't know him?" Key asked Darwin.

"They're not from Mercy," he answered.

The truck had lifted dust as it bounced north on the ranch road.

"Well, Diff must have offended them too." The men stood and reassumed their packs. There was now a single line of blue along the western horizon where the ceiling had broken. Key sent Ronnie back to tie two orange construction streamers on the base of the sage at the landing site, so they could shoot it with the transit exactly from the ramp site. Now the men turned to face the unrelenting wind in the harsh brightness and started kicking dust-flashing footsteps toward the distant road.

TEN

A T THE ANTLERS, the three men sat in the window booth. There had been a discussion in the truck about hurrying to the site. Ronnie was hot to get back, maybe catch the intruders, intercept them on the farm road, "kick their asses," then inspect the damage at camp, clean up, fix stuff. He waved his arms as he went through it. It was his camp and he was mad. But Darwin had prevailed: "Those two are gone and they aren't coming back. Let's have some supper in the town like we planned and then go back. There's plenty of daylight."

Art had parked the big flatbed truck behind the wooden building in a weedy gravel lot and they had entered that way, past the small kitchen deck and into the bar and dining room which faced the street. There were two men sitting at the dark wooden bar in shirtsleeves watching the news on the elevated television on the cornice of the backbar. Sitting down in the dark room, they all could feel their faces burned by the day. It was disconcerting to be out of the wind. They put their sunglasses on the varnished tabletop and let their eyes adjust.

Ronnie fingered the salt and pepper shakers which were two small Corona bottles with perforated caps.

"We've got salt and pepper," Key told him.

"I wasn't going to take them," Ronnie said.

The bartender came over, a woman in Levi's and a faded blue turtleneck with the sleeves pushed up to her elbows. "Hello, Darwin," she said. "Hi, Ronnie, where you been? Where'd you run to the other week? You just now missed Traci."

"Working," Ronnie said, looking at where he bumped his thumbs together on the table.

"Good, good. She said you're quite the cook."

"He's altogether skillful," Darwin said. Ronnie held still.

"This your whole crew?" the woman asked Darwin. She was looking at Arthur.

"It is," he told her. "This is Art. How have you been, Marion?"

"I'm fine, same old. I'm trying to figure a way to raise the price of beer and blame it on someone else."

Arthur Key looked once at the woman, her natural ease, her shape in the shirt and her smiling eyes, and he looked away. All of a sudden the day seemed full of women.

"To hear it around here, it's an invasion. There's forty of you raising hell out at Difficulto."

"It's just a summer project," Darwin told her. "Diff gets everybody riled up. He likes that."

"I know it," she said. "And he's done it. You'd think the federal government was out there building a god knows what. You guys eating?"

"You got any of the sirloin tips?"

"Yes sir."

"That's me," Darwin said. "With that little salad and some ranch dressing."

She looked at the other men. "You want menus?"

"No, ma'am," Arthur said. "I'll have the same."

"Cheeseburger," Ronnie said. "I've been waiting for a cheeseburger with the fries."

"And could you bring us two pints of the Old Mill Dew?" Darwin said, looking to Arthur for his approval. It was an Idaho brewery. "And some lime Kool-Aid for this young chef."

"Coke," said Ronnie. "We're in town."

Outside the streaked and tinted front window of the Antlers, the bright day still flared, the traffic in town desultory and sparse, though the quiet street scene was a strange dimension to the men who had been out on the plateau for weeks. Each passing vehicle seemed an incursion, and the people crossing to the pharmacy or walking by talking or holding the hand of a child invaded the men's attention. It all might as well have been a movie. Opposite such an active diorama, the little elevated television flickered its blue and red lights, faces eclipsing one another as the voices rang tinny and disconnected. Ronnie looked up at it.

When Marion returned with the silverware and the beverages, she said to Darwin, "That's Hector in the kitchen, if you want to say hello. He saw you come in."

"I will," Darwin said, rising. "I'll be right back."

When he disappeared into the back, Key and Panelli could hear the two men speaking Spanish loudly for a minute, a laughing greeting, and then the voices subsided.

"Could you live in a town like this?" Ronnie asked Key.

"Nice town," Key said back. Arthur touched Ronnie's glass with his own. The beer was a creamy bitter and Key felt it open his throat. "Why not?"

"Too small. Don't you think? I've never been in a small town before. Bunch of guys here already know me."

"Ronnie," Arthur said. "You didn't waste any time cutting a wide swath through the single women in town."

"I passed out and hit my fucking head on the floor." He pointed. "I was sitting right there and I went down hard."

"After being told to rest in the clinic."

"And Traci and her mom took me over to their place."

"That's how it always starts," Key said. He was now surprised again to be able to kid this way. His range of motion was growing. His worry about the campsite had subsided.

Ronnie leaned up on the scarred wooden table with both elbows. "But, seriously, this is a weird little place, isn't it?" He turned and nodded at the five mounted antelope heads on the old dark paneled wall of the Antlers. "I have never in my life seen that before. Something about that is not exactly right."

"This is the West, Ronnie. There's some stuff."

"You know what they look like? I saw them in the mirror the day I came in here, and they scared the shit out of me. I thought they were watching it all, like judges. I've dreamed about them, these five guys. When I was hurt, I saw them watching."

Key examined his friend for moment over the top of his glass, the bitter beer wonderful in his mouth. It was a privilege to sit like this in a restaurant booth and know that sometime soon the food would come. It was good to have a chair with a back, and he leaned back now.

"She's a nice girl," Key said. "And you've been good about it. You keep on and see what happens. This could be a very fine town for you. We'll have a little supper here and then find her so you can give her your note, and we'll go back to camp and work another week." The sentence sounded like good work itself, sane and filled with promise.

Darwin came back out with his buddy Hector. The man was somewhere in his thirties and wore a short white cook's hat and an apron. Key and Ronnie stood to shake his hand. After the introductions, Hector said, "His wife taught me the secrets of the culinary trade at Diff's place. Did you ever see the kitchen out there?"

"We haven't."

"Diff's old man had the right idea," Hector went on. "That kitchen is the largest room on the entire place except for the barn. We cooked."

"Hector's part owner here," Darwin said. "His wife teaches school."

"Shall we talk or shall we eat?" Marion said from behind them. She balanced the three large white oval plates before her as well as a basket of hot rolls in a folded checked cloth.

"Next time have some Mexican or the Chinese," Hector told them as they climbed back into the booth while their plates slid onto the table. "I've got an Idaho fu yung that will make you well."

"Will do," Key told him. Darwin and Hector shook hands, and the cook went back around the bar.

Arthur Key ordered one more beer and looked at the steaming plate of gravied steak before him. His plate had exactly twice the mashed potatoes and meat that Darwin's did. "This looks a little customized," he said.

"The cook's a friend of ours," Darwin said.

"He is now."

In the window booth of the Antlers Bar and Cafe, the three men ate without talking. Ronnie ran a big circle of ketchup onto his fries and dusted them with salt and ate them four at a time when he wasn't tearing at his sandwich. The two other men worked knife and fork into their steaming dinners. The sirloin tips were fall-apart and savory.

Finally, a faint parenthesis of ketchup at each corner of his mouth, and his mouth full of French fries, Ronnie said, "What we should have done is got a boxful of those black-eared rabbits and brought them with us to our side of the canyon. Kick that gene pool in the ass. Get some superrabbits on the old mesa."

Arthur Key considered his remark and then made it. "I'm not sure we want to play god with the rabbit tribes."

"How old is that river gorge?" Ronnie asked.

There was no answer but the door yawned open behind them and the two people they had seen in their campsite came into the Antlers. They were speaking noisily, the girl saying, "And the rest is just so much bullshit and you know it since you are a expert in the bullshit department, King Bullshit is who you are." She laughed. Darwin put his hand over onto Ronnie's arm and pinned it to the table to signal the younger man to stay quiet. Arthur Key saw him and turned to see the boy and the girl take stools at the bar. The men stopped eating.

"Nothing is going to happen here," Arthur said to his table.

Marion came out of the kitchen and stood before the two. "Buster, this young lady is not old enough to sit at the bar."

"She might be," the boy said. "She's got her ID now."

"She might be two weeks older than when I told you guys this same thing two weeks ago. Now, you can take a table or you can drive up to Concept where they'll serve children, or so I hear."

The girl stood and squirmed a hand into her cutoff jeans pocket.

"Don't bother, honey. I don't care if it cost you a hundred bucks and came all the way from Boise. I'm not serving you."

Now the girl had a driver's license in her hand, but Marion wouldn't look at it. The girl was tapping the card on the bar, one-two, one-two.

"Don't do that, Gina," Buster told her.

"How much bullshit is this?" she said.

"Let's just sit over here." He tried to guide her back past the window booth to a table by the wall, under the line of mounted pronghorns.

"I'm still having a beer," the girl said, loudly.

"Not in here, you're not," Marion said, grabbing two menus.

"We got whiskey in the truck anyway," Gina said to the room. Buster had guided her to a chair which she kicked at and it barked on the old hardwood floor. Key had watched the kid, noting that he didn't have a belt or knife or anything large enough to be a firearm in his pocket. He had resumed eating, though it was all different now.

"What you looking at?" the girl Gina said.

Darwin still pressed Ronnie's arm.

"Nothing," Ronnie said. "I wasn't looking."

Marion came and stood at the table, her bartender's face on, weary but ready to do what might be next. "You guys want some of Hector's pie?"

Behind her the boy Buster was trying to get the girl to quiet down.

Darwin had his wallet out and told her to wrap half a pie so they could take it. They had to get back. The room was very small now.

Stepping out the back door was relief and Art took a breath, and then walking to the truck was also a relief and the men kicked their feet without talking.

"What are we doing?" Ronnie said. "They're right fucking there."

"We've got work to do," Arthur said. "And as sweet as it might have been to hear you comment on that girl's tattoo, it would have changed the day for us."

"I was going to compliment her dancing ability and ask her to stay off the table."

"Same," Arthur said.

"Ronnie," Marion called from the back door, motioning him over. Arthur followed the young man returning to the building. He had to. "I hear you are quite the gentleman," she told him. "I just want to say good for you."

Ronnie looked at her. "I appreciate that."

"We'll see you soon, I hope," Marion said.

Ronnie nodded. Arthur Key stopped him with a hand on his arm. "Give her the note."

"What?" Ronnie said.

"He's going to give you something, but you've got to promise not to read it."

Ronnie squirmed, but Arthur held him.

"What is it?" she said.

Ronnie stood still finally and quickly fished the creased paper out of his back pocket and handed it to the woman in her apron behind the old cafe.

ELEVEN

THE FOURTH OF JULY passed unnoticed on the plateau and without remark. A week later, Arthur asked Darwin when it had been, had they missed the Fourth, and they narrowed it to one of three nights when they had sat at Ronnie's table after dinner in the charcoal twilight under the clouds of bats emerging from the vermilion canyon walls. As always in some ebony quadrant of the sky there were ghosted flashes of an electrical storm blooming like small stars and some nights two storms north and south so far distant as to seem tricks of the eye. They decided that one of them may have been the fireworks at Mercy, perhaps.

By mid-July they'd skirted the tent, tying up the sides and fastening the door flaps open. From time to time, they'd lower the windward side if there was a storm or just a blow, but mostly it was warm until midnight and the open air helped. Darwin set up his big yellow Igloo cooler on a short square stand Ronnie had made from two-by-four scraps (and painted blue with the last of the gallon), and twice a week he'd drop a block of ice in the cooler, and the men drank the cold water from insulated mugs with their initials inked on the sides. At night with the tent open in the dark, they heard the varmints moving in the sage, the rabbits as they settled, always one being taken by a coyote or a hawk, a quick scream or two, but nothing that could slow the train of sleep that claimed them in the same order: Ronnie, Darwin, Arthur Key, though now his mind worried him only a minute after he had reclined.

When the mornings came up now, the sky was bifurcated by the electrical wires that Idaho Power had erected on the trunk line. The black cables ruined a little something for Key, made the place smaller. Tamed it. They'd come with a cherry picker truck and run the wires through insulators on each tall post right up near the tent. When they'd arrived, the two guys in khakis and white company T-shirts drove up to the tent yard. Their toolbelts were jammed with devices of their trade and heavy insulated pliers.

"How long you guys living here?" the driver asked Darwin.

"Through August."

"This is that television deal," the other man said. "You guys are the motorcycle program, right? That little girl who wants to be the new Evel what's-his-name."

Hearing about it this way, being called out of the dream of the project, bothered Arthur Key, and he went back to the canyon where he had been helping Ronnie dig small-diameter postholes for the chain-link fence which would line the rim. Their challenge in this regard was to find the solid ground still close enough to the edge to afford a view. Key had already decided to have the steel posts only ten feet apart. He'd spent his whole life looking at balcony rails with too few supports. This fence was going to keep people from falling; they certainly were going to lean on it. Ronnie was in the seat of the little Farmall tractor, backing to each spot, and Arthur guided the small auger where he wanted it.

"When is August?" Ronnie asked him.

"You don't know your months?'

"I don't know what day it is."

"I don't either," Key told him. "It's late June. July. August." The big man guided the steel blade into the spade hole he'd made. "Go," he told Ronnie, and Ronnie switched on the auger motor and the drill turned into the dirt. Each hole was three feet deep, which would leave a five-foot pole.

"You ever build a fence before?" Arthur asked him.

"You know I haven't."

"This is hardly work," he told Ronnie, pointing at the rolls of chain link, the bales of pipe, the boxes of fittings. "It's a kit. Like an Erector set."

"Okay," the boy said. "You ready to move?"

"Go."

Ronnie motored the tractor forward and then backed to the next marked spot.

"You don't know what an Erector set is, do you?"

"Is it like a toy?"

"What'd you play with as a kid?"

"I wasn't a kid. I'm a kid now."

Key pointed at Ronnie. "You're not a kid now. You're a journeyman in the construction arts. But your dad didn't get you an Erector set."

"Just tell me what it is. My dad wasn't exactly around."

"Ever?"

"I might have met the man."

"This was down in Joliet?" Arthur had spray-painted a yellow dot on the auger at three feet and he watched it now. The thick red dirt rolled out of the hole in waves.

"Not in but all around. We moved some."

Key waved at Ronnie. "That's enough, lift her out." Ronnie raised the auger and turned it off. Arthur walked the canyon edge to the next mark. Below him a hundred yards two small eagles rode their wings in the glassy air. Today he could smell the river, the water on the rocks, the topmost spill of a hundred tons of air slowly bumping and roiling down the vivid gorge.

Ronnie drove out into the sage twenty feet. He had become expert with the standard transmissions, and he reversed fluidly and backed again to where Key now waited, his arm out to receive the post digger. "Good. You're good."

"What grade did you finish?" He set the blade and said, "Go."

Ronnie started the auger. "Tenth, eleventh."

"You got to high school?"

"Ninth."

Every time the rotating drill would strike rock or shudder, Key would shake the armature until it broke through or freed itself.

"When did you first get arrested?"

"Come on, Art. Let's make a fence."

"We're talking."

"Okay, when'd you get arrested? Just what the fuck is your sad story, big man?"

They could hear the blade rankling rock and the motor groaned. "Shut it down," he told the boy. They lifted the steel post digger from the ground and Arthur went back and picked up the six-foot St. Albans bar. He dropped it into the hole and tapped a few times experimentally. Then he assumed a grip and lifted the heavy steel bar straight up. He drove it into the hole and Ronnie felt the tump it made striking sandstone. Arthur instantly pulled the bar out and dropped it into the sand. He folded his arms and stuffed his hands under his arms and looked at Ronnie. "Don't ever do that without gloves." He walked off a little ways, breathing through his nose. He could see the two guys from the electrical company move their cherry picker to the next pole and begin again. A two-man crew like that was good to watch; they knew the drill and did three hours' work in one. Still, the two heavy black wires looked odd to Key, out of place. He drew a breath and pulled his leather work gloves out of his back pocket and put them on.

"You okay?" Ronnie said.

"I should have had my gloves on. Put your gloves on."

"I'm just driving."

"Put them on." Ronnie pulled his gloves on.

Arthur Key picked up the steel bar and again drove it into the shallow posthole. Then twice and three, four, five, six times. He finally stood and dropped the bar to the side and guided the auger back in. "Let's see what we see," he said. This time when Ronnie started the auger there was another noise as it engaged the ground, a grinding snap, and pieces of broken red rock began to spill over the lip as the bit went down. At three feet, Arthur signaled and Ronnie hoisted the turning auger up into the air.

They continued down the line, the fresh atmosphere of the river rising over Arthur Key as he worked the precipice. The fence was to be one hundred and ten yards in a winding line along the edge, thirty-two holes. When Darwin whistled them for lunch, there were ten to go. Arthur Key lifted the auger armature and locked it in place so Ronnie could take the tractor and gas it after they ate.

The two linesmen were finishing the outlet boxes at the base of the last pole, two boxes: 110 and 220. They drilled the boxes fast against the wooden post, and then they stood and opened and closed the latched doors.

"You're all set," one of the men told Darwin.

"Why do we need that?" Ronnie asked Arthur Key. They had removed their gloves and were working at their hands in the whitewash bucket.

"We don't," Key told him. "It's for the show. There's going to be some lights and some cameras and such. More than generators could do."

"Is he going to build a permanent structure out here?" the company man asked Darwin. He was looking at the stacks of plywood and lumber. His partner had walked over to the edge of the gorge and now returned appraising the various features of the construction site.

"I don't think so."

"This all smells a lot like money," the man said.

"It's like those temples where they sacrificed the virgins," his partner said. "It's going to be something. I may drive down from Boise. You going to build a ramp?"

"Too much community college for Brad," the driver said to Darwin.

"The Incas had a whole temple for it. A hundred tons of stone so they could cut some girl's throat."

"Enough with the Incas," the driver said. "Those are hot now," he told Darwin, indicating the electrical boxes. "You're good to go."

"Thanks," Darwin said. "You want to stay out and have some lunch?" He was cutting thick ham sandwiches diagonally with the butcher knife and tomatoes protruded.

"No, thanks. Whenever we get down here, we swing back up through Theron and eat at the Black Cat. If you haven't been up there, it's worth the trip. If you're crazy for curly fries and buffalo burgers."

After the power company truck drove away, the men took the paper plates laden with the sandwiches thick with cheddar and purple onions and romaine and mustard and sat at the blue table. Darwin had a jar of potato salad and Ronnie coated his with black pepper the way he'd learned that Arthur Key ate his. Art set the two-gallon glass jar of giant dill pickles on the blue table and speared one out with the long knife, slicing it quickly lengthwise and dropping half onto Ronnie's plate.

"This is a handsome picnic," Arthur Key said. "You want a pickle, Darwin?"

"None for me," he said. He finished pouring their mugs full of lime Kool-Aid.

"You ever go on a picnic?" Arthur asked Ronnie. "Take your girlfriend to the park?"

Ronnie's mouth was full, chewing. Finally, he answered: "I might have. I ate in the park."

"Is eating in the park a picnic?" Arthur asked Darwin.

"A picnic is no casual matter," the older man said. "A picnic is a serious endeavor."

"There's the planning. This isn't a bag of burgers in the car."

"To eat a lunch in the daylight out-of-doors on a blanket with a young woman," Darwin said, "is courtship. You would only do such a thing with your intended."

"You two are so full of shit that it is a wonder of nature." Ronnie drank his Kool-Aid greedily.

Darwin slid his milk crate stool back and stood up. He went into the tent and returned with a folded blanket of green plaid. He gave it to Ronnie.

"Nice," the young man said. "This is for my big picnic?"

"Be careful with it," Darwin said. "But, yes, it will be a good start."

"Now all you need is some fried chicken and some napkins."

"Wine, glasses, silverware, pasta salad, salt and pepper, brownies," Darwin said. He had made them a pan of swollen brownies in his Dutchoven the night before and pulled the bag from the foodbox now and set it on the table.

"I don't like wine," Ronnie said.

"It's not about you. Take the wine in case. You can drink Kool-Aid."

He stood and refilled each of their mugs with the sweet green drink. "I will."

"Ronnie," Art said. "Don't feed the rabbits." All during their lunch Ronnie had been tossing bits of lettuce over near the corner of the tall bundle of lumber. He'd been feeding a dozen or so of the bravest rabbits for weeks.

Ronnie stood up now. "They've never seen lettuce before. Not for a thousand years, as you'd say." He picked up the ruins of his lunch, the plate, his crumpled napkin, tossing his fork in the washtub and the paper in the trash barrel. "This is the best job I personally have ever had, but that does not mean you two are not just full of shit." He grabbed his gloves out of his back pocket with a flourish and pulled them on. "Now I'm going to gas the tractor and drill ten more holes."

As he walked away, Arthur said, "Don't bring her out here. It won't be a picnic out here." Ronnie didn't turn to the remark.

When the postholes for the steel fence were dug, each dark spot circled by perfect rings of the rusty earth, Arthur removed the power takeoff from the tractor and took Ronnie out near the gate, where they changed the oil. Arthur guided the young man through the process, removing the fine-threaded plug and catching the thick black oil in a plastic vinegar bottle which he cut in half with his pocketknife. Using the top of the bottle as a funnel, Ronnie poured four quarts of fresh oil into the vehicle.

"You ever watch television?" he asked the big man.

"No," Arthur said.

"I used to watch a lot of television. They had sets in the dayrooms at juvie, and I watched it."

"What did you see?"

"That's what I was thinking. I don't remember. God, day in and day out."

"You want us to get a television now that we've got power."

Ronnie was pouring the oil carefully and looked up at Arthur. "Oh god no. I was just talking." When he looked up from the last quart, Ronnie said, "Somebody's coming."

Key listened and then said, "That's the river. The wind changed."

"No, listen."

Twenty seconds later Key heard it too, a vehicle approaching, which became a green pickup truck. Arthur walked up the dirt road, spilling the dirty oil in a stripe up the middle of the white gravel. "You got ears like a rabbit," Key told the boy. "There's some real-life traffic today."

The green and white carryall pickup slowed and eased up beside Key and Panelli. "Dudes," the driver said. He was a small man with a razor-line mustache, and he had a worn-out piece of paper pinched in his fingers. He held it out the window to Arthur Key, who saw it was a penciled map. "Just where are we, then?" It was the telephone company.

TWELVE

THE TWILIGHT THICKENED until the two men nailing the brace on the two-by-four guardrail became a pair of silhouettes with hammers. They worked without talking. The entire camera platform had been cut and measured all afternoon: the decking which they screwed down with the power drill and the gated rail, sixty uprights and the top bar. They'd been setting and nailing these cut pieces for two hours now, and like people who read as the day fails, they didn't see that they'd lost the light. At close range, they could see everything they needed. At three, Darwin had driven Ronnie into town for dinner with Marion and Traci. The young woman would drive him home later. Off south half a mile, a coyote had been calling and then gave off calling. That was when Darwin looked up and saw the stars burning through the dark. The encampment had gathered itself in such failed light into five dark blocks.

"This day is tipped over," Darwin said.

Arthur Key stepped off the deck and pulled the last five

sections of railing onto the boards. "Let's save these for Ronnie. It'd be bad luck to finish this tonight. He can polish off this little crow's nest."

Darwin had the drill. "Where's the case for this?"

The two men saw how dark it had become and they stood and scanned around their feet.

"Don't let me kick it into the river," Key said. He found it on the single entry step they'd erected, and he handed it to Darwin.

"You believe in luck?" Darwin said.

"I believe in everything," Arthur Key said. "I believe in work. I believe in day and night and whatever this is called when the day's over but it won't get dark."

They walked back toward the tent and now felt the chill that had been working along the canyon for the past hour.

"But that's not what you were asking."

"I don't know. I think I was asking if you wanted a little whiskey."

"I believe in having a little whiskey. Just to clean out my old coffee cup." Key felt good. His head was empty. He put his hammer and gloves in his toolbox and grabbed his Levi's jacket from the peg above his cot inside the huge tent. Darwin lit the candle lanterns on the blue table and he poured a lick of George Dickel into the two cups.

"You want some ice?"

"I don't," Key told him. "I don't want to get started on the niceties."

"No sense in that." Darwin touched his cup to Key's and took a sip. The two men sat in the quiet dark. The river was just a whisper now and the sky continued to bloom with stars. Silent on the sage mesa, they felt the whiskey warm in their throats, and the silence seemed to Key to be a kind of balance between one thing and the next, a fulcrum of some sort, as solid and substantial as the weight of whatever it carried. In any section of the tricky night sky, satellites slid, and other lights moved at intervals. It was for a moment like he was in his own head, Key thought, everything was so far away, pinned against the far wall of knowing, the distances between him and the next thing were vast and still opening. He felt the cold air behind his ears and down his neck.

"Were you ever in a fight?" Darwin asked him. "A big man like you. Didn't people want to fight you?"

"Sort of. I mean yes. It happened a couple of times when I was in the wrong place, a bar. Early on when we'd close a job down, I'd go out with the guys to celebrate and if I stayed say until ten or eleven, some smartass would come for me, bump me, call me a name, like that. I wanted to throw these guys around, but I never did. Sad, isn't it?"

"You'd leave the bar," Darwin said quietly.

"I wasn't much of a bar guy."

"What did you do to celebrate?"

"Not too much. It was enough for me to have done the job right." He lifted his cup for another splash. "Now that is sad. But I was pleased and didn't feel the need to go anywhere or buy something or whatever. Most times, almost all the time, I had a new job to plan, and that felt real good. I thought sometimes of my dad, how much he would have liked some of the work I had, but mostly I'd make my notes on what to do better next time, what to do again, what not to do again, and go home."

Darwin had fired up the two-burner propane stove which they had begun using as the nights warmed up, and he had their pot of stew out. He was cutting an onion into it, letting the pieces drop into the simmering mixture. "You want toast?" he asked his friend.

"Let's fry up some bread on the skillet," Art said, handing

him the flat tray from their wooden galley cabinet. Darwin sliced two thick pieces from the sourdough loaf while butter melted and pooled on the warming steel. He tossed the bread there and moved the pieces around in the butter with his knife.

"I know you didn't have a wife. Did you have a dog?"

"No dog."

Darwin drank down his whiskey. "Now that's pathetic right there."

Key laughed softly.

A minute later they could smell the bread browning at the edges. Darwin stirred the stew. "The onions are stiff, but this stew is ready."

They let the bread burn a minute more and then Darwin turned off the stove and ladled out two enameled bowls of stew.

"I like the bread burned a bit like this," Darwin said. The bowls of stew were beautiful on the blue table in the lantern light. The lanterns hissed faintly and the stove ticked sharply cooling down.

"It's good enough for who it's for," Darwin said, sitting opposite the big man. They ate the evening meal and wiped their bowls with the final crusts.

"My wife always left a bite of bread," Darwin said.

"I've seen it that way," Art said. "My dad would do it."

"Why'd she do it?" Darwin said. "Even when we were still hungry, young I mean. We'd eat and she'd leave a bite, a corner."

"Did you ask her about it?"

Darwin sat still. The men's faces were above the lightfall from their lamps, and Arthur could not discern his friend's expression. "No," he said finally. "I didn't get the chance."

"Maybe it's in the Bible," Arthur said. "I don't know that book, but could it be in there?"

"Goddamn Bible anyway," Darwin said. He drank his whiskey off and poured another inch. He stood up and took their dishes to the washtub.

Arthur joined him and took the bowls, wiping them out and then rinsing from the clean barrel. "I sense you want to argue about this, Darwin, but it's not my argument."

"You think there's a god anywhere near this poor place?" Darwin said. He wasn't speaking loudly.

"That also is not a discussion I can have," Arthur Key told him. "You'll have to contact the professors on that one."

"No I won't," Darwin said quickly.

Now under the whirring of the river there was another sound or something like a sound which became a faint rhythm like breathing and then a shadow drifting along the farm road toward the camp. The figure turned in at the gate, and both Arthur and Darwin knew it was Ronnie Panelli. He didn't see them and when Arthur called his name, he stopped.

"What time is it?" Ronnie said across the yard.

"Come on over. We're having a drink," Darwin said.

"That's okay."

"What did you do? Where's Traci?"

"It's okay."

"Come over."

"That's fine. I walked back. I'm going to hang out for a while." Ronnie turned, faltering, and then moved back toward the lumber stack. A moment later, they saw the cab light of the flatbed truck go on and then off, and the sound of the door shut.

"Oh, for godsakes," Darwin said. He lifted the whiskey bottle. "One more?"

"That's a long walk," Arthur told him. "You better go over there."

"We're drinking here." Darwin put a short splash in his own cup. "In this I'm no good," he said. "I can't talk."

"No," Art said. "I cannot. I'm no good."

"I'm worse, my friend. It would be a mistake for me to go over there."

The two men sat in the dark, touching their cups down in moist circles on the heavy blue table.

Art reached the bottle and poured himself a touch, drinking it right down. "We're drinking. You go over and talk to him and if it won't go, I'll try it."

"He's in the truck for the night," Darwin said. "Something went bad in town. I wouldn't know where to start, where to take it or how to get out. You go. I'll save you some whiskey."

Arthur Key breathed in and then out. "I'll give it one shot." He stood in the gloom and immediately felt the pull of the sky. He was out of place, too large, a long way from the ground. He seized a water bottle to hold him down, and he walked to the old truck.

Ronnie had the windows rolled up, and he was smoking in there. Arthur knocked on the driver window. Ronnie wouldn't turn his head. Arthur rapped again. "Hey, you don't smoke."

The young man blew a stream of smoke into the windshield. He would not look at Key. The larger man gave it a minute and then took the door handle and stepped very close to the glass. "You don't want me to do this."

Ronnie finally looked at his friend. "I smoke. I can smoke."

"What happened?"

"I walked home. I don't belong over there."

"All the way?"

"I've been walking. I got a ride from some geezer to the bridge cutoff."

"Is Traci okay?"

"I'm okay. I'm going to sit in here for a while."

They were still speaking through the glass. "What did you fight about?"

"No fight. Really, Arthur, no fight. I don't know what I was thinking."

"Where'd you go?" Art's breath bloomed on the window and the cab filled with the smoke from Ronnie's cigarette.

"We were at her house. Marion came home. We were cooking."

Arthur Key just waited. He stood still by the window and put his hands in his pockets in a posture of eternal waiting. "Did you tell her what you were doing out here? About the job?"

"She knows about that."

"Roll down the window. You're going to choke."

"I told her where I was from, about my mom, about running away." Ronnie looked at Arthur, his face a ruin. He rolled the window down and spoke softly now. "I told her I'd been in jail."

"How'd she take it?"

"Why did I tell her that? What the fuck is wrong with me? I'm nuts since I've been out here." His short laugh sounded queasy. "I'm fucking upside down out here. Christ, Arthur, I told her I'd been in jail."

"And what did she say?"

"We were cooking some spaghetti and she went in the other room, and when I was alone I figured out what I had just told her. We were just talking about how her dad had been rough, and I'm nuts anymore and I told her that I'd been in jail. When she left the room, I went out the back door. I was insane to tell her. She's only known bad guys. What is the matter with me? Talking? I walked about a mile and some old guy lifted me to the cutoff. I've been walking." Ronnie had put out the cigarette and was rubbing his face with both of his hands. He went on. "I'm not going to go through chapter and verse of my little life with that girl. I could for a minute imagine telling her about breaking and entering, about stuff I took. I'm not even here right now. I'm a crazy man for acting this way."

Arthur Key stood and looked down, breathing, and then

up at the stars in their clusters. He looked over at Darwin in the shadows, the little yellow candle dots. "You want some stew?" Arthur Key asked him.

"You guys eat?"

Key opened the truck door and Ronnie climbed down. His hair was gone, cut to a buzz, and Arthur Key put his hand on Ronnie's head. "She cut your hair."

"Art," the boy used the name as if it was part of his terrible logic, tearing to a new page in their book. "I screwed it up. This is important. This is only the second important thing I've even been close to. The first was running and I knew it, when I got out of bed in the middle of the night in my mother's house and I dressed, I knew it wasn't the same old bullshit, small-time stupidity. I knew I'd be this sorry for it forever, but I went. I ran. My mother doesn't even know where I am and it's seven, eight months. I could have stayed and gone to court and then to jail again. I'd still be in jail; it was going to be two years. Two fucking years." Ronnie Panelli shook, a young man not a hundred and sixty pounds, a month away from twenty. He bit at it for a while but then just cried, standing and shaking.

"Ronnie," Arthur Key said. They stood in the thick dark, the air simply nothing, a host for shapes. "You were a thief. It was a shitty little thing. No one expects you to go and put everything back."

Ronnie's shoulders were rolled as far forward as shoulders go and his hands thrust deep, tight in his pockets could not still his crying.

Key went on. "Listen, son. Take a deep breath right now." Key took the boy's shoulders and pulled them back as Ronnie inhaled. "Now blow it out and get over it. You'll see her again. You'll talk. The world still waits on you."

Ronnie shivered. He let his shorn head fall against Key's chest for the briefest second. "I walked out here."

"I know you did."

"You guys in bed?"

"You tell her that you were a thief, but you let that life go. Tell her the truth. You're a carpenter."

"I am not."

"You better be. We've got some work out here tomorrow."

"Right, I know," Ronnie said. He was weary now. Key could hear the kettle over on the cook shelf in the dark as Darwin stirred the leftover stew.

"You want some toast? That was a walk."

"I'd eat it. I saw some deer. Four bucks right by the road."

"You see any snakes on the road?"

"Why do they do that? That's the kind of bullshit I can't stand about this place. Some goddamned snake right in the way." Ronnie sat down at the table. The two candles lit the edge of everything. "I appreciate it," he said as Darwin dropped one of the heavy spoons by the enamel dish.

"That's a smart haircut," Darwin said. "Looks good." Ronnie put his hand up, remembering it, and he smiled against his will.

Key sat at his corner of the table and did what he could to avoid Darwin's look, but late on such a day it was going to come, the solid recognition. Ronnie was at his stew. With the short hair and his face a plate in the yellow candlelight, he appeared a child. Darwin nodded to the big man and said, "You did good. I'd still be over there talking to the truck." When Arthur looked up, Darwin added, "Take a deep breath. The world still waits."

THIRTEEN

THE PHONE SOUNDED at 3:30 A.M. Arthur Key, who had
been waiting again under a thin membrane of sleep,
swung his legs out of his cot after the first short ring. All
of his sleep was like a waiting and it did not restore him. He
had been wired tight from when he was a kid, a kind of alert-
ness, readiness for the day, but this year had climbed into that
without relent. His work and the long days on the plateau
helped him sleep an hour and then two every night, but he
rose too quickly through the dark and lay waiting every dawn.
Now it was full dark in the tent, fresh but not cold and he
quickly pulled on his trousers and then his boots, barefoot. He
loved stepping into the world every day, and even now with
the phone's noise, the ring sounding like a cup of pennies
falling in a glass jar, he stood under the great wheel of stars
and breathed until his shoulders rose. In the corner of his eye
he caught some movement and turned to the mess table. In
the dark no shapes moved, and Key himself stood rigid. The
phone rang again, and Key saw a shadow turn as a coyote there
under the table stepped into the starlight and regarded the

man. Another emerged and the two walked without sound in a quick circle out and around the lumber stacks, disappearing.

Arthur Key stepped to the phone and lifted the receiver to his ear. The plates of stars at this hour had broken and slid upon one another, tilting, and he saw the bent handle of the Big Dipper standing straight out of the distant black horizon.

"Dean?" a voice said on the wire. It was a woman and Arthur Key could sense the room she was in for there were people talking in the background and music somehow. He didn't answer. He worked his eye sockets with two fingers and then looked again at the sky, an impossible array. Leaning his head against the rough telephone pole, he used it as a marker to measure the drifting satellites: four, five, six of them.

"Dean. You there?" The woman's voice was distorted, and Key understood she was probably drunk.

"Hello," he said. "You've got a wrong number. I'm sorry."

Before he could hang up, she said, "Take a minute." Key could hear her inhalation, choking back a sob. "Allow me this favor. Do me just this one good deed. Call Dean to the telephone and instruct him to speak to me. It's Pam."

Key listened to the room, some man across the space giving someone instructions, laughter, the lyric percussion of the music.

"I'm going to hear his voice."

"He's not here," Arthur Key said. "You've reached Idaho."

"Idaho," the woman said as a fact. She laughed. "You are sweet. Idaho. That is the biggest lie I've heard tonight. Did you understand that I need to talk to Dean?"

"Listen," Key said. He hadn't talked on the telephone for a hundred days.

"I'll beg," the woman said now, and her voice spiked and broke. "He knows I'll beg. Please. Can you hear me begging?"

Key put the receiver against his leg. He turned and saw the

coyotes trot through the gate onto the farm road and cross into the open world. It was still dark east to west, the canopy netted with stars in flotillas. A fire blinked from sixty miles north on the horizon. He quickly raised the telephone again to his ear and said, "Dean went to Sacramento for a wedding. He'll be back Friday. He wants to hear from you." With the last word he set the receiver back on the hook and closed the metal cover of the phone box. The first light breeze lifted his hair warm in the fresh night smelling of the clay dust and dew. He didn't like having his boots on without socks. He would get some clean socks and get properly dressed and put the coffee on. It was early, but he would start the coffee.

Of the Los Angeles days, there was almost a year of Alicia and Gary coming by Arthur's loft two and sometimes three times a week, with better wine than Arthur drank (because he drank very little, usually just a whiskey at the end of the day with Harry) and presents for him, fresh flowers, Alicia taking a proprietary hold of his place, and two Oriental rugs they couldn't afford, and even once a pair of Gucci loafers, Gary saying, They're Alicia's idea of you getting with the program. Later, the times when he wore them, she stood closer to him. They liked Los Angeles and Gary was doing well as a sales rep, and Arthur had that thought: Gary was made to be a sales rep, a standout; he made a great first impression and later his name would come to mind first.

But Gary wanted in. He had the film bug, and Arthur saw he had it. For a while, Arthur thought that maybe including Gary in a few gigs, taking Alicia and Gary to the parties, might be enough. They'd go somewhere and on the terrace would be three movie stars and Gary could use that in phone calls for a month, more than a month. So, Arthur stopped throwing the expensive paper invitations away. He got them every week, silver envelopes containing some packet of material that folded out or pinwheeled or became figures from a film or card castles or a gilded treasure map, sometimes a musical chip or a hologram. Invitations with fifty man-hours in them. So he started reading them; if Paramount wanted to throw a carnival on the lot, he'd go and take Gary and Alicia. Once there, Arthur found a station and stayed, talking to the three or four studio executives he dealt with regularly; sometimes an actor would come up and remember sitting in the upside-down train that he had suspended, things like that. It was at a party on Mulholland Drive, an actress's house, that Gary got the introduction he'd wanted.

The man who respected Arthur more than anyone in town was the oldest stuntman in the business, Damon Sloan. He had started as a kid in the late forties and once had ridden the wing of an airplane holding only a belt. He didn't do that anymore, but he made it look like he did, and his mind in these matters was exactly parallel to Key's. The man's weakness, then, wasn't safety: it was women. It was late afternoon in the tiered backyard on Mulholland Drive that Sloan met Alicia, by her design, and she held his arm (though she didn't need to do anything to hold him except wear her white sweater with the polo stripes, which she had done very much on purpose) as they drank their drinks, her champagne and his dark beer. Gary and Alicia knew about Damon Sloan; his website was an absolute film archive. He was on the board of Sundance, and he was connected with every real independent filmmaker working. They laughed there in the smoggy late-day sunlight until Gary came up and introduced himself, and another drink later, they made plans to go out to dinner once Penn & Teller had finished their magic show promotion for the two hundred people who had helped make this recent film.

Arthur Key stood to one side. He hated Penn & Teller, and

he considered it a weakness to dislike them. When Alicia and Gary had heard they would be at the party, she'd gotten on the phone and started buzzing. But Arthur hated magic. It made people careless and hopeful, and he had a low tolerance for anything that disregarded cause-effect. Today, it was all glass. They were playing with glass, throwing it, putting their arms through glass. Arthur Key shook his head at himself; what an idiot he was, what a pathetic sad idiot. It was just a magic show, but he wanted to grab Penn and then Teller and say, Stop playing with the glass. Tell a funny story and just stop. Arthur Key could work on the films, but he hated the parties.

Alicia came up and took his arm and told him they were going on with Damon Sloan. He didn't say anything. He told them he'd see them later. He didn't trust his own advice and knew he was missing something fun loving. That had been the phrase. Fun loving. He'd thought of that moment at that party many times during this summer on the high dry desert plateau in Idaho.

It was the moment that he first knew, or so it seemed to him later. One of the blocks holding him up had slipped and he let it slip. He had earned his life and now something, Alicia, had appeared and she was not earned and he was unable to get it square in his mind. At the Hollywood party, the sun lit the side of Alicia's beautiful face. She turned to him and said, "I like your shoes," and she lifted on her toes and kissed him on the mouth goodbye, and he had felt it start there. He watched Gary and Alicia leave with Damon Sloan, and he knew what Gary was going to do and what it would lead to, or so it seemed to him later. He knew about Alicia against him and the heartbeat it cost him, or so it seemed to him later. When this moment came to him in memory, he was frozen in it, unable to stop the rest, and his inability took his breath.

Alicia was tender and comical and spoke to him close up in whispers with such forceful familiarity that he could only believe she knew him better than anyone else. For a month she had been playing what she called her cardiac research, searching for his heart and fumbling his shirtfront, saying, "Where's your heart, mister? Where is it? Come on," and she'd frisk him front and back. "Give it up. It is so mine. I definitely plan on having it, now where, exactly, is that thing?" He was not good at games and had no answer for her but held and turned as she went at him. She'd smile, her hands now on his face, a closed-mouth smile that Arthur could interpret only as confidence, surety, knowledge.

At his place Alicia acted as the unacknowledged hostess. She knew Art's news, his projects, said so. She talked like his partner in these things. Alicia set the table, adjusting anything a visitor might touch. Alicia spoke for Art if there was a chance, as if his opinions were understood only by her. Alicia herself knew she was doing it but could not help it. Even Gary cautioned her and she would do it again the next Friday. She had a key to his loft and would be there sometimes when Art and Gary would arrive.

One night, Gary joined them late at Arthur's place, breathless. He wore the high grin that Arthur had seen before; it always meant he'd quit his job. He carried a white shopping bag in which were two bottles of Dom Pérignon.

"I want to explain this carefully," Gary said, joining them over the seafood pasta dinner, "because we are in the company of my brother, the engineer." He poured the champagne glass by glass. He set the bottle down and lifted his glass until they all touched it. "To my illustrious new career," he said.

They waited.

"Did you see Damon Sloan?" Alicia asked.

"I did. And, you are looking at the newest member of the

ancient and venerated guild for stuntmen and actors, the temporary card of which I carry now in my wallet."

"What did you do?" Arthur said. He was already distracted by the proximity of Alicia, his feelings for her which he knew nothing about, and he wasn't ready for his brother to flake out.

"What I do is this," Gary said. He held his hand out over the table. "I drive a black 1966 Mustang convertible between the avocado trees. This takes two days at least, depending if they use a helicopter shot, and by the time I enter the ranch yard, I've made more money than I made this past month." He now moved his hand through the candle flame. "Then I drive through the flaming fence." He was smiling and he looked at them all. "Through the flaming fence, which takes a day at least, and then I drive through the flaming house . . ." His hand slid over the second candle. "And this takes four days, because there are six setups before I come out the other side with a backseat full of chickens, roasted, of course." He drank his champagne. "It is a dream and I am in it. My career has begun."

Art said quietly, "Whose film is it?"

"It's an indie. These guys are from Texas. They've done two beach movies down in Corpus Christi."

"What's the name of the movie?"

"*The Golden Road.*"

"Wow," said Alicia. "Congratulations."

"Is Damon involved?" Arthur asked.

"He knows the guys, one of them."

"When is it?"

"Tomorrow."

"I'll go out there with you. What are they using for the fire?"

"Art," Gary said, and he put his hand out on his brother's

wrist. "Don't worry. Let me have this. I'll go over everything with them, double. I promise. I can't show up there with my big brother. This is a real good deal and it could lead to all the other good deals." He put his arm around Alicia and pulled her to him. "Let me take care of it, big boy. Wish me the best, because this is the best." He tapped Key's hand and lifted his glass again, holding it until Arthur raised his own. Arthur Key wanted to say something, but he had a flaming fence in his head and was unable to get past it.

Before he could call her, it was all achieved. Gary took the job and was up near Sacramento, filming his car stunts, when Alicia came for dinner and doing the dishes together, she and Arthur fell into an embrace. He was tired and anxious and in a moment he was lost or found, grateful to be not thinking. In his arms she said, "He's used me up." She reached to kiss him. "I want something now. Don't talk." Measurement was long past; all he knew was the desire to have this woman against him again, more fully than ever. It was like magic, he knew, worse than magic. His hands felt right on her back, and there were other things that seemed natural somehow, and at some point he made the decision to go ahead with her and take this.

The next day, before he could regroup and gather how he felt, she came to his office and took him back to her apartment, and there it was again new and familiar, so far from the gravity he knew and lived in. It was heedless, as was the day before, acts like none he had committed, acts without regard for the tolerances or distance from safety. They were together there when the phone calls came.

FOURTEEN

D ARWIN KNELT IN THE DIRT with the drill motor, screwing the uprights into the ramp railing. Each section was ten feet long, the top and bottom two-by-fours, and he had the outside rungs in place and was working toward the middle as if constructing a ladder. These would be hinged to the ramp perimeter at all sides. It was noon on a dry day in August and the raw wood was dotted with his sweat. He thumbed the perspiration from his eye and looked up to see the last sheet of plywood from the stack on the plateau walk by toward the wooden ramp on Rio Difficulto. The round white thermometer that Darwin had hung on the telephone pole indicated it was eighty-eight degrees. Ronnie had the last sheet of wood now, the way he'd carried each piece over the days, and to Darwin it appeared to be a beautiful sheet of grained material, a glove on top and one below, going to the canyon edge on two legs. There was no wind now, and the wind had played with Ronnie all week, pushing him over into the ground and pulling him powerfully, until he had become an expert sailor of plywood, reading the pressure and slicing into it at whatever tack was required not to be blown down. The sky was a flat eye, a stark pool of blue at the center rimmed by the gauzy pale horizon in 360 degrees.

Arthur Key lay facedown in the flat sunlight on the ramp deck marking with a thick red carpenter's pencil the vertical walls where the hinges for the railings would go. He had designed the collapsible rail, and sections of the thing lay in the sandy sage. Darwin worked the last piece. When he saw Ronnie approaching, Key arose and went to him and took the leading edge of the board in his hand and guided Ronnie up onto the platform, where they laid it on their expansive floor, adjacent to the last open space. The four-by-eight slot of bare ground looked to both men like the last piece in the puzzle of the summer. They had screwed down the two outer pieces, because Key had wanted it perfect: left side, right side and then the perfect middle sheet. It was a challenge, and when they'd finished drilling home the two framing plywood sections, Arthur Key had said, "Now we'll see what we're made of."

"You say some stuff," Ronnie told his friend.

Ronnie kicked it around so it would be ready and then he stepped up on it and said to Arthur Key, "Let's wait for Darwin and have him set it in."

Key nodded at the young man.

"He should have to do some of this," Ronnie added. "I'm about tired here."

"You better not be," Key told him. "You've got asphalt coming tomorrow." He pointed back along the smooth bladed approach that ran to the ranch road.

"Heavy equipment is my specialty," Ronnie said. "This ramp is going to make it tough to put their little steamroller into the river."

"Don't underestimate yourself." Arthur stepped off the

long wooden floor and lifted a section of the railing. "Let's drill these out so we can finish up tomorrow."

They had sheeted the entire ramp from the canyon edge back: twelve feet by forty-eight feet, squaring and leveling as they moved back toward solid ground. Arthur had taken two days to set the first three sheets. They got the leading lip absolutely level on the massive railroad tie frame, but the angle back was wrong. Arthur shot it with the transom twice from each side, adjusting the slant until he had twelve degrees exactly. It meant shimming a bright new one-by-six on top of the substructure railroad ties, but as the dark came up that night, he saw it was right, and Ronnie drove the screws home. They drilled two dozen four-inch screws into each plywood section, buttressing the sides into a seamless flooring.

The cantilevered undercarriage was composed of fitted ten-foot railroad ties, notched and cut exactly, each piece custom-made from the drawing that Arthur Key had been composing all summer. It was his from top to bottom. He had walked the canyon edge until he found the place where they could purchase as much cantilever as possible. He'd staked the place a month ago, and then they had gone into the canyon ledge and dug eight four-foot holes or as close to four feet as they could get through the rock. The digging required three days, and when the holes were clean and lay ready, Arthur Key spread all the railroad ties out on the ground, dragging them in an open grid like a diagram. Ronnie had coded each upright and crossbar, horizontal and diagonal, with spray paint, yellow and red, and the entire assembly appeared a kind of monstrous kit, twenty long dark ties cut with clean and formal housing joints lying about the sandy plateau. The men had their ten-inch carriage bolts in two galvanized buckets.

Ronnie had finished putting the excavation tools away, washing the shovels and parking the little tractor where their lumber stacks had stood. He went to the cook table and drew a glass of water. The dirt was driven into his hands and crusted around his sore wrists and he wanted to wash up. He had come to love the end of the day, the big bar of Lava soap on the sill of the washpan, the warm water lather and the cold water rinse. An evening wind had come up in short gusts and the rabbits lay in the sage with their ears down. Summer seemed stalled and the late-day weather now was laden with cumulus clouds bumped into haystacks and the false afternoon dark, lit by lightning in the black barrels so far away there was no thunder, just the periodic flashes. Some nights the storm broke, though, over the gorge and the lightning would step toward and then above their tent, the storm like a mob, the rain ripping up the night, big drops, an hour of crashing and then gone and the clean slate smell in the humbled sage. The sky was four shades of blue from east to west—a tipping plate— and in the north the sky was black and ticking with lightning in the distant mountains. It was eight o'clock and wouldn't be dark for an hour. Ronnie saw Darwin look up from the strip steaks crackling on the griddle. They watched Arthur Key stepping among the prepared sections of the undercarriage, bending from time to time to strike one of the railroad ties with the large rasp he carried in his hand.

Ronnie said, "Those look good."

Darwin covered the steaks with sliced potatoes and then overlapped all of it with the enameled lid of his roasting pot.

"He's got the thing a little perfect," Ronnie said. "But I'll go over. He's going to want to test fit it again."

"Let's go see."

Arthur walked among the parts, knocking splinters off with his boots and sometimes running the rasp a stroke or two on the cut corners. The men were all tired and none had drunk enough water. They'd worked since noon finishing the holes in the cliffside and they had worked without speaking. When

Ronnie came up, he stood behind Arthur and waited. When Arthur bent and turned a notched piece, Ronnie would lift the partner tie and make the fit. They checked every piece. Ronnie's wrists were striped with scratches from his work with the splintered timbers. He had cut the receiver grooves with the crosscut saw and then knocked out the material in the wide notches with a steel wedge and a sledgehammer. None of them had knocked out cleanly, and Arthur had shown him how to use the wide chisel to clean each joint. The sections came together square and tight, so that when they laid the timbers down, Arthur Key had to kick them apart.

"You won't need to bolt it," Darwin said.

"Ronnie's cut it right," Key said. He knew Darwin was kidding. "But we'll bolt it just in case."

"I want to get at that big new socket wrench."

The three men stood in the field of scattered lumber in the dark like figures in a nocturnal puzzle. The only sound now was the chuffing wind and the steady sizzling from the frying griddle. They were waiting for the word from Arthur that the day might be over.

"You wanted this right," Arthur said to Darwin.

"We all did. It's a good job."

"You'll want to go easy with that big wrench," Arthur said to Ronnie. He heard it as he said it, the first unnecessary sentence in a hundred days. They all heard it.

Ronnie started to answer, and Key told the young man, "You know what to do. Let's eat. We'll put this all together tomorrow."

That was last night. Now, in the flat blank hot center of the summer, Arthur Key could not help himself. He kicked the last sheet of pretty plywood around square and slid it into place.

"We'll make him screw it in."

The board knocked against the far piece and stuck. It was flush top and side but hung up on the facing sheet.

"Oh oh," Ronnie said to Arthur. "Is this what we're made of? Get out your arithmetic."

Key dropped to a knee and eyed the fit. "Check it," he told Ronnie.

Ronnie knelt and saw that it was almost a quarter inch. "Still," he said. "You were close. Shall I kick it in? I'll grab a bigger hammer."

"No. No way," Arthur said, pulling Ronnie up and taking in the whole expanse, the blond flooring of the ramp at Rio Difficulto. "Leave it and we shall see."

Ronnie watched Key's face.

Arthur pulled a yellow construction crayon out of his pocket and made a wavy line across the footing of the ramp, two feet from where it met the ground. "Tomorrow, you run the asphalt up to here and we'll smooth this edge until you can't feel it with your bare fingers. We don't want this poor girl and her motorcycle to have their last memory be a bump."

They had lifted a section of the railing and were going to commence attaching it where it would fold down when Ronnie said, "Car." They both stood and looked, but there was nothing on the ranch road all the way to the hills. "It's a car." Ronnie stepped over and pulled his black T-shirt from the camp table and put it on.

A moment later a vehicle broke into view, trailing a little powdery dust, approaching the plateau. "Your ears," Arthur said. It was a black Escalade SUV. "It's the money," Arthur told Ronnie. "Don't expect to be appreciated for the next few minutes."

Darwin came out of his truck and waved at Key and Pan- elli. Two men dressed as if for golf got out of the SUV, and then a petite woman with terrific dark hair stepped from the passenger seat. As with everyone, the men and the woman stood turning their heads for a moment, taking the place in, cautious to move in such a space. It was the time of day when everyone walked exactly in his own shadow, and Darwin ushered them over toward the canyon.

"Here's the first folks to use your fence, Ronnie," Arthur said. He and Ronnie now sat on the edge of the ramp and watched the visitors approach the open gorge. The men stood at the metal fence, making a space for the woman between them. They leaned on the top bar with their elbows, stilled by the spectacle. In the noon light, the panorama was pale red, pale green. Arthur Key was now sure he recognized the woman. She had starred in a spectacular credit card commercial three years before, and the project had been a Ferris wheel that he had made to roll down a suburban street before the computer graphics guys finished it off. Her name was Gabriella Smith, and she had since become very famous as the darling of world wrestling, where she was featured as a sort of virgin queen, the girl, better than the rest, for whom they all fought. She was thirty-four or -five but looked nineteen.

"She the rider?"

"She is," Key said.

"She's tiny. She doesn't go a hundred pounds." Ronnie was staring across at her. "Arthur, she might make it."

Arthur Key watched Darwin now as he pointed out where the bleachers would be erected. He pointed down to the camera platform and then back to the ramp. When he did that, the two men each raised a hand in a wave and Arthur and Ronnie nodded back. The young woman still stared into the chasm.

"If she's going ninety-five miles per hour when she's right here"—Arthur tapped the wooden decking—"then she'll go out with the proper velocity and she'll be up one hundred and ten feet above the plane when she is exactly two thirds the way across, and then she'll fall with her machine onto the far side with a margin—depending on winds of less than five miles—of exactly thirty-five feet, at least, and she will not stay on the machine at all but hit as if she'd jumped from a nine-story window."

Now Darwin was leading the group across the worksite to where Arthur and Ronnie sat. Arthur spoke quietly. "Her bones are small, but she'll break them all."

"Jesus," Ronnie said. "Really."

"It's not fate, Ronnie." Arthur handed the young man his notebook. "It's science."

As the group neared, Gabriella Smith stepped forward toward Arthur Key and extended her hand. "Mr. Key," she said.

Arthur spoke to Darwin. "We've met." Everyone shook hands now. The two men were Brent Goodall and Adam Embry, the two producers.

"We have indeed," Gabriella went on. "This is a man who can roll Ferris wheels."

"Looks like it," Brent Goodall said. "This is incredible what you've done here." He waved his hand over the ramp, the area at large.

"I didn't know we had Art Key on the job," Adam said.

"No one did," Ronnie said.

"Well, I feel better." Gabriella had not let go of Arthur's arm. He stepped back a little and said, "You shouldn't."

"You're really going to do this?" Ronnie said to the visitors.

"Barring an act of God," Goodall said.

"He doesn't act out here," Arthur Key said. "It's just us."

The task of telling the short narrative of what was supposed to happen the day after Labor Day fell to Adam Embry and he explained the hour they had planned. It would not be live but taped live, he called it. They would bring in two and maybe three of the largest wrestling stars in the world—and he named their names—and there would be a helicopter camera as well as the one on the platform and a handheld. There was some uncertainty about the bleachers and the live audience since this was hell and gone from anyplace and the locals were uncooperative and uninterested and more than uncooperative and, frankly, more trouble than they were worth.

"We'll erect them," Key said. "The risers will be here tomorrow along with the asphalt for the runway. That'll go here."

Mr. Embry was still talking about the interviews they'd already taped, almost forty minutes, which they would intersperse with the taping from the site. Key took Gabriella's elbow and led her back along the graded dirt runway. They walked all the way to the ranch road.

"You are an experienced rider," he said.

"I have been training."

"What is the bike?"

She told him. They were standing on the two-lane dirt ranch road. They could see Embry stepping around now on the ramp, talking to the three other men.

"You'll need to be at forty when you make the gate turn," he told her. "We'll bank it for you, a little."

"I can do that."

"There needs to be no wind, not four miles an hour in any direction. If there is any wind . . ." He shook his head.

Gabriella Smith turned slowly in a full circle. She gave the impression of never being still, ready for the next minute before this one was finished. Her hair worked in the sunlight as she moved about, five different browns all shining. He wanted to read something from her that was careful or afraid, but it wasn't there. Talking to this person on the real road magnified the summer for Arthur Key; it affected his stomach. Here it was and he saw the panorama just like every project he'd turned down for reality television.

"What a place," she said. Arthur Key stood now with his hands in his pockets in the hot sun. "Have you done all this?" she asked him. "How long have you been out here?"

"Have them strip the bike. They can take everything off and paint it silver, but have them strip it."

"I have some gear, you know. A little chute, if I need, and I know how to use it. Everything is padded."

"You've never jumped this far."

"But I could have. And here, there is nothing in the way. No junk to jump, no cars, no fires, no crowd."

He looked at her, the kind of woman he'd met again and again in Los Angeles: beautiful in a unique way, smart and ambitious for stardom. Finally two things at once: cheap and special. It was what had confused him about California the most, the people who wanted to be famous. He'd lived his life such that every time someone he didn't recognize came up and knew his name, it unnerved him. His brother had wanted it, and his brother Gary had the looks for it.

"No," he said, again looking down at the petite woman beside him. "There's no junk and no fire. Just the river."

FIFTEEN

A T FOUR-THIRTY IN THE MORNING, Ronnie heard a strange wheeze as if someone had stepped on a squeeze toy, and he sat up in the dark tent and then he heard a pan clatter and a scream. The cry was unmistakable, one they'd heard every third day for the season, a rabbit under an eagle or a hawk, but now in the blue light from the east, Ronnie stood in his boxer shorts on the wooden apron of the tent in the granular gray predawn and watched the coyote, gray and yellow, lope back up the entry road as if it were a path made for him, a rabbit in his jaws.

"Goddamnit," he said. He pulled on his boots and began to walk through the sage to pee against the two-strand wire along the ranch road.

"Goddamnit is right," Darwin said, coming into the day, buttoning his chambray shirt. Sleeping was finished.

From inside the tent, Arthur Key called, "If you wouldn't fatten them up like that, they might have a chance to get away." Darwin had put the coffee on, the blue flame on the propane stove hissing, when Key came out of the tent.

Ronnie walked back, kicking his boots, throwing the laces. "You've pissed on every corner of this property by now," Arthur told him. "Those coyotes must smell welcome in it. You could bottle it and use it as a hunting lure."

"You bottle it," the young man said.

"We got a job for you, D," Arthur told his older friend. "Bring that drill motor and a handful of those four-inch screws." Arthur Key was dressed for the day in a flannel shirt the sleeves of which had been cut off a month before. He walked off toward the ramp.

"What?" Darwin said. "Now we're starting before coffee?"

"You're the foreman."

Ronnie cut over through the brush still in his green plaid boxers, taking those long steps in his work boots. His arms were folded over his bare chest in the fresh morning.

"That's got to be wonderful for that coyote, having a bread-fed rabbit like that. You're changing the food chain top to bottom, Ronnie. Did you know that bunny's name?"

"Goddamn coyote," Ronnie said. He stood at the ground edge of the massive wooden ramp. The night's dew lifted around them smelling of sage and dust and now the sky changed every minute, paler, paler, more pale.

"You shouldn't have returned that rifle," Key told him. "You could stand guard."

"And I'd shoot the sonofabitch," Ronnie said. "These rabbits aren't hurting anything."

"There's an argument," Arthur said.

"What am I doing now?" Darwin said. "Is this the last sheet did you say?"

"It is. This last one." Arthur Key tapped the plywood with his toe. "We saved it for you."

Ronnie stepped closer. "Look at that." The sheet of plywood was snug in place. It fit now. Key looked at him. "I got it. It shrunk in the night. Congratulations, you genius."

Darwin, on a knee, was driving the screws along their partners in the neighboring sheets, each fastener squealing as it cinched down and dimpled. When he drove the last screw, he stood.

"Ta da," Ronnie said quietly. The plate of the ramp appeared a theatrical stage, a dark low square against the million facets of the pink rocks of the far canyon wall.

"We've still got this rail and the painting and the asphalt and those bleachers."

"And we can do that," Ronnie said. "I say 'ta da.' This is the biggest thing I ever did."

Key reached and shook the young man's hand. "Good work too," he said. They all shook hands in the early light and then the three men walked up onto the wooden structure. They took small steps to the canyon lip. Halfway, Key instructed Ronnie to tie his boots.

"Come on."

"You're on the worksite. Safety first. I'm not climbing down to pick you up. Tie those laces and we'll take a look."

The view from the protruding edge was difficult to fix, stabilize. The twisting rope of the river deep in the gray morning shade seemed now straight below and it kept nudging the men, pulling their knees, or so it seemed, and Ronnie had to step back.

"What do we do after this? What have I got, two more checks?"

"Or three," Darwin said.

"Go back to Pocatello to that grange hall with that hammer and that toolbelt, and you'll be building garages all fall; that'll lead to something, that'll lead to the next thing for you," Arthur told him. "You could start a table outlet."

"The next thing. Is that what it comes down to?" Ronnie looked across at the tent, the campsite, the table.

"That's the whole lesson, I think."

Ronnie backed another six feet. His two friends now appeared statues in the sky. A smudge took Ronnie's eyes and he rubbed at it and focused again on the thing which became a flock of birds at the rim of the atmosphere. "What are they?" he pointed.

The men turned and Darwin said, "Cranes. They'll be in Canada by noon."

"Canada," Ronnie said. "I forgot about that. What's the next thing for you? What are you going to do?"

"I'm going to finish the rail," Arthur said. "And paint this pretty plywood so the weather can't have it right away, and then I don't know. It's been a summer."

"We're going to eat first, right?" Ronnie said. He was still watching the distant flight.

"You going back to California?"

"I should." Arthur Key looked at Darwin. "It's probably time to do what I should. I think I'm almost able, ready for the next thing." He was experimenting with the words, and they weren't exactly right, he noted, but they were close. Since telling his story to Darwin on the way to Idaho Falls, Arthur Key had felt simplified and quiet.

"It's a solid piece of work," Darwin said. "Your footings are tight." They had assembled the railroad ties, sledging the housing joints firm and flush and then securing them each with two of the ten-inch carriage bolts. When the entire assembly was bridged, they leveled each side with tire jacks and poured concrete into the eight footing holes.

"Yes, they are."

"Those treated ties will outlast the rock face," Darwin said. "You ever build anything to last?"

Ronnie had retreated from the edge and was now standing halfway back, contiguous with the cliff line.

"Not like this," Arthur Key said. "Most of my work goes up and we take it down. I never once built a house. Years ago, we did a film in Aspen. We made a sliding roof on a cabin, so you could look down in, like a dollhouse. It was a sort of joke; you could see the folks in there in their pajamas, like that. It ended up being about nine seconds in the movie, but it took us almost four weeks, and then when we were done, we took it apart and put the roof back right. That place still doesn't leak. But while we were there we built a pretty big deck out of flagstone and redwood for the producer's mountain house. That'll be there five hundred years, snow or sun. Is that coffee ready?"

They could see the corridor of steam coming from the big enamelware pot. Key loved the sight of that steam. He knew it had been part of what had saved his life. Now, for Arthur Key the mornings were slightly different than they'd been for almost a hundred days. He knew he was sleeping now, because he woke ready to dress and get his boots, and it wasn't until the second hour when the floor dropped and the friction of his memory began. But even then, there was daylight in the day, and sometimes not even the work, just a coffee or a talk could keep him there. He knew he was less of a ghost, but he didn't know the measure.

The men walked down the grade of their creation and back onto the sandy earth, across to the cook table. Ronnie went in the tent to dress. The sky had blanched and patterned out in a checkerboard of insubstantial white clouds now, appearing in sections and fading as the day opened. Ronnie looked east and west for more birds, but there were none.

Darwin poured the coffee and cracked eggs onto the skillet. He quickly sliced four potatoes and started frying them in butter.

"Cream in coffee is a privilege and double out here," Arthur Key said. He said this every day at the river gorge.

"Amen," Ronnie said.

"What about you, Mr. Darwin?"

"I built a house, as you well know. I believe you've seen it."

"You did? Where?" Ronnie asked. "That house at Diff's ranch?"

"Did you go from the ground up?"

"I bladed the hillside with Diff's little D-six, a war surplus antique."

"I'll bet that was fun." Arthur Key sat across the blue table now. Ronnie sliced three thick pieces of bread and laid them by the griddle for Darwin.

Darwin's face lit a little and he said, "It was. It took all day to start that old diesel and then only ten minutes to cut our site. That machine is still out back of Roman's shop somewhere."

"But you did the plumbing and electrical?"

"Who else was coming out? There's not much to it, and we had time."

"Where'd you mill the logs?"

"Right there in the back of the shop."

Arthur Key spoke to Ronnie. "He notched them just like we did, right?"

Darwin said, "We did."

"Did you number them?" Ronnie asked.

Darwin smiled. "We did."

"God, that's good work. A house."

"Did you build the place for your wife?"

"She wasn't coming out from Elko if it was life in a tent. She'd lived in a tent and had had enough. You should see that place inside, what she made there."

"It's a fine property," Arthur Key said.

His friend understood him and answered: "I can't go back there."

"You can do the next thing, like everybody else. Diff needs you and it's a good place."

Darwin turned the nine eggs over one at a time and dropped the bread onto the hot surface. He waved his spatula at the ramp. "What do you think they're going to think about it in a thousand years?"

Arthur Key looked off toward the massive wooden ramp and after a moment he said, "What do they think of it today?"

By noon they had the rail erected, except for one ten-foot section, and the sun had polished Ronnie's shoulders a remarkable high brown.

SIXTEEN

T HEY MADE THE QUICK TRUCK RUN for firewood early
in the day. At dinner the night before, Darwin had said
that with the ramp construction complete it was about
time for a turkey. They were eating spaghetti, which steamed
in the dark. Darwin had opened a bottle of Chianti and poured
them each a coffee cup of the thick red wine. "We'll dig a pit
and throw in a turkey and bake some potatoes."

"And this is Idaho," Key remarked.

"And what does that mean?" Ronnie said. He was sam-
pling his wine experimentally, his first taste all summer.

"What does it mean?" Key said right back to him.

The spaghetti was too hot and Ronnie pulled it apart with
his fork. "This is the dinner lesson again?"

"People associate Idaho with potatoes," Darwin told him.
"You knew that."

Ronnie tore a fistful of bread from the end of the French
loaf, waving it in a half circle, over the rocky river gorge, the
sandy plateau, the sage in random squadrons to the hori-

zon. "Potatoes," he said. "With this place?" He took a bite and, chewing, continued: "No offense, but I saw more potatoes in Illinois. This, if in fact it is Idaho, is the rabbit state. I associate this place with rabbits." He threw a corner of his bread at the corner of the lumber pile and the five rabbits that crept near every night anticipating what he'd treat them with dashed away.

"Don't feed them, Ronnie."

"Do you like a baked potato?" Darwin asked the young man.

"Yes, I do. And I like this spaghetti."

"Your mother could cook," Arthur Key said to him.

"She could. But she didn't have much time. She worked two jobs all the time I was a kid. But she made some stuff." He looked at his two friends. "Cannelloni."

"That's beyond us."

"She made lots of bread."

"You should have eaten some," Darwin said. "Although you're plenty strong for a skinny guy." He continued: "Tomorrow's Sunday and we're baking a turkey. We'll need wood."

"In what oven?" Ronnie said. His mouth was ringed with red sauce. Catching the two men looking at him, he added, "Or do I want to know?"

Now in the daylight, Ronnie Panelli held the big truck in second gear and drove with his hand on the vibrating black Bakelite shift knob as he steered slowly along the packed dirt farm road. He and Arthur Key had been south along the two-track for firewood, which now was piled—half a cord—in a knit interleaf on the center of the broad truck bed. If they went twenty miles an hour, it wouldn't scatter, and it was only a four-mile trip. They'd found a section of twenty jack pine standing dead from beetle kill, and Arthur had oiled up Darwin's well-worn chainsaw and shown Ronnie how to drop a tree.

"We'll leave the ones with nests," Arthur told him, pointing to the large straw balls where ospreys had claimed the top forks of three of the pines. He chose a tree at the perimeter and started the saw and knelt to his work. He talked over the saw as he went through each cut, notching the front fall line and kicking out the pretty wedge of wood, oddly yellow against the flaking gray trunk. Ronnie stood away twenty feet. "Why doesn't it just fall down?"

"Stand over here," Arthur said. "You're safest right near the base, unless there's other trees already down." Then with Ronnie behind him, he drew the backcut down at forty-five degrees and the tree stood and Arthur put his finger where the kerf widened a quarter inch and then a half as the dead tree cracked and dropped exactly where he'd said it would. He handed Ronnie the sputtering saw and had him limb that tree and buck it up to get accustomed to the saw, its weight and the centrifugal drag. Ronnie later knelt and cut down a tree then, cut by cut, hanging up only on the wedge, which wasn't cleanly met and which he had to kick and kick until Arthur took the idling saw from him for a second and notched it out.

Each of the fallen deadwood sections came apart with a single ax blow, and the two men split about half the logs, enough to make their temporary load ride well. They piled the slash by the farm road, a small haystack of sticks which would be a home for field mice until it was burned in the winter.

In the truck Ronnie checked his unbound freight with every short dip in the road, and Key noted the care he took. Ronnie stopped twice to jump out and re-sort some of the pieces drifting to the edge. He had wanted to figure a way to use the comealong, but Key had talked him out of it, pointing back to the plateau and reminding the boy it was only a few miles.

Ronnie had a way of overdoing all the things he'd just learned. They drove with the windows down in the warm day, and Arthur Key saw even in the late morning that the light had shifted, and the cant of the shadows of the sage and the waving block shadow of the truck as it pressed along the broken margin of the old road made him feel that summer had crested and would recede now even by inches.

When they topped the rise south of camp, Ronnie honked the horn twice. "My god," Ronnie said. "Look at that. Just what the hell is that?" The raw wooden flying ramp jutted out over the canyon like some rectangle the artist had forgotten or mistook. "Who did that?"

Arthur Key scanned the installation as they approached. They were at the point in the road where the girl would sit and adjust her helmet, both legs on the ground and the motorcycle idling.

Ronnie hauled the large truck through the open gate on the plateau and eased it up to where Darwin stood with his shovel. He had spaded a five-foot circle in the soil well away from the campsite.

"Lumberjacks," Darwin said, appraising the load.

"Where do you want it?" Ronnie said. He lifted himself onto the flatbed by stepping in the rear tire.

"Right here," Darwin said, stabbing the ground with his spade.

Ronnie kicked the tangled load back a stitch at a time until it fell in tangled bunches into a pile. He sat quickly on the edge of the truckbed and pulled off his workboots one at a time and poured half a cup of yellow sawdust from each. As the flakes fell he looked at Darwin and said, "We're rich." Tying his boots up again, he jumped to the ground and pulled on his work gloves. He took Darwin's shovel and said, "Okay. Now, about this hole."

He dug a round pit almost four feet deep at the center

in the red-brown earth, standing in the thing at the end, scooping the last crumbs as if making a big cup. Then he walked over to the blue table where Darwin was closing a second layer of heavy foil on the turkey. There were six double-wrapped potatoes glistening silver on the table.

"This is key to this operation," Darwin said, going to the little jeep and bringing back a loose-rolled sheet of chicken wire.

"Okay," Ronnie said.

"Lift our bird onto this," Darwin told him, opening the screening on the blue table. Ronnie laid the shiny package in the center, and Darwin began to coil it in the wire. "We're going to need a way to get this guy out of the fire." He crimped a metal paintcan handle into two segments of the chickenwire and held it all aloft.

Arthur Key was at the fresh pit filling it with the firewood, tepeeing the longer limbs to contain the stacked split wood as the mound rose. "This is your deal, Darwin," he called. "Come say if we're good."

The two men joined Key, and Darwin said, "Let's burn it."

Ronnie retrieved a paintcan of kerosene from their five-gallon bucket and laced it in loops around the base of the firewood. Key handed him the box of kitchen matches. "This is going to be some little fire," Ronnie said.

"Stand this side, Ronnie," Arthur told him, "or you'll singe your outfit."

Ronnie lit the match and dropped it on the wooden pyramid, and in a minute a clean yellow flame stood before them seven feet tall, flashing in the daylight, and after the black kerosene burned off, the conflagration was almost without smoke, just a white afterthought shooting from the flames.

"People are going to think we've been struck by lightning," Ronnie told Darwin. "You are going to burn that little turkey right up."

"We shall see," he told the young man. "We shall see."

As the fire burned for the next half hour, Key and Ronnie added limbs and logs to it, consuming most of their wood. Between times, they cleaned the tent, and Darwin loaded the back of his open jeep with three and then four bags of laundry, including the sleeping bags and pillowcases, detergent and bleach.

When the firepit brimmed with pulsing red coals, glowing white and swollen, Darwin brought the turkey over, holding it by the handle he'd clipped in the chicken wire frame. Arthur shoveled a space in the middle by scooping the knotted embers out onto the dirt bank. When the cavity was sufficient, Darwin speared the paint-can handle with the pitchfork and leaned over quickly and set the wrapped turkey onto the coals. Key packed coals around and over the bird, four and then five inches, until it had disappeared in the glowing fire pit.

"Let's bury it now," he told Ronnie and he threw a shovel of dirt onto the fire and then another until they both moved the spaded earth back into a dome over the hot pit.

"It's got to be perfect," Darwin said. "When you finish patting it down, wait and watch."

The men had sealed the pit and tamped it with their shovels.

"Rest in peace," Ronnie said. "You cowboys know some things. If this works, I'll eat it."

"There it is," Darwin said, pointing to where a fissure had appeared and white smoke streamed from it. "One of those and we'll have nothing for dinner but cinders."

Ronnie shoveled and patted it closed. "What about those potatoes, those famous Idaho potatoes?"

"I'll dig them in at four o'clock," Darwin said. "For now we are all set." He took Ronnie's shovel and handed him the keys to the open jeep. "It's laundry day. You be back by five-thirty," he said. "That bag of quarters is under the seat."

Ronnie looked around the camp. It was noon and he was going to town. It felt like a holiday. He walked to the jeep and climbed in. "Don't go off from the Laundromat to see that girl and get all our gear stolen." Arthur Key pointed at Ronnie. "Go to her house first and she can come and have a nice visit downtown while you both watch our clothes tumble dry."

"And don't you eat down there," Darwin added. "We're having a turkey."

SEVENTEEN

THEY'D EXTRACTED THEIR TURKEY from the baking sand, along with six roasted potatoes, at half past six, taking their time. Arthur Key had never seen it done this way before, and they lifted the bird with a pitchfork tine thrust through the paint-can handle. Darwin set it on the cutting board still wrapped and covered it with a dishtowel. He had his red-handled wire cutters right there and he showed them to Key. "Any meal you start with the wire cutters is top drawer. We'll wait for Ronnie." The boy was already an hour late.

They sat and poured a glass of the George Dickel as the sky gave up light and the ground began to glow. They had another half glass. Arthur Key felt well. Through his arms and chest, he owned a new ease, and for a week or two his eyes had been open wider than before, or so it seemed. His thoughts came but they did not assail him. And now he opened a discussion with Darwin, one he had been waiting for. They had been talking about Ronnie, what he was doing, how he was vexed at the Laundromat, still pairing the socks, folding the shirts, or how he was having Traci help him, the kind of help which would take twice as long. "You ever fold clothes with a woman?"

"Many times. I am highly skilled in the domestic trades." Darwin watched Arthur's face in the gloaming. "Oh my. You never have."

"No, I have not. I came close a time or two, I think." He smiled. That he could make a small joke again pleased him, but he corrected it. "I was never close."

They were silent in the changing light; the particularity in the evening shadow was distinct. The two men sat six feet from the turkey that marked the end of their summer, and Key asked Darwin what really he was going to do and added, "Roberto's off and running in Idaho Falls. You're going back to the ranch, certainly."

"Certainly," Darwin said with only the lightest touch of bitterness. "You say certainly."

"Look, Darwin, I can't measure what happened to you. My life has no equivalent. I'm sure it broke part of you. All I know is what we've done out here, and talking to Roman and Diff. That ranch feels right. The days there." He looked in his glass and shook his head slowly. "You aren't serious about this argument with God."

"You aren't serious about it," Darwin said. The twilight allowed the men to turn toward each other and talk across the table, using their glasses to touch the blue wooden surface as they spoke.

"Just tell me of it," Arthur Key said. "Forgive me, but I think it is a bad idea."

"It is not an idea." Darwin looked at his friend. "It is what I was left with. It was a life and then it was taken, and there was no help. There is no help. You think I haven't thought about fixing it? I was surprised myself as if struck from behind. It is all a surprise now, but it is real." Darwin drank his whiskey off. "You're a man who thinks he can fix things, I guess. I don't know you very well. Maybe you are strong enough to hold God up, but I am not. And I will not. I don't know what I'm going to do. You're right about Roberto; he's on his way. I don't really like the way they act around me when I'm up there. Arthur Key, maybe you can hold things up while they get fixed. I found out; there is nothing to hold up. That's all."

"But your house, the ranch."

Darwin folded his arms and leaned upon them. He put his head down and rocked slightly. "What a year," he said quietly. "You don't want to eat without the boy, do you?"

"Let's go find him," Arthur said, standing up.

They had to lock the turkey in the pantry chest to keep it away from coyotes, and they went to the truck.

At ten minutes after nine o'clock, Darwin turned off the old ranch road and crossed the railroad tracks at the end of Main Street in Mercy, easing the big white flatbed truck over the rails wheel by wheel and throwing the headlight beams across the side of the two-story mercantile, the building standing in their sight as if wakened.

"Cut through the alley, Darwin." Arthur Key pointed right. "Let's see if he's at the Antlers."

Ahead they could see the blue and white lights of the Antlers sign pinning the town to the night, three cars in front, all pink on one side from the beer lights in the window. There weren't five other vehicles parked the length of the old street. The two men hadn't been in town after dark all summer.

Darwin hauled the truck in back of the first row of buildings and slowed behind the Antlers. Marion's Blazer and a motorcycle stood alone in the gravel lot. They continued in the alley of the dark garages and buildings of the hamlet, weeds growing from every cornice and volunteer willows sprouting behind the sheds. In the dark it all reminded Arthur of his old neighborhood in Dayton, his father, his mother, Gary. Darwin drove back to Main and across to the freestanding Laundromat, a small block building full of white light. Through the big front windows, the two men could see the room was empty.

"I guess we should go over to the girl's house then," Darwin said. It was one of the strangest moments of the summer, the two men up in the front seat of their truck looking in at the two rows of washers and dryers. There was a huge calendar stuck up on the rear wall by a white clock which read 9:20, and a sign in red letters: OVERALLS, GREASE AND ASPHALT— WASHERS 1 AND 2 ONLY.

"You worried or just pissed off?" Darwin asked.

"I'm hungry," Arthur said. "He's in love. He doesn't need to eat."

Though all the dryer doors were open, Arthur Key stepped down from the truck and went into the bright laundry. It smelled like powdered bleach and Arthur walked down the row of washers and dryers. The back door was half open and when he looked out to check for the jeep, Arthur Key saw their laundry scattered in trails throughout the dirt parking there. He picked up two shirts and smelled that they had been washed. Everything was damp and had been thrown on the ground.

He went quickly to the truck and told Darwin. Then Art jogged across Main Street and stepped into the Antlers. One table of three guys watched a baseball game on the elevated television. He went behind the bar and slipped through to the kitchen where Marion was filling a rack with pint glasses.

"Arthur Key," she said. "In town? How can I do you for?"

"Did you see Ronnie tonight?" he asked her.

"I saw Darwin's jeep over at the laundry. I think Traci was going to help him with it, right?"

"Who is that kid who is after Ronnie?"

"Darren. He and his buddy Buster were in here about five. You want a beer?"

"Later, we need to find Ronnie." Arthur smiled at the woman and went out the front where Darwin waited in the truck running.

"Was it all over the place?" Darwin asked him.

"It was more than Ronnie dropping the socks," Arthur Key said. "He had some assistance making this mess. It is going to be something, if we can find him."

The lights were on at Marion and Traci's house, but there was no jeep in front. Darwin went to the front door and opened it and hollered in, and in fact went inside the little bungalow and called for Ronnie and for Traci and hearing nothing he came out. "The door wasn't locked, but they don't lock their doors." He was back in the truck and the truck was idling.

"That feels funny," Arthur said. It was more than a funny feeling for him. He, as much as any time in the entire summer, was ready for the immediate moment; he wanted with all his teeth and arms and fingers to find something and fix it. "Where are they?"

Darwin's face was serious. "This town," he said. "Let's go get the laundry. I don't want to go back out tonight, until we find him."

The spotlight over the back screen door of the Laundromat was riddled with frantic moths, hundreds churning and bumping the beacon. It took Darwin and Arthur one minute to gather all the clothing from the ground and bring it inside the facility. There on the two tables they picked the garments that needed to be washed again, and Arthur went across the wide old Main Street to the Antlers for two beers and forty quarters. The old barroom was empty now, ten o'clock on a weeknight in Mormon

Idaho, and Marion said she'd finish cleaning the grill and come across to take their ironing. "When was the last time you wore an ironed shirt?" she asked him.

"That would have been the old me," Arthur said, and he heard it as being true.

"I wouldn't mind meeting that guy," she said. "If you knew him."

He looked down. "I did."

"Well, look for me across the street. This will be ten minutes tops." When he pushed out the front screen, she was at his arm and gave him a small box of Tide and a bottle of bleach. "Ten minutes."

Striding back he saw the old pickup truck with the one wrong door which they'd seen at their camp was now parked in front of the laundry, and inside the building he could see the girl, her dirty blond hair up in a clump, talking to Darwin. She was agitated in her white tank top, and when he entered the space in the bleached light, he saw there were muddy finger stripes across her shirt, which he knew were blood.

"Ten o'clock P.M.," she was saying again to Darwin. "No fucking way."

Arthur walked past them to where the washers waited and he charged them with detergent and bleach and lodged the quarters and started the machines.

"Don't be doing that," she said. Her face was oddly patched and red, and there was silver sweat in her hairline.

Arthur Key turned his attention to her. "Where's your boyfriend, Gina?"

She started at her name and then went to the washers, opened them behind him. "Look at the sign, mister. We close at ten o'clock P.M."

Key took her by the arm and lifted her around to face him. He shut the washers with his other hand. "You'll be open late tonight. We had a problem, but you know about it, don't you?"

"Let go of me," she tried to yell, but her voice cracked.

"What's going on tonight?" he asked her, pointing at her shirt. "Who's bleeding, Gina?"

"I have to close up and get home. It's ten o'clock P.M." She pulled away and he let her go. "I'll call the sheriff on you assholes."

"The phone is right here," Darwin said, pointing to the payphone on the wall.

As Gina went to the door, Arthur Key saw Darwin's jeep go by on Main Street. Marion came jogging in, clutching three bottles of beer in her arms. "Ronnie and Traci just drove by," she said, putting her cargo on the laundry table. "They've gone down to the clinic." She was at the payphone. "I'll call Randy." Key turned and followed Darwin half a block up the street to the dark clinic.

Darwin was there first and had Ronnie's face in his hands holding it up, a spectacular raspberry on one cheek that ran with a kind of grain onto the corner of his forehead. There was black blood down his nose forming a small goatee on his chin. His eyes were bright. Traci got out of the passenger side of the vehicle and came around. Her jeans were bloody in two patches, the size of a hand or a face.

"What are you guys doing in town?" Ronnie said. "Where's that turkey?"

Darwin turned to Arthur. "He's okay. He's all cut up, but he's okay." Marion had his wrist now and she looked into his eyes.

She turned to Traci. "Are you all right?"

"They didn't touch me," Traci said.

"They stole all our clothes," Ronnie said. Now he folded his arms. "Darren and Buster came by and started a bunch of trouble and they stole our clothes and threw them all over the place and made a mess. We went and got all of it."

Key saw the other figure now, in the back of the jeep below the spare. Ronnie reached in and pulled him up. "This is Darren. He was in our camp last week with that piece of work." He pointed at Gina where she stood glowering in the laundry doorway. "He broke his nose and has been passed out and he may have a broken rib. That's why we're here at the clinic. He's been bleeding on our laundry for about six miles, which is where we fought. About two miles from the bridge. Buster has gone home. Gina and Buster left about the time that Darren went down. Does this make sense? Can you hear me?" Ronnie bumped his left palm against his ear. "I didn't kick him. I never kicked anybody, not once."

Darren had now helped himself out of the vehicle and sat on the cement step of the clinic walkway, elbows on his knees. Darwin knelt before the boy and checked his nose carefully with his thumb and forefinger while Darren sat still. Finally the man stood and said, "It's not broken."

"I'm going home," Darren said.

"You wait here for Randy," Marion told him. "I'll stay with him," she said to the group. "Traci, take the jeep and go get the Easy Wash and we'll send these guys back to camp in good shape."

The group stood in the gravel parking lot of the village clinic, five people above the defeated boy. Arthur saw that Traci had Ronnie's hand, and she let it go and said, "I'll be right back."

She took the jeep and the three men walked to the Laundromat. Gina had fled. "I know where there's a turkey," Darwin said. He opened the door of the flatbed and pulled himself in. He backed out. "You guys start the wash." As he eased onto the roadway, Randy's Subaru passed him, the stick-on blue light flashing above the driver's door.

"Did you cook it okay?" Ronnie said. They were in the white room. He ran the water into the oversize laundry tub and began to rinse his face.

"God knows," Arthur said. He could see their reflection written on the expanse of the front window, two ghosts in a stark tableau. Arthur hadn't been in a room at night in this lifetime, but before he could founder Traci was back and hauling in the great loads of laundry and sleeping bags and solvent. Arthur helped her and then, lifting the last load from the jeep, he turned and saw in the theater of the lighted room, Traci washing Ronnie's face with a rag, her hand on his bare shoulder as a brace as she scrubbed up behind his ear and around his neck, under his chin, rinsing the rag and then his face and the other ear and his chest as he stood with his eyes closed. It was love. Arthur stood transfixed. Love had been no friend to Arthur, and even now seeing it in others alarmed him in a way he could never explain—with a kind of sickening hope.

Marion arrived and the bloody clothes were soaked, and the five big utility washers began to churn heavily. A short while later the white truck nosed up to the bright building and Darwin climbed out with a metal bucket full of wrapped potatoes and in the other hand the turkey in its ashen wrapper of wire and foil so that when he entered the large soap-smelling room he appeared the survivor of a disaster.

"Let's get this man a shirt," Darwin said of Ronnie, who stood arms folded leaning against the bank of washers. "So we can eat."

From the truck he also brought the plaid picnic blanket and spread it over the large laundry table in the back. Marion crossed to the Antlers and returned with a box of silverware and plates and salt and pepper and a stick of butter and napkins and a maroon Antlers T-shirt with a silver antelope screened onto the chest which she handed to Ronnie to wear. "Those are ten bucks," she said. "Credit. Thirty days same as cash."

"Thirty days," Arthur said. She looked at him.

Darwin had given Ronnie the wirecutters and the boy clipped the chickenwire end to end. Darwin pulled the foil layer away and then the next, and steam twisted off the brown bird in spirals.

"It's a turkey," Traci said.

"And potatoes," Darwin said, handing them around.

Darwin lifted a drumstick onto Ronnie's plate and the turkey shifted and fell apart, revealing the onion and the orange inside and the smell of the arrangement hovered over the table. Marion bowed her head and Traci followed, so the three men exchanged a glance and looked down while she said grace. When she looked up she said, "It smells amazing."

Traci started to tell the story while they sorted their plates and began to eat, how Darren had come into this very room wanting to fight Ronnie and hit him from behind, just once so as to start the thing, but when Ronnie turned, Darren stood in the door and told them that he couldn't fight in town. "Ronnie and I were just starting the laundry and Ronnie said, No way, he didn't have time, that he'd meet him tomorrow, anywhere."

"We thought he had gone," Ronnie said. "That's when his buddy and the girl and he came back and tore through here taking our stuff and throwing it around." Traci cut a thick pat of butter and spread it on Ronnie's potato.

Marion had opened the beer and the bottles stood amid the dishes on the green plaid blanket while everyone ate and Darwin lifted spears of the turkey and dropped it onto their already full plates.

"These potatoes are good," Ronnie said. "That fire must have been about right."

"So you went after them," Arthur said to the boy.

"I had to," Ronnie said. "You sent me to do the laundry. We followed them out past the four corners and on the far side of the four-way, they threw our stuff in the ditch and they were waiting in the dark. Traci told Buster to stay back, that it was just Darren, and he did and the whole thing didn't really last that long."

Traci told how Darren had run at Ronnie, tackling him on the asphalt and climbing him with his knees and standing quickly up. "He kicked him and Ronnie rolled over and got up." Traci looked from face to face. "I thought he'd hurt you and there was blood."

"It was the damndest thing," Ronnie said. He looked at his plate, the drumstick.

"Use your fingers," Marion said. "Pick it up."

He did and he continued. "He swung at me at the same time I swung, but he brought his head with it and there's no reason for it and I didn't intend it, but he just nailed his face onto my fist. Arthur, I mean, I wasn't exactly looking, but I felt it." Ronnie looked at his hand.

"We all felt it," Traci said, "and there was blood everywhere in a second. Buster and Gina just took off. Darren was in the road."

"We picked up the stuff and asked him if he wanted a ride to town."

"I never kicked him."

There was a shuffle in the front of the room, and two backpackers stepped in the front door of the Laundromat. "You open?" one said. They were both about twenty.

"Go ahead," Marion said. "It's all night tonight."

They came in and shucked their packs against the first tier of washers and began to pull out their dirty clothes. Arthur got up and threw two loads of clean wet laundry into the dryers. Now the reflection of the dinner party in the big windows looked like an old photograph at a wedding, and he stood to the side for a moment before rejoining the table.

Darwin rolled the carcass of the turkey and forked slivers of meat from the sides and bottom; it was almost all gone.

Ronnie pointed at the remains with his drumstick and said to Traci, "Did these guys tell you how they cooked this bird?"

"I've got a brand-new quart of vanilla in the freezer across the street," Marion said. They all looked at her. It was eleven o'clock, near the end of the first turkey dinner in the Mercy Laundromat.

EIGHTEEN

RONNIE WAS CAUGHT. He opened his eye and the light knifed him like a stick, and now blind he woke without a sound and sat on the cot, barefoot and silent, his breath stopped in the dark. His heart was in his face, and the air in the tent was heavy. He listened and could hear only the blood chugging in his neck. He'd been dreaming of his mother in her kitchen and he'd been waiting to hear what she would say. Ronnie looked down and saw in the hollow of his shoulder the point of light which had stabbed him, and he bent his eye there and saw the ray of moon shooting through the bullet hole in the canvas wall. He knelt and put a hand on Arthur's cot and it was empty.

Outside, the moon had just cleared the eastern horizon skylighting the echelons of ruined hills at the rim of the world, and flashing all the rest of the sage and the lumber and the campsite into two dimensions like a graveyard set in a comic play. The black shadows of the utility poles and the wire angled out in a stark chart on the ground. Ronnie stood and pulled on his workshirt, making a shadow that startled him, and he went to the table and put his fingers on it and listened. The night was warm. He was going to call when he saw the ash of a cigarette and the two figures at the roadgate.

He walked out barefoot in the cool loam, barelegged in his boxer shorts, entering the perimeter of the low voices, Arthur's and Darwin's. They watched the boy's approach printed like a black-and-white film in the lit night. "Who's smoking?"

Darwin lifted a cigarette from his shirt pocket and struck a match.

"I thought you quit," Arthur said.

"I smoke with ghosts. What is this meeting? Are we working two shifts?"

"It's a night," Arthur said. He was also barefoot wearing his sweatpants and an undershirt. "Darwin was going for a walk. I believe he does it every night."

"Some nights," Darwin said. He was moving in a slow pace south along the track.

Ronnie stood a moment watching their backs. "I might as well tell you boys, there's nothing down this road this way or that." He then followed after Arthur, the fine dust on the smooth hardpack a strange pleasure on his bare feet. "Is this overtime?" Ronnie said.

Arthur Key turned to him. "You don't need to talk. We'll just walk out a ways."

The moon had now left the rust of the atmosphere lifting off the earth, and the men and their shadows ahead of Ronnie made fabulous jointed contraptions drifting over the granulated plain. Ronnie was glad to have Darwin ahead with his boots on if there were snakes.

After twenty minutes, they came to the first bend beneath the first low hillock, and Darwin stopped and stood, his hands in his pockets. The light and the angles had continued to shift and shorten, but the effect was powerful and quieting. "It's funny to have company," he said. Ronnie and Arthur waited to see if they would walk on or turn toward camp.

"Why can't you guys sleep?" Ronnie asked. He was almost whispering. "Is this going to happen to me?"

Darwin turned to the boy, his face only a shadow.

"I had a crazy roommate at juvie two years ago and he was always waking me up. 'Are you asleep? Are you asleep?' Like that, and bumping me. 'Are you asleep?' But except for him, I can sleep. If I start thinking, I just play some golf. I set up in the thick rough, a bad lie under a tree and all I've got is a three-iron, and I take my time and I'm asleep before I make the backswing. I've done some things I'm sorry for now, and I've fucking disappointed everyone I've ever known, but my mother told me that God also loves the wicked. I don't know, *wicked* is tough, but I'll take it."

"You're not wicked," Darwin said. He lifted his hands and started walking back to their summer quarters. Ronnie turned quickly; he did not want to be last in line now with nothing behind him except the thousand forms of the sage, if that was what they were. He fell in step with Arthur and they walked abreast behind the older man. Their shadows were cut with precision into the dusty road.

"I'd like to tape up where that asshole shot the tent," Ronnie said. "Have we got something for it?" Arthur Key put his hand now on Ronnie's shoulder, a moment, and then the three men swung their legs without talking toward the moonstruck camp.

With daylight, they painted the sides of the ramp park service brown, including the fold-down railing, and Ronnie painted the platform white. He rolled a first coat on before noon, walking back from the cliff edge like a man mopping a floor. He was tentative at first, near the lip, reaching with his pole and roller, then after that was established white in a three-foot margin, he relaxed and didn't miss a spot, striping each section once and twice so no wood or the shadow of plywood showed through, not a single holiday. While the huge white surface was still wet, he and Arthur fanned a light spray of sand over the whole thing.

At lunch, Ronnie couldn't stop looking over at the construction. The paint had changed it utterly, magnified its oddness in the natural world. Now, finally, it looked anomalous, brand new and out of place. Ronnie drank a huge tumbler of lime Kool-Aid down steadily without stopping. He'd taken the kerchief he'd worn all morning and tied it around his forehead, but still the sweat ran into his eyes. His brown shoulders shined wetly as he chewed on the large roast beef sandwich Darwin had set before him. He ate as if thinking about the next big thing to paint. The sandwiches over the summer had only gotten bigger, messier, as Ronnie had learned to like lettuce and then the grainy mustard and then onions, white and purple, anything that Arthur had, and now this sandwich brimmed with tomatoes and strips of Gruyère cheese and dripped green salsa and mayonnaise. Darwin filled Ronnie's glass again.

"The second coat won't take you an hour and will only be three gallons," Arthur told Ronnie. "You can use the same roller. This isn't fine work; we want to leave a surface." He took the young man's chin and turned his face up to see the bruise beneath his eye, and then he splayed Ronnie's fingers to see where his knuckles had been blue, but now they were spotted with white paint, and Ronnie smiled. He put his feet out and showed his painted work boots.

"You're a workingman, all right."

"This is what you want to see," Ronnie said, standing. He pulled his faded blue denim shirt out of his pants and showed Arthur the blue stain under his heart. "The first thing he did was kick me right here." It was the size of a football. He put his finger in the purple center and made a white spot. "That was when I started fighting."

Arthur Key put his hand on Ronnie's lowest rib and moved it along with an even pressure. "Anything sharp?"

"All sore, nothing sharp."

"You want some coffee, Arthur?" Darwin asked.

"Somebody's coming," Ronnie said. The men all looked north and before Darwin had poured the coffee, they saw Curtis Diff's big blue Suburban come over the low hill.

"It's the landlord," Arthur said.

"And he's about to see the biggest white thing in Idaho," Ronnie said. "I'll take some of that coffee." He was tucking his shirt in. "Do the laundry, fight, paint." Ronnie sat down to the last bite of his lunch and cocked his head. "And listen. There's somebody else coming. Bigger."

Roman Griffith was driving the Suburban and Curtis Diff got out of the passenger seat. "Oh shit, Roman," he said loudly. "We've missed lunch."

Roman waved at Darwin and came over and took the man's hand. He looked all around. "Good," he said. "You're close. Get this done, because I've got some genuine projects back at the ranch." He looked at Ronnie. "Who got paint all over this welder?" Now all the men shook hands and Darwin gestured with the big enameled coffeepot.

"Sure sure," Diff said. He sat down at the table. "We saw your asphalt go through town and thought we'd come for an update."

Now a red semitractor appeared on the hill pulling one and a half oval bins. There was a neon green two-wheel roller on a derrick behind the cab.

Ronnie stood. He'd been waiting for this. "Are we ready, Art?"

"We're good right now," Art told him. "You bladed that perfectly a long time ago. Watch this guy back these trailers."

Arthur Key walked out to the ranch road and spoke to the driver for a minute and then the huge rig pulled past the gate forty yards and started backing. Art stood by the fence gatepole and whistled every ten seconds or so, and soon the half trailer rolled in the yard, just like a baby carriage, and then the larger bin followed and straightened as the driver brought the assemblage back along the bladed dirt runway, with Key walking beside it, an arm on the rear corner, until it was tangent with the great white wooden ramp.

The driver came around and climbed up to snap open the comealongs and attach the cables so his little lift winch could lower the steamroller. The hydraulics groaned as the strange-looking device was lifted free and swung into the air. Key guided it down until it sat in the sand.

"LeRoy!" Diff called, standing. "Get some of Darwin's coffee before we do any road building."

LeRoy waved and walked over to the campsite with Arthur Key. "Well, I'll be damned," the driver said. "It's the big boss. They're talking about this deal all the way to Canada." He turned to Darwin. "That was some party at New Year's, Darwin." He lowered his voice and pulled his old ballcap off his head. "I heard about Corina, and I'm sorry for your loss."

"It's a new year," Darwin said. He looked at Key. "Sit down, LeRoy."

"I don't want this load to cool too much, but I could have a half."

Ronnie had already uncoiled the hose from the well pump and was laying it over to the green steamroller. Key saw the big crescent wrench in the young man's back pocket, something he would have forgotten a month ago. They all drank coffee and watched Ronnie loosen the threaded steel plugs from each of the big drum wheels.

"This year about got away," LeRoy said. "I was working that water plant above Jackpot, all that Idaho water for the

Nevada casinos, and am only back with my rig for a month. Let's have that party again, and this time I'll bring an antelope. My brother and I are going to Wyoming in October. I mean if you want to."

Ronnie saw the men watching him as he fed the hose into the front wheeldrum and walked back across the yard in the steady sunlight to the pump. He pulled the handle up and they could hear the water hissing. "A gallon of water, according to Mr. Arthur Key, the mastermind up here, weighs eight pounds." He crossed now over to the table. "How's the oil in that thing?" he asked LeRoy.

LeRoy smiled. "Brand new," he said to Ronnie. "This kid's ready to go."

"We are having that party," Diff said. "Come a day early, so we can start cooking. And bring your brother, LeRoy. These years. We've got to start them right."

LeRoy went to the steamroller and sat in the metal tractor seat and started the thing, choking it and then setting the idle. He showed Ronnie the two slotted gears: forward and reverse.

"We're in the way of progress," Diff said to Roman. "Let's go back to the ranch before we get in trouble." He'd been watching Darwin and now simply nodded and said, "We'll see you around."

"Come by," Roman said, and the two men climbed in their vehicle, circled, and drove south.

LeRoy showed Arthur how to work the chute chains and lever on each of his trailers, and they began laying the steaming black asphalt. LeRoy ran a line of the black stuff in a conical stripe from the lip of the ramp out until the long trailer was empty and then using the second smaller load, they ran the bead evenly to the gate and in a short turn onto the ranch road itself. Arthur Key had made an elemental dray out of a railroad tie and the big chain, and he now dragged that over behind their little Farmall tractor, a machine that had done so much of the season's work. Key had Ronnie stand on the railroad tie as he dragged it slowly out the same route. Then they turned and bladed it slowly back into a smooth broad cake, six feet wide, grainy black and glistening.

They had LeRoy run the steamroller, now at three thousand pounds, up onto the waiting surface and he showed Ronnie the graduated steering and told him to do the center first. Ronnie conducted the bright green machine the length of the roadway out the fencegate and around the short corner, making a shiny ribbon of the middle, and then he reversed, grinding slowly toward the wooden ramp, rolling the heavy drum wheel just onto the platform, ironing a seal there.

He then rolled the north edge of the road up and back and then the south edge. The camp was clear in the bright day. It was ninety degrees and the sky had blued out to a high white. Arthur dismantled his homemade plow and walked out to talk to LeRoy by his idling semitractor. The truck's rhythmic purring and the crunch of the steel rollers were the only sounds in the world. Ronnie rode the two heavy rollers up and down the brand-new pavement, shining it like an apple.

When it was perfect and pronounced perfect by Ronnie, the men drained the water from the drums and reloaded the little road press onto LeRoy's truck. After the asphalt man had departed, Ronnie found his paint roller where he had left it wrapped in wet plastic and commenced the second coat on the flying ramp at Rio Difficulto. He was now black tar and white paint and well into the day. It was still and hot. Ronnie roped each side of the folding rails and lowered and raised them to paint each side. They were heavy and he leaned into it. When each rail was erect, it formed a secure brace, and Arthur planned to bolt the three sides permanently in place when the show was all over. People would have to try to fall off this thing.

Arthur used the hour to measure and mark the middle of their smooth asphalt approach, so they could stripe it later

with spraypainted white dashes. They would mark the platform with black dashes. Darwin had waved and gone into the
tent to nap.

The air had stopped. The plateau smelled of the baking oil
road. Ronnie was on the ramp coiling the rope. It was when
the next vehicle, Marion's Explorer, came up the old ranch road
that Arthur Key saw what he saw. Marion turned into the camp,
and he waved for her to stop short of the tent yard. He walked
over and she slid down and retrieved a small blue cooler from
the backseat along with two shirts, ironed on hangers.

"That was a great dinner and a long night last night, and
it's too early for these"—she showed him the brown bottles of
beer on ice in the cooler—"but they'll be good later. And you
could wear one of these shirts anytime you please, Mr. Key."
She was handing him the shirts when he saw something.

NINETEEN

ARTHUR KEY KNEW what he had seen, but even then he put his hand up as if to grab Ronnie, grab the world beyond. The breath went out of him as if drawn by a kick. For some reason, he laid the shirts down on the ground and he turned and looked again. He must have looked at Marion, because now he could remember the fear on her face. Then he loped over to the flying ramp, and he ran across its perfect floor solid to the edge and the abyss below. While he ran, the air, the white air became the sky in a dream, in his morning thoughts and his stomach felt it all. He could see where Ronnie had been marking with the yellow wax crayons so they could paint the center line. The friction song of the river met him as a surprising noise. Ronnie had not cried out. Arthur scanned the cliffs below and the variegated broken palisades, and the great spillages of red rock, all magnified in the terrified air now, shimmering and hard to read. He could not see Ronnie. Behind him he heard Darwin shout from the campsite. There was another voice, maybe Marion's. Key stood still and looked hard into the confusing depth and distance of the inscrutable canyon wall. Darwin called again, and Key's hand now pointed down, although there was nothing he could perceive. He moved quickly deftly down the ramp and over onto the ground below, weaving through the shaded under-carriage in the timbers. He knew where the footing was, and he followed the trail out into the daylight again toward the three sandstone terraces where the men had sometimes lunched. He was trying to move carefully and said it aloud, "Move care-fully. Watch these steps," but he was not moving carefully and he knew he was running. "Don't run," he said. From the last stone table, Key could assume an angled look back at the rock face.

He saw the rope.

Without measuring, he started down a scree fall they'd never stepped in. There was no footing beneath this; they'd ex-amined it. Leaning back in the broken rocks, he dug with his heels, sliding two and three feet with each footfall. He lost con-trol of his descent, even stepping backward and kicking back for purchase, and his speed increased as in skiing, and he knew if he came to the lip of this spillage, he was going to fall. Arthur steered himself with his outspread hands in the frac-tured sandstone talus. He had to lie back completely to stop. Then he was sliding again without recourse. Now he heard Darwin call his name, and he could see the man above him on the ramp. His boots came to a rock the size of an easy chair and he did stop.

Key stood carefully and looked straight down into the dis-tant silver-green river. He waved up at Darwin and pointed south and began to feel the rock on which he stood begin to slide. He was lost now and turned to face the fall when he came past a shelf and he stepped onto it, his heart kicking. There was room here for a minute, not two, and he heard the concussion of his last rock blasting itself against the canyon floor. He toed along the stone ledge, his hands grappling into the mountainside for any help. This route took him fifteen feet to another boulder which offered him no choice. He had to jump even to get a leg started and he climbed the protrusion, crawling full body on the sunheated sandstone. Then another boulder which he pulled himself over and then another on his knees. He could see the rope, two taut lines thirty yards farther. It hung straight and still. There was weight on it, he could tell. He could not see above to what it was snagged on. Key had to ascend through a wide crevasse riven in the red rock and then go across a narrow sill, which crumbled with each boot step. The old river was louder now, and its modulations seemed distinct; it sounded to Arthur Key like a loud and frightened conversation.

When he came upon the rope, he could not reach it. It was ten inches beyond his hand. In a moment of clear vision—free from thought or hope—Key waited. The two lines hung tightly about a foot apart and he could reach neither. Now he could not see Darwin. Neither could he see by what means the rope was suspended. He could not get farther down from here, and there was no up. He could only go back. The river was talking now, and the discussion was like his breathing, and he drew a breath and when he let it out, it led him into the air. He was surprised to be in the air like that. He leaned out from the earth until the overbalance claimed him, and he closed a hand on each length of the rope where it hung. He was now at forty-five degrees, and his feet could not gather him back to the world. He stepped one foot from his ledge and then carefully lowered his weight onto his hands, and he stepped out into the air with the other. He was hanging above the talking river gorge. Then he slowly brought his hands together and clenched both strands and using his boots to grasp and drag a coil of rope, he descended hand by hand twenty yards to where the rope ran against the rock. Here he found purchase with his feet on a chiseled outcropping. He sat on the rough stone and looked over. Ronnie Panelli dangled ten yards below, upside down.

His first words were a broken whisper, and then his voice arrived and he said, "Ronnie." Arthur Key kicked a heel hold into the granular canyon wall. His hands could get no tighter around the rough rope and he tested the weight, pulling it all up a foot. He'd felt the tipped pressure of vertigo, but now it rinsed away and settled and the air seemed as substantial as the rock. He wasn't sick and he was not afraid. He would just do this. "Ronnie," he called now, and he leaned against the broken rocks and he pulled, each lift an armlength. He did not know how Ronnie was caught in the rope, and he moved as a fluid, without stop and without jerking or hoisting out of time, just hand over hand bringing the boy back. The fluctuating sound of the river was his heartbeat in his ears. He had only one thought and that was: This is why I was made so big, so I could lift this boy.

It took two minutes, and by the time Arthur seized Ronnie's belt in his right hand and pulled him up into his arms, Darwin was back above him, calling from where he lay supine on the ramp. Arthur Key held the boy first and the earth next; he didn't care, he could fall now. Having Ronnie in his arms stopped the day. Darwin was calling directions or something in a steady beat, but the crazy words were taken by the wind and the river and the rock, except for one and that was *helicopter*.

TWENTY

THERE WAS STILL half a pot of coffee cold on the propane stove and Arthur Key filled his enameled cup and added the cream to it and he sat at the blue table and then rose again in the punishing daylight and walked with the cup around the tent, slowly, and sat back down and then pushed up and stood again and sat at the table now and saw that his hand was in a fist and it was a big fist, and he laid that on the table and watched until it opened. The plateau was empty and the wind was still. It was hot, still over ninety degrees, but there was moisture in the air. He looked around again and was going to stand and he resisted the impulse. He had already walked the entire encampment and retrieved the clothing and papers and cups that the helicopter had blown through the sage; some of the debris, dishtowels and some of his paperwork had been scattered in the fence he and Ronnie had built the month before. Arthur went into the tent and straightened the sleeping bags on the cots and lined up the boots there and the personal gear in its duffels, and he unrolled the tent sides and tied them at the corners.

The pilot had set down on the narrow band of asphalt half-way between the ranch road and the ramp, and he had done so with a gentle precision that was remarkable. The aircraft was small. Key didn't know how long it had taken to carry Ronnie, over his shoulder, up the cliffside and he was mad now that he hadn't looked at his watch. It might have been half an hour. He knew that when he reached the top, the helicopter appeared in twenty minutes. Ronnie had the rope tangled around his wrist and shoulder and his neck and an ankle. He had been breathing strangely, a slow periodic chuff, and Arthur had tried not to move him too much, but he'd had to cut the rope and haul the younger man out like a bag of cement. Twice in the steep scree, the big man had pushed up too fast and come away from the earth, Ronnie's weight wanting him backward, the two of them out in the air, and both times he felt a terrifying relief of the beginning of the last fall. At the top it was bad, because Arthur had laid him carefully on the ground and Ronnie had issued a high slow groan with a wispy cry in it and bent his neck back and away in a distorted stretch. They opened his shirt and saw his chest was crushed, a gray depression, darkening as they watched. They covered him and checked his heartbeat and his shallow breathing. Key waited by the boy, ready to do mouth-to-mouth.

As soon as the medical aircraft lifted away, Darwin laid it out: he and Marion would go to Twin Falls in her car. "I'll stay," Arthur said. "You can call. Later. Go."

Marion came to him and sat him on a milkcrate. "His eyes," she said back to Darwin.

"Are you in shock?" Darwin asked him.

"I'm good. I don't want to be in the car. Go. Call me."

Marion handed him a tumbler of water. "Drink this. Lie down."

"Go," he told them. "I'll be here."

It wasn't shock, but it was something. Everything he'd put together for weeks was now loose in his heart and the pieces were sharp. He tried, as was his custom, to think of the next thing. For some reason he could not remember the climb, and when he closed his eyes he saw only the red and gray grid of Darwin's plaid shirt. Arthur Key's mind was empty. It was a double-pocket shirt and Darwin wore it without ever rolling the sleeves. Arthur tried to calm himself, to breathe, and he sat and took each of his boots off and banged them clean of sand and he peeled his socks off and shook them, and still as he sat and lifted one foot and then the other, putting himself back together, his heart was jangled.

He stood up.

Arthur Key had never done a project without a drawing, even from his schooldays. He went in the tent and found his notebook. On the blank page, he penciled freehand the ramp: top, side and front. For some reason he printed the date at the top and lettered in his name and the lowercase phrase *not to scale.*

Alone at the table, he sipped the cold coffee and he worked at his drawing. The rabbits in the new silence moved through the campsite, up under the table, tame and curious. He looked at his watch. It was almost five o'clock. He held the paper still and freehand drew perfect circles where the auger would go.

It cut across his grain to use a tool for the wrong purpose. Arthur Key had never used a wrench as a hammer once in his life or a pliers as a hammer or a pliers where a fitted wrench was the right tool. He backed the Farmall tractor onto the wooden ramp over the distant river. He'd already drawn the six circles in the painted white surface with his yellow marking crayon. He knew exactly where the uprights were; he'd built this thing. Still he drilled the pilot hole with the one-inch hand auger and then he started the posthole drill on the tractor power takeoff and set its spinning steel against the wood. The blade was dull and the broken steel edge rankled, not taking a bite. He pressed it down, pushing the little hydraulic lever all the way forward until the auger bit and ripped in one exploding second through the thick plywood deck, a jagged hole. He raised the bit and moved the tractor above the next yellow circle. It didn't take an hour. The six openings were ugly ripped holes in the platform, each lined with splinters and each looking down alongside a standing railroad tie, and the voices of the river now came up through these torn places.

He parked the tractor where it had been kept all summer, by the diminished lumber pile and he took the time to tap out the cotter pin and remove the heavy worn steel bit and lie it up off the ground there. All summer long it had done them well.

Now he was committed, so he ate.

He opened a bottle of Diff's red wine and filled a mug with it. He sawed the heel off the sourdough bread and cut a hefty wedge of the cheddar cheese, and he sat down in the camp chair and put his feet on a milk crate. To the north, the clouds had banked and were brown and yellow, a storm that wouldn't come this way.

It didn't matter to him; this was already an act of God, regardless of the weather.

Way west the wall of nimbus which had shaded him all afternoon was now dispersed in a low boundary with one golden soft spot, the sun. He started to talk to himself, the things he had done, but gave it off. The bread and the cheese and the wine were good and he threw bits of crust to the rabbits, who came forward now like house cats. There was a little breeze and he was grateful for it; it would be useful later.

Arthur Key had not been drunk all summer, and he wasn't drunk two hours later. He was into the second bottle of wine and he watched the last birds cross in the small light. He'd been out to the ramp once with the kerosene, and he had drizzled it generously down each of the holes he had broken into the thing, saturating the thick wooden supports. Now he went out with the gasoline and fed it along the sides, and down, but not before he had pulled up the collapsible rails and latched them in place, shaking each. How well they fit at the corners. It was the kind of thing Harry would take a picture of for next time. He had hundreds of computer file photographs showing joints and connectors, and below each the date and the dimensions and the name of the job. These were beautiful rails.

Key watched the river which was only a white line now in the black canyon, a crooked reflection of the last sky light. The air lifted his hair.

He clambered underneath the construction in the dark and found the first support. It lit with one match, gently and easily, a small fire licking the kerosene. Every tie ignited with one match. By the time he climbed out and had ascended the plateau, the ruined holes in the ramp glowed yellow and then, as the flames came through each new chimney, the sides caught and yellow flames lifted there like pulsing flags. To the north he could see the chambered lightning in the humped hills. In a moment the sound of the river was overtaken by the fractioned ripping of the flying ramp as it rose into flames and stayed there. The yellow fire coned above the ramp thirty feet, forty. It was a well-designed fire, and Key was glad to have such fuels.

His heart was empty.

He poured another mug of wine and went over to the telephone.

Key put his forehead against the splintered telephone pole and ran his fingers over the metal numbers on the face of the old field telephone. It was just eight o'clock on the luminous dial of his old Bulova, a watch that had been his father's, and when Key opened his eyes, his shadow vibrated on the pole and the shadow of the pole ran into the dark world.

The connection sounded like a hollow chamber. Harry answered on the third ring, and Arthur Key took a shallow breath and said, "Harry." There was a silence on the line and then something was set down and then Arthur said again, "Harry. I'm alive." He knew it was the strangest thing he'd ever said, and he knew that he meant it.

"I know you're alive," Harry said, his voice as familiar as a hand on the shoulder, Harry's voice. "Oh, Arthur, I know you're alive, goddamn it. I've got too many things to show you for you not to be alive. Where are you, Oregon? No, don't say. Oh, Art."

"You've been working?"

"We have. We're busy. It's like you told me: I'm becoming an engineer. When you come back, you'll see. I'm a walking, talking engineer. You're coming back? No, don't say. We did the paddlewheel film."

Arthur Key watched the lovely fire pull at the wooden ramp, beating and snapping as if in a hurry, as if enraged. "Did you get the thing to turn over?"

"Arthur, it was like dancing. Five tons and it turned like a dancer. I should tell you, I'm an engineer. I'm glad to hear you."

"I couldn't call."

"Don't say it. Arthur, it's okay. I knew about it. You don't have to call. We've got work if you want, but you need to take your time. Don't say anything. We've got a calendar through the year. We're fine."

Arthur turned and the fire was a steady stream of flames coming up the front and through the deck in roiling columns. The shadows of the tent and the tractor shook and rattled on the dark sage plain. Everything now in the night had gone brittle, only two sides, one white, the other black.

The voice of his old friend. Arthur sat on the milk crate in the new dark. The blade of the distant mountains was subsumed in the skyblack. "Arthur, I need to tell you that Alicia went back. She went home about six weeks ago, right?"

Key listened in the friction of the fire.

"She came over twice and brought some of your brother's stuff and she talked to me as you must know, and you know also that she said for you not to—how did she say it?—not to punish yourself. Like that. She said that. And Art, she was serious. I know she was."

The two men were silent. Arthur Key worked the back of his head against the splintered wooden pole.

"Oh, Art, she also said to say that she's okay and that she's going to be okay and to tell you that."

"I appreciate the message, Harry."

"We picked up two small jobs at Columbia this month, each three weeks this fall. I've started on the drawings."

"That's good, Harry. You sound good."

"You sound good, Art. God, I'm happy to hear you." Key closed his eyes. "What's it like where you are, Art? Are you okay?"

"There's five skies, Harry."

"Five skies."

"There's five skies every day."

Harry was quiet and the chamber echoed, and then Harry said, "Be careful, Art. We're here. I'm getting to be an engineer, but we're just here."

"Take care, Harry."

"We will. You take care."

"Harry," he said. "I'll see you in a few weeks. I'm coming back."

Arthur Key set the receiver back in the cradle and put his head down for a minute and closed his eyes, finding the fire waiting, beating there.

Two hours later, Arthur Key sat at the north end of the fence that he and Ronnie Panelli had built that summer, a steel structure that would outlast everything else they'd constructed on the high desert plateau. He sat on the ground looking into the river gorge which was lit as never had it been in a millennium of midnights, a box of flaring rocks and the river white and calling. The fire worked steadily and was undiminished. He had a cup of wine in his hand but he hadn't lifted it to his mouth in an hour.

The vision was in his mind. Arthur Key had seen it one other time at a festival job years ago in Colorado. They had been cleaning up and had already loaded the heavy seating. Key was on top of a semitrailer of the bundled supports, straightening out the load bands and dropping them to a co-worker so they could be cinched. The crew was clearing the stage, and in a minute they would dismantle the thing and load it too. Key watched one man coiling the long black power cord, rolling it around his folded elbow. It was the way he'd seen a hundred times: the man making a neat job of it as he slowly walked backward. The men always walked backward coiling cord or rope. He did it himself. There was something careful in it maybe, something unconscious. Key cleared the last thick strap and had the man below tighten it, and when he looked back at the stage, he saw the man with the now thick bundle of black cord step backward off the stage and disappear. It was ten feet. The man fell into a rolled snow fence they'd used in the arena, breaking his collarbone.

Suddenly blooming dust furrowed in the blasting light beyond the fence, a rumbling, and the head of the snake became Marion's Explorer, as facets catching glass and chrome. It was going too fast and reeled into the yard too fast and Arthur heard it crack the far gatepost as it entered. The vehicle stopped short and the door flung open, gathering the following train of dust, and Darwin came into the pulsing void, a man standing against the sheet of light in that shirt, gray and red. Arthur was up now and stepped to him, his shadow capturing the older man.

"You dropped Marion in town."

"Goddamn day." Darwin's eyes were full of the white fire. He held both his hands out toward the blaze. "What did you do?"

"Woke up."

Darwin stumbled past him, walking as if into the wind, as if there were something to be done about the inferno. Glowing splinters from the vertical ties streaked into the darkness and flakes from the layers of plywood rose glowing and went dark in the continuous fountain of cinders.

Darwin was transfixed. The two men could see the far wall of the canyon, red rocks in the torchlight.

"You didn't call."

"That's right."

"So I know."

"You know." Darwin turned the golden plate of his face to Arthur Key. "He didn't wake up, Art." Darwin's voice was injured: "What was he doing?"

"Coiling rope."

"He had a driver's license and Marion found his mother."

"His mother," Key said quietly. "Is there any insurance out here?"

"Some. The ranch, of course. There'll be some."

"I've got some money," Arthur said.

"I know you do."

"Goddamn it."

"Goddamn it."

They were wary of each other in the heat of the fire. The flames towered steady and unabated, though the decking glowed whiter now and sagged in white-orange undulations which heaved and wavered. The broken holes opened and closed like mouths and there were other apertures in the vanishing structure. Arthur turned about and walked back to the camp and went into the tent. Spotted shadows played against the white canvas wall. Inside he gathered Ronnie's sleeping bag and his old shoes and his duffelbag kit, and then also he grabbed up the folding cot. When he stood, Darwin was behind him in the shelter. "What are you doing?" Darwin took hold of the sleeping bag. Arthur tugged it and backed toward the tentflap. Darwin's voice was still different. "What are you doing? Leave it." He pulled hard at the sleeping bag, tearing it away from Key, who was now out again in a world lit by fire. Darwin came out and pushed Arthur enough and swung his fist at the man, striking his neck, and following with his left to Key's chest. "Stop," Darwin said. "Fight me." Arthur Key waited to see if Darwin would hit him again, his eyes plainly saying it: hit me. And then he pulled away and he did not stop but strode toward the fire, each step into another band of heat, doubling, and he hurled the gear, cot and all, onto the burning platform, raising great ghosts of cinders. When he spun around his shirt was steaming and he felt his eyebrows singed to stubble.

Darwin sat hard on a milk crate and folded the sleeping bag on his lap, and as he did papers fell out onto the ground. "Get back," he said to Arthur Key.

"What is it?"

Darwin sat at Ronnie's table, looking at the white sheets. It was light enough to read everywhere on the mesa and into the depths of the river canyon. The world was a lit room. Arthur stood above Darwin while the older man looked at page after page, dozens. Even here they could still feel the heat. The men did not move except for Darwin's hand turning a page and then another page. Then he was still and then he pushed the sleeping bag away onto the ground and then he laid the white papers on the table and then he leaned over and put his head onto his folded arms on them so the gusting wind would not have its way.

Arthur watched his own shadow shake and flutter out across the country. He had been waiting for Darwin to hit him again, and now his heart subsided as the feathers of burning debris lifted through the night. There was a polished shelf of flames now peeling up from under the lip of the ramp, seamless and mesmerizing, and the stage was thin as paper.

Arthur Key drew two tumblers of water from the cistern and handed one to Darwin. There were ashes in their hair and the white tent was covered with the dotted ashfall. They heard a cry now which became a groaning crack and the deck of the flying ramp folded and plunged away, the front—and then in another flurry of a million burning tickets, the back. Where it fell away from the earth the asphalt had been consumed and forty feet of it shone slick as oil. Darkness came over the encampment like a canopy and the black smoke was visible only as a blank roadway cutting through the stars. Two of the railroad tie uprights still stood, narrowed to withered posts which burned like the last weary sentinels of a lost city.

Darwin sat up when he heard the thing collapse, and he stood and walked with Arthur over to the precipice where they stood out of the thinning smoke and saw the glowing litter down the rockside cliff, scattered embers and the red edges of paper-thin wood the size of a hand. Their eyes were out and unadjusted, but they knew the canyon was dark again under the starlight, and now they could hear the river chanting again as it would chant tomorrow and in the season to come.

Darwin had his hands in his pockets. "You got it all," he said.

Arthur Key watched the flickering remnants below them die bit by bit.

"Let's go down to the ranch tonight," Darwin said. "I don't want to stay out here. Do you?"

"I don't."

The men assembled their kits and they tied the tent closed and cleared up their kitchen, putting everything away. Darwin drove them slowly out of the campsite and south on the ranch road. Arthur tapped the overhead light in the cab and looked at Ronnie's papers. They were drawings. He had drawn each project: the tent, the utility poles, the runway, the ramp, the fence, even the camera station. There was a sideview of the canyon with a dimension arrow in it and a question mark in the middle. He'd put his name on each page and at the top of each had marked "Not to scale."

IN OCTOBER of the year on the abandoned plateau above the deep river canyon, a vehicle approached along the hard dirt of the old ranch road. It was the white flatbed truck, and the driver slowed at the gate and turned into the weed-grown campsite. What remained was a short inventory of the summer story: the camera platform which had now three colors of spray paint on it, graffiti names and figures, and the wooden rail was broken out and in pieces on the ground; the pallet floor where the workers' tent had been; a short stack of lumber and plywood; a steel fence along the canyon perimeter; and the dozens of cement circles scattered in the larger mesa; they would have been footings for the stadium seats. The asphalt path was now bleached gray and lined with bright green bunchgrass thriving in the runoff. The ramp site was a pocket of charred red rock also now dotted with the green thistles and weeds of fall. When locals came out here, one would point at the burned rock and use that hand in the air to try to exaggerate the size of the great wooden ramp. Then the lightning strike, also with the hands lifting spread, as if they'd been eyewitnesses, as if they'd stood here on the very night.

Now the old white truck drove up and circled and stopped, throwing a spavined autumnal shadow, and Roman Griffith slid out of the passenger seat and walked over to the bare tent flooring. Darwin was driving and he came around the back of the truck and pried the first pallet loose with his shovel handle and threw it onto the truck. In a minute after loading the debris, Darwin drifted over to the chain-link fence and looked again into the chasm, now crisp, deep red and blue in the October light. Today he could barely hear the river. When he went back over to the truck, Roman had stacked the pallets and loaded most of the lumber. Darwin told him, "We can take the particleboard, but I won't work with it."

"We've got planking for the roof," Roman said. "We'll just get this out of here before somebody throws it in the canyon or burns it up. We can use it for a walkway if it rains." He was securing his chains now and slid the hook end over to Darwin, who set it in the truck sleeve. "Let's cruise," Roman said. "We're done here."

Darwin pulled himself up into the truck and shut the door. He wheeled the vehicle in a large turn through the sage, not bothering to back up. He stopped at the ranch road and the two men took half an hour and sistered a section of two-by-four to the broken gatepost with two screws and three wire cinches. Then they tied two strands of barbed wire across the gate gap. It wouldn't stop anybody who knew to come out here, but it would no longer be an open invitation.